NEW ENGLAND
GHOSTS

Volumes in the American Ghosts series:

NEW ENGLAND GHOSTS

Haunting, Spine-chilling Stories
from the New England States

Edited by
Frank D. McSherry, Jr., Charles G. Waugh,
and Martin H. Greenberg

Rutledge Hill Press
Nashville, Tennessee

Published in Nashville, Tennessee, by Rutledge Hill Press, Inc., 513 Third Avenue South, Nashville, Tennessee 37210

Typography by Bailey Typography, Nashville, Tennessee
Cover design by Harriette Bateman

Library of Congress Cataloging-in-Publication Data

New England ghosts : haunting, spine-chilling stories from the New
  England states / edited by Frank D. McSherry, Jr., Charles G. Waugh,
  and Martin H. Greenberg.
     p.   cm.
    ISBN 1-55853-091-6
    1. Ghost stories, American—New England. 2. New England—Fiction.
I. McSherry, Frank D. II. Waugh, Charles. III. Greenberg, Martin
Harry.
PS648.G48N49   1990
813'.08733083274—dc20   90-43189
                                  CIP

Manufactured in the United States of America
1 2 3 4 5 6 7 8 — 96 95 94 93 92 91 90

Table of Contents

Bon Apparition!

Welcome to New England—six states of historical importance and haunting beauty. Home of the Pilgrims, birthplace of Thanksgiving, and point-man for the American revolution, New England has indeed justified its feisty resemblance to a clenched-fisted arm. The lush foliage, covered bridges, lighthouses, and coastline have dazzled visitors from before the days of Currier and Ives. Mount Desert, Newport, Nantucket, and "old Cape Cod" have all, at one time or another, sandboxed the rich and famous.

Welcome also to *New England Ghosts*—thirteen stories of historical importance and haunting beauty. Part of Rutledge Hill Press' American Ghosts Series, *New England Ghosts* joins *Dixie Ghosts, Western Ghosts, Ghosts of the Heartland* and *Eastern Ghosts* as one of five books of regional ghost stories covering the United States.

Authors tend to set ghost stories in locales that are obscure and lonely, and Maine, for example, with its eight-five percent forestation and low population density holds much potential for isolation and unfamiliar territory. New England has thus proved fertile ground for great numbers of ghost stories, even at the beginning of our nation's history. Boston-born Benjamin Franklin apparently fathered America's first ghost story, "To Madame Helvetius." Nathaniel Hawthorne, one of America's most influential nineteenth-century writers, was born in Boston and lived mostly in Massachusetts and Maine.

As American literature moved into the twentieth century, writers of supernatural stories continued to have a deep involvement with New England. H. P. Lovecraft, the most influential twentieth-century horror writer until Stephen King, was born and spent most of his time in Providence, Rhode Island. And King, a native Mainer, is the most successful horror writer of all time.

In addition to home grown talent, many writers visit New England, fall in love with it, and either immigrate, as did Dahlov Ipcar, or regularly return as summer people. New England's natural splendor, strong educational system, taciturn people, and wholesome life styles make it exceptional real estate—attractive to writers even if they're allergic to seafood.

The authors in this volume include some of America's best. More than half of these stories have been filmed or have won significant awards. Several target provocative issues, such as Donald Westlake's "This is Death" and Joyce Carol Oates' "Night-Side," which use life to examine death. Barry Malzberg's "Safety Zone" and Rod and Anne Serling's "The Changing of the Guard" use death to examine life.

Finally, some of the stories, such as Dana Burnet's rage of despair or Stephen Vincent Benét's classic campaign for the votes of a "previously hung jury," are simply unforgettable.

So sample these stories. Bon apparition! They're just a shade different, but hauntingly good.

—Charles G. Waugh
Winthrop, Maine

NEW ENGLAND
GHOSTS

When Ed thought that by committing suicide he was putting an end to his troubles, he didn't realize that his real problems were just beginning.

ONE

This Is Death

Donald E. Westlake

It's hard not to believe in ghosts when you are one. I hanged myself in a fit of truculence—stronger than pique, but not so dignified as despair—and regretted it before the thing was well begun. The instant I kicked the chair away, I wanted it back, but gravity was turning my former wish to its present command; the chair would not right itself from where it lay on the floor, and my 193 pounds would not cease to urge downward from the rope thick around my neck.

There was pain, of course, quite horrible pain centered in my throat, but the most astounding thing was the way my cheeks seemed to swell. I could barely see over their round red hills, my eyes staring in agony at the door, *willing* someone to come in and rescue me, though I knew there was no one in the house, and in any event the door was carefully locked. My kicking legs caused me to twist and turn, so that sometimes I faced the door and sometimes the window, and my shivering hands struggled with the rope so deep in my flesh I could barely find it and most certainly could not pull it loose.

I was frantic and terrified, yet at the same time my brain possessed a cold corner of aloof observation. I seemed now to be everywhere in the room at once, within my writhing body but also without, seeing my frenzied spasms, the thick rope, the heavy beam, the mismatched pair of lit bedside lamps throwing my convulsive double shadow on the walls, the closed locked door, the white-curtained window with its shade drawn all the way down. *This is death,* I thought, and I no longer wanted it, now that the choice was gone forever.

1

My name is—was—Edward Thornburn, and my dates are 1938-1977. I killed myself just a month before my fortieth birthday, though I don't believe the well-known pangs of that milestone had much if anything to do with my action. I blame it all (as I blamed most of the errors and failures of my life) on my sterility. Had I been able to father children my marriage would have remained strong, Emily would not have been unfaithful to me, and I would not have taken my own life in a final fit of truculence.

The setting was the guestroom in our house in Barnstaple, Connecticut, and the time was just after seven P.M.; deep twilight, at this time of year. I had come home from the office—I was a realtor, a fairly lucrative occupation in Connecticut, though my income had been falling off recently—shortly before six, to find the note on the kitchen table: "Antiquing with Greg. Afraid you'll have to make your own dinner. Sorry. Love, Emily."

Greg was the one; Emily's lover. He owned an antique shop out on the main road toward New York, and Emily filled a part of her days as his ill-paid assistant. I knew what they did together in the back of the shop on those long midweek afternoons when there were no tourists, no antique collectors to disturb them. I knew, and I'd known for more than three years, but I had never decided how to deal with my knowledge. The fact was, I blamed myself, and therefore I had no way to *behave* if the ugly subject were ever to come into the open.

So I remained silent, but not content. I was discontent, unhappy, angry, resentful—truculent.

I'd tried to kill myself before. At first with the car, by steering it into an oncoming truck (I swerved at the last second, amid howling horns) and by driving it off a cliff into the Connecticut River (I slammed on the brakes at the very brink, and sat covered in perspiration for half an hour before backing away) and finally by stopping athwart one of the few level crossings left in this neighborhood. But no train came for twenty minutes, and my truculence wore off, and I drove home.

Later I tried to slit my wrists, but found it impossible to push sharp metal into my own skin. Impossible. The vision of my naked wrist and that shining steel so close together washed my truculence completely out of my mind. Until the next time.

With the rope; and then I succeeded. Oh, totally, oh, fully I succeeded. My legs kicked at air, my fingernails clawed at my throat, my bulging eyes stared out over my swollen purple cheeks, my tongue thickened and grew bulbous in my mouth, my body jigged and jangled like a toy at the end of a string, and the pain was excruciating, horrible, not to be endured. I can't endure it, I thought, it can't be endured. Much worse than knife slashings was the knotted strangled pain in my throat, and my head ballooned with pain, pressure outward, my face turning black, my eyes no longer human, the pressure in my head building and building as though I would explode. Endless horrible pain, not to be endured, but going on and on.

My legs kicked more feebly. My arms sagged, my hands dropped to my side, my fingers twisted uselessly against my sopping trouser legs, my head hung at an angle from the rope, I turned more slowly in the air, like a broken wind-chime on a breezeless day. The pains lessened, in my throat and head, but never entirely stopped.

And now I saw that my distended eyes had become lusterless, gray. The moisture had dried on the eyeballs, they were as dead as stones. And yet I could see them, my own eyes, and when I widened my vision I could see my entire body, turning, hanging, no longer twitching, and with horror I realized I was dead.

But *present*. Dead, but still present, with the scraping ache still in my throat and the bulging pressure still in my head. Present, but no longer in that used-up clay, that hanging meat; I was suffused through the room, like indirect lighting, everywhere present but without a source. What happens now? I wondered, dulled by fear and strangeness and the continuing pains, and I waited, like a hovering mist, for whatever would happen next.

But nothing happened. I waited; the body became utterly still; the double shadow on the wall showed no vibration; the bedside lamps continued to burn; the door remained shut and the window shade drawn; and nothing happened.

What *now*? I craved to scream the question aloud, but I could not. My throat ached, but I had no throat. My mouth burned, but I had no mouth. Every final strain and struggle of my body remained imprinted in my mind, but I had no body and no brain and no *self,* no substance. No power to speak, no power to move myself, no power to *remove* myself from this room and this suspended corpse. I could only wait here, and wonder, and go on waiting.

There was a digital clock on the dresser opposite the bed, and when it first occurred to me to look at it the numbers were 7:21—perhaps twenty minutes after I'd kicked the chair away, perhaps fifteen minutes since I'd died. Shouldn't something happen, shouldn't some *change* take place?

The clock read 9:11 when I heard Emily's Volkswagen drive around to the back of the house. I had left no note, having nothing I wanted to say to anyone and in any event believing my own dead body would be eloquent enough, but I hadn't thought I would be *present* when Emily found me. I was justified in my action, however much I now regretted having taken it, I was justified, I knew I was justified, but I didn't want to see her face when she came through that door. She had wronged me, she was the cause of it, she would have to know that as well as I, but I didn't want to see her face.

The pains increased, in what had been my throat, in what had been my head. I heard the back door slam, far away downstairs, and I stirred like air currents in the room, but I didn't leave. I couldn't leave.

"Ed? Ed? It's me, hon!"

I know it's you. I must go away now, I can't stay here, I must go away. Is there a God? Is this my soul, this hovering presence? *Hell* would be better than this, take me away to Hell or wherever I'm to go, don't leave me here!

She came up the stairs, calling again, walking past the closed guestroom door. I heard her go into our bedroom, heard her call my name, heard the beginnings of apprehension in her voice. She went by again, out there in the hall, went downstairs, became quiet.

What was she doing? Searching for a note perhaps, some message from me. Looking out the window, seeing again my Chevrolet, knowing I must be home. Moving through the rooms of this old house, the original structure a barn nearly 200 years old, converted by some previous owner just after the Second World War, bought by me twelve years ago, furnished by Emily—and Greg—from their interminable, damnable, awful antiques. Shaker furniture, Colonial furniture, hooked rugs and quilts, the old yellow pine tables, the faint sense always of being in some slightly shabby minor museum, this house that I had bought but never loved. I'd bought it for Emily, I did everything for Emily, because I knew I could never do the one thing for Emily that mattered. I could never give her a child.

She was good about it, of course. Emily *is* good, I never blamed her, never completely blamed *her* instead of myself. In the early days of our marriage she made a few wistful references, but I suppose she saw the effect they had on me, and for a long time she has said nothing. But I have known.

The beam from which I had hanged myself was a part of the original building, a thick hand-hewn length of aged timber eleven inches square, chevroned with the marks of the hatchet that had shaped it. A strong beam, it would support my weight forever. It would support my weight until I was found and cut down. Until I was found.

The clock read 9:23 and Emily had been in the house twelve minutes when she came upstairs again, her steps quick and light on the old wood, approaching, pausing, stopping. "Ed?"

The doorknob turned.

The door was locked, of course, with the key on the inside. She'd have to break it down, have to call someone else to break it down, perhaps she wouldn't be the one to find me after all. Hope rose in me, and the pains receded.

"Ed? Are you in there?" She knocked at the door, rattled the knob, called my name several times more, then abruptly turned and ran away downstairs again, and after a moment I heard her voice, murmuring and unclear. She had called someone, on the phone.

Greg, I thought, and the throat-rasp filled me, and I wanted this to be the end. I wanted to be taken away, dead body and living soul, taken away. I wanted everything to be finished.

She stayed downstairs, waiting for him, and I stayed up-

5

stairs, waiting for them both. Perhaps she already knew what she'd find up here, and that's why she waited below.

I didn't mind about Greg, about being present when he came in. I didn't mind about *him*. It was Emily I minded.

The clock read 9:44 when I heard tires on the gravel at the side of the house. He entered, I heard them talking down there, the deeper male voice slow and reassuring, the lighter female voice quick and frightened, and then they came up together, neither speaking. The doorknob turned, jiggled, rattled, and Greg's voice called, "Ed?"

After a little silence Emily said, "He wouldn't— He wouldn't *do* anything, would he?"

"Do anything?" Greg sounded almost annoyed at the question. "What do you mean, do anything?"

"He's been so depressed, he's— Ed!" And forcibly the door was rattled, the door was shaken in its frame.

"Emily, don't. Take it easy."

"I shouldn't have called you," she said. "Ed, *please!*"

"Why not? For heaven's sake, Emily—"

"Ed, *please* come out, don't scare me like this!"

"Why *shouldn't* you call me, Emily?"

"Ed isn't stupid, Greg. He's—"

There was then a brief silence, pregnant with the hint of murmuring. They thought me still alive in here, they didn't want me to hear Emily say, "He *knows,* Greg, he know about us."

The murmurings sifted and shifted, and then Greg spoke loudly, "That's ridiculous. Ed? Come out, Ed, let's talk this over." And the doorknob rattled and clattered, and he sounded annoyed when he said, "We must get in, that's all. Is there another key?"

"I think all the locks up here are the same. Just a minute."

They were. A simple skeleton key would open any interior door in the house. I waited, listening, knowing Emily had gone off to find another key, knowing they would soon come in together, and I felt such terror and revulsion for Emily's entrance that I could feel myself shimmer in the room, like a reflection in a warped mirror. Oh, can I at least stop seeing? In life I had eyes, but also eyelids, I could shut out the intolerable, but now I was only a presence, a total presence, I *could not* stop my awareness.

6

The rasp of key in lock was like rough metal edges in my throat; my memory of a throat. The pain flared in me, and through it I heard Emily asking what was wrong, and Greg answering, "The key's in it, on the other side."

"Oh, dear God! Oh, Greg, what has he done?"

"We'll have to take the door off its hinges," he told her. "Call Tony. Tell him to bring the toolbox."

"Can't you push the key through?"

Of course he could, but he said, quite determinedly, "Go on, Emily," and I realized then he had no intention of taking the door down. He simply wanted her away when the door was first opened. Oh, very good, *very* good!

"All right," she said doubtfully, and I heard her go away to phone Tony. A beetle-browed young man with great masses of black hair and olive complexion, Tony lived in Greg's house and was a kind of handyman. He did work around the house and was also (according to Emily) very good at restoration of antique furniture; stripping paint, re-assembling broken parts, that sort of thing.

There was now a renewed scraping and rasping at the lock, as Greg struggled to get the door open before Emily's return. I found myself feeling unexpected warmth and liking toward Greg. He wasn't a bad person. Would he marry her now? They could live in this house, he'd had more to do with its furnishing than I. Or would this room hold too grim a memory, would Emily have to sell the house, live else-where? She might have to sell at a low price; as a realtor, I knew the difficulty in selling a house where a suicide has taken place. No matter how much they may joke about it, people are still afraid of the supernatural. Many of them would believe this room was haunted.

It was then I finally realized the room *was* haunted. With me! *I'm a ghost,* I thought, thinking the word for the first time, in utter blank astonishment. I'm a ghost.

Oh, how dismal! To hover here, to be a boneless fleshless aching *presence* here, to be a kind of ectoplasmic mildew seeping through the days and nights, alone, unending, a stupid pain-racked misery-filled observer of the comings and goings of strangers—she *would* sell the house, she'd have to, I was sure of that. Was this my punishment? The punishment of the suicide, the solitary hell of him who takes

7

his own life. To remain forever a sentient nothing, bound by a force greater than gravity itself to the place of one's finish.

I was distracted from this misery by a sudden agitation in the key on this side of the lock. I saw it quiver and jiggle like something alive, and then it popped out—it seemed to *leap* out, itself a suicide leaping from a cliff—and clattered to the floor, and an instant later the door was pushed open and Greg's ashen face stared at my own purple face, and after the astonishment and horror, his expression shifted to revulsion—and contempt?—and he backed out, slamming the door. Once more the key turned in the lock, and I heard him hurry away downstairs.

The clock read 9:58. *Now* he was telling her. *Now* he was giving her a drink to calm her. *Now* he was phoning the police. *Now* he was talking to her about whether or not to admit their affair to the police; what would they decide?

"Noooooooooo!"

The clock read 10:07. What had taken so long? Hadn't he even called the police yet?

She was coming up the stairs, stumbling and rushing, she was pounding on the door, screaming my name. I shrank into the corners of the room, I *felt* the thuds of her fists against the door, I cowered from her. She can't come in, dear God don't let her in! I don't care what she's done, I don't care about anything, just don't let her see me! *Don't let me see her!*

Greg joined her. She screamed at him, he persuaded her, she raved, he argued, she demanded, he denied. "Give me the key. Give me the key."

Surely he'll hold out, surely he'll take her away, surely he's stronger, more forceful.

He gave her the key.

No. *This* cannot be endured. *This* is the horror beyond all else. She came in, she walked into the room, and the sound she made will always live inside me. That cry wasn't human; it was the howl of every creature that has ever despaired. *Now* I know what despair is, and why I called my own state mere truculence.

Now that it was too late, Greg tried to restrain her, tried to hold her shoulders and draw her from the room, but she pulled away and crossed the room toward—not toward *me*.

I was everywhere in the room, driven by pain and remorse, and Emily walked toward the carcass. She looked at it almost tenderly, she even reached up and touched its swollen cheek. "Oh, Ed," she murmured.

The pains were as violent now as in the moments before my death. The slashing torment in my throat, the awful distension in my head, they made me squirm in agony all over again; but I *could not* feel her hand on my cheek.

Greg followed her, touched her shoulder again, spoke her name, and immediately her face dissolved, she cried out once more and wrapped her arms around the corpse's legs and clung to it, weeping and gasping and uttering words too quick and broken to understand. Thank *God* they were too quick and broken to understand!

Greg, that fool, did finally force her away, though he had great trouble breaking her clasp on the body. But he succeeded, and pulled her out of the room and slammed the door, and for a little while the body swayed and turned, until it became still once more.

That was the worst. Nothing could be worse than that. The long days and nights here—how long must a stupid creature like myself *haunt* his death-place before release?— would be horrible, I knew that, but not so bad as this. Emily would survive, would sell the house, would slowly forget. (Even I would slowly forget.) She and Greg could marry. She was only 36, she could still be a mother.

For the rest of the night I heard her wailing, elsewhere in the house. The police did come at last, and a pair of grim silent white-coated men from the morgue entered the room to cut me—it—down. They bundled it like a broken toy into a large oval wicker basket with long wooden handles, and they carried it away.

I had thought I might be forced to stay with the body, I had feared the possibility of being buried with it, of spending eternity as a thinking nothingness in the black dark of a casket, but the body left the room and I remained behind.

A doctor was called. When the body was carried away the room door was left open, and now I could plainly hear the voices from downstairs. Tony was among them now, his characteristic surly monosyllable occasionally rumbling, but the main thing for a while was the doctor. He was trying to

9

give Emily a sedative, but she kept wailing, she kept speaking high hurried frantic sentences as though she had too little time to say it all. "I did it!" she cried, over and over. "I did it! I'm to blame!"

Yes. That was the reaction I'd wanted, and expected, and here it was, and it was horrible. Everything I had desired in the last moments of my life had been granted to me, and they were all ghastly beyond belief. I *didn't* want to die! I *didn't* want to give Emily such misery! And more than all the rest I didn't want to be here, seeing and hearing it all.

They did quiet her at last, and then a policeman in a rumpled blue suit came into the room with Greg, and listened while Greg described everything that had happened. While Greg talked, the policeman rather grumpily stared at the remaining length of rope still knotted around the beam, and when Greg had finished the policeman said, "You're a close friend of his?"

"More of his wife. She works for me. I own The Bibelot, an antique shop out on the New York road."

"Mm. Why on earth did you let her in here?"

Greg smiled; a sheepish embarrassed expression. "She's stronger than I am," he said. "A more forceful personality. That's always been true."

It was with some surprise I realized it *was* true. Greg was something of a weakling, and Emily was very strong. (*I* had been something of a weakling, hadn't I? Emily was the strongest of us all.)

The policeman was saying, "Any idea why he'd do it?"

"I think he suspected his wife was having an affair with me." Clearly Greg had rehearsed this sentence, he'd much earlier come to the decision to say it and had braced himself for the moment. He blinked all the way through the statement, as though standing in a harsh glare.

The policeman gave him a quick shrewd look. "Were you?"

"Yes."

"She was getting a divorce?"

"No. She doesn't love me, she loved her husband."

"Then why sleep around?"

"Emily wasn't sleeping *around*," Greg said, showing offense only with that emphasized word. "From time to time, and not very often, she was sleeping with me."

"Why?"

"For comfort." Greg too looked at the rope around the beam, as though it had become me and he was awkward speaking in its presence. "Ed wasn't an easy man to get along with," he said carefully. "He was moody. It was getting worse."

"Cheerful people don't kill themselves," the policeman said.

"Exactly. Ed was depressed most of the time, obscurely angry now and then. It was affecting his business, costing him clients. He made Emily miserable but she wouldn't leave him, she loved him. I don't know what she'll do now."

"You two won't marry?"

"Oh, no." Greg smiled, a bit sadly. "Do you think we murdered him, made it look like suicide so we could marry?"

"Not at all," the policeman said. "But what's the problem? You already married?"

"I am homosexual."

The policeman was no more astonished than I. He said, "I don't get it."

"I live with my friend; that young man downstairs. I am—capable—of a wider range, but my preferences are set. I am very fond of Emily, I felt sorry for her, the life she had with Ed. I told you our physical relationship was infrequent. And often not very successful."

Oh, Emily. Oh, poor Emily.

The policeman said, "Did Thornburn know you were, uh, that way?"

"I have no idea. I don't make a public point of it."

"All right." The policeman gave one more half-angry look around the room, then said, "Let's go."

They left. The door remained open, and I heard them continue to talk as they went downstairs, first the policeman asking, "Is there somebody to stay the night? Mrs. Thornburn shouldn't be alone."

"She has relatives in Great Barrington. I phoned them earlier. Somebody should be arriving within the hour."

"You'll stay until then? The doctor says she'll probably sleep, but just in case—"

"Of course."

That was all I heard. Male voices murmured a while longer from below, and then stopped. I heard cars drive away.

How complicated men and women are. How stupid are simple actions. I had never understood anyone, least of all myself.

The room was visited once more that night, by Greg, shortly after the police left. He entered, looking as offended and repelled as though the body were still here, stood the chair up on its legs, climbed on it, and with some difficulty untied the remnant of rope. This he stuffed partway into his pocket as he stepped down again to the floor, then returned the chair to its usual spot in the corner of the room, picked the key off the floor and put it in the lock, switched off both bedside lamps and left the room, shutting the door behind him.

Now I was in darkness, except for the faint line of light under the door, and the illuminated numerals of the clock. How long one minute is! That clock was my enemy, it dragged out every minute, it paused and waited and paused and waited till I could stand it no more, and then it waited longer, and *then* the next number dropped into place. Sixty times an hour, hour after hour, all night long. I couldn't stand one night of this, how could I stand eternity?

And how could I stand the torment and torture inside my brain? That was much worse now than the physical pain, which never entirely left me. I had been right about Emily and Greg, but at the same time I had been hopelessly brainlessly wrong. I had been right about my life, but wrong; right about my death, but wrong. How *much* I wanted to make amends, and how impossible it was to do anything any more, anything at all. My actions had all tended to this, and ended with this: black remorse, the most dreadful pain of all.

I had all night to think, and to feel the pains, and to wait without knowing what I was waiting for or when—or if— my waiting would ever end. Faintly I heard the arrival of Emily's sister and brother-in-law, the murmured conversation, then the departure of Tony and Greg. Not long afterward the guestroom door opened, but almost immediately closed again, no one having entered, and a bit after that the hall light went out, and now only the illuminated clock broke the darkness.

When next would I see Emily? Would she ever enter this room again? It wouldn't be as horrible as the first time, but it would surely be horror enough.

Dawn grayed the window shade, and gradually the room appeared out of the darkness, dim and silent and morose. Apparently it was a sunless day, which never got very bright. The day went on and on, featureless, each protracted minute marked by the clock. At times I dreaded someone's entering this room, at other times I prayed for something, anything—even the presence of Emily herself—to break this unending boring *absence*. But the day went on with no event, no sound, no activity anywhere—they must be keeping Emily sedated through this first day—and it wasn't until twilight, with the digital clock reading 6:52, that the door again opened and a person entered.

At first I didn't recognize him. An angry-looking man, blunt and determined, he came in with quick ragged steps, switched on both bedside lamps, then shut the door with rather more force than necessary, and turned the key in the lock. Truculent, his manner was, and when he turned from the door I saw with incredulity that he was *me*. Me! I wasn't dead, I was alive! But how could that be?

And what was that he was carrying? He picked up the chair from the corner, carried it to the middle of the room, stood on it—

No! No!

He tied the rope around the beam. The noose was already in the other end, which he slipped over his head and tightened around his neck.

Good God, *don't!*

He kicked the chair away.

The instant I kicked the chair away I wanted it back, but gravity was turning my former wish to its present command; the chair would not right itself from where it lay on the floor, and my 193 pounds would not cease to urge downward from the rope thick around my neck.

There was pain, of course, quite horrible pain centered in my throat, but the most astounding thing was the way my cheeks seemed to swell. I could barely see over their round red hills, my eyes staring in agony at the door, *willing* someone to come in and rescue me, though I knew there was no one in the house, and in any event the door was carefully locked. My kicking legs caused me to twist and turn, so that sometimes I faced the door and sometimes the window, and my shivering hands struggled with the rope so deep in my flesh I could barely find it and most certainly could not pull it loose.

I was frantic and horrified, yet at the same time my brain possessed a cold corner of aloof observation. I seemed now to be everywhere in the room at once, within my writhing body but also without, seeing my frenzied spasms, the thick rope, the heavy beam, the mismatched pair of lit bedside lamps throwing my convulsive double shadow on the walls, the closed locked door, the white-curtained window with its shade drawn all the way down. *This is death.*

One of the masters of the hard-boiled detective mystery, Donald E. Westlake was born in New York in 1933. Educated at the State University of New York, Plattsburg, and Binghamton, he started writing full time after two years in the Air Force. In 1962, he be-gan the sixteen novels of the Parker series, starting with The Hunter, *and including* The Mourner, Deadly Edge, *and* Butcher's Moon. *His comedies include* God Save the Mark, *which won the Mystery Writers of America's Edgar. Westlake has also written works of fantasy and science fiction, including this one.*

The monotony of the endless rainfall emphasized the dreariness of Allie Baird's life. If only she could be with the one man she truly loved.

TWO

Rain

Dana Burnet

The rain had fallen for a week; steadily, monotonously, relentlessly. There had been no storm; no bluster of wind.

The sky was a grey mask covering the face of God. In all the world there was no sound but the drip, drip, drip of rain.

Allie Baird stood at her bedroom window, clad in nightdress and faded calico wrapper, her long yellow hair falling over her shoulders. In the distance lay the little Maine fishing village, huddled against the sky, and beyond it the drab reach of the sea. Out of the cluster of wet roofs a lone steeple stood grimly aloft, like a tombstone dominating a graveyard. Allie regarded that steeple with an especial hatred. It belonged to the church she had been married in. . . .

As she stood there shivering with the cold, a desolate picture composed itself in her mind. She saw again the naked wooden altar; heard once more the voice of the lugubrious minister pronouncing sentence upon her soul; felt the cold hand of Jim Baird fumbling for her hand, and the colder embrace of the ring upon her finger. It had rained that day, as it was raining now. Eighteen years! And in all that time only three things of importance had happened to her; first, the birth of her child; second, the death of her child; and third, a trip to Portland for a minor operation. Except for these events, her life had been a barren desert of days.

In the bed behind her a man stirred and grunted. She turned quickly, gazing down at her husband with a new and critical interest. His huge body bulked large beneath the tumbled coverings; his florid face, with its inevitable stubble of beard, seemed unusually hideous against the untidy pillow. His small eyes leered up at her with that maddening lifelessness, that phlegmatic stare which had begun to sicken her.

"Still raining, Allie?"

"Still raining."

He had asked that question every morning for a week, and she had answered it in the same way; but this morning her voice trembled. He heard, and scolded her peevishly for her incaution of dress.

"You'll catch your death, goin' about in that wrapper. Why don't you get your clothes on like a sensible woman?"

She did not reply, and he settled into his wallow, with a ponderous groan.

"Ain't no use my gettin' up awhile. This rain's a fust-rate jailer. Call me when breakfast's ready."

"I'll call you, Jim."

She dressed listlessly, and in silence. The man in the bed began to snore; she went swiftly out of the room, with a little indrawn breath, her hair still hanging loosely down her back.

Entering the kitchen, she laid the fire, lighted it, and set about the business of getting breakfast, only pausing to sip a cup of coffee. This she drank standing at the window, her eyes fixed upon the distant grey blue of ocean that formed the horizon of her world. Suddenly her gaze grew more intent; a dull light flickered in her eyes. She had seen a sail upon the far water, a draggled moth struggling through the rain—

"There, now, Allie, you've burnt the bacon! Thought I smelled it scorchin'."

Jim Baird, in shirt, trousers and grey cotton socks, stood sniffing in the doorway. Having justified his suspicions, he shuffled forward, grumbling.

"Just like you," he muttered, "always lookin' out the window and not mindin' your housework—"

She did not seem to hear the familiar arraignment. Her eyes were still bright with looking out of the window.

"I thought I saw a sail, Jim."

"Pshaw! What if you did? Ain't nothin' to get excited about, is it?"

Still she did not heed the indictment in his tone.

16

"Look, Jim, isn't that a schooner out there—off the Point?"

Jim looked, obviously to arm himself with a denial.

"I don't see no sail," he stated, positively. Allie smiled, a slow terrible smile.

"You never see the things I see, do you, Jim?"

"I don't see no schooner off the Point, not in this weather. And you don't neither, though you're always sayin' you do. Soon's you get a little mite fidgety, you begin seeing ships off the Point. Ain't you never forgot—"

He stopped, sobered by the expression on her face, and returned querulously to the first charge against her.

"You always was careless and wasteful, Allie," he complained, prodding the defunct bacon with a mournful forefinger. "Careless and wasteful—with bacon costin' what it does."

"It doesn't cost as much as whiskey!"

"Now, Allie—"

"Whiskey's the thing that has ruined you, Jim Baird; not my carelessness."

"Well, now, I ain't allowin' that I'm ruined, Allie. The farm still pays expenses, and a little mite over. And as for what you said—you know I ain't no heavy drinker."

"I wish to God you were! I wish you'd go out and get drunk like a man, and come home and beat me—if you wanted to! It's this everlastin' takin' it, takin' it, takin' it behind my back—and then lyin' to yourself to ease your conscience."

"Now, Allie, you know that ain't true. You know I'm subject to colds. The doctor said a drop or two wouldn't hurt me—"

"He didn't say to drink a bottle a week!"

"I ain't drunk a bottle. There's some—Now, Allie, you know I need a tonic. This house's chilled through. The weather's murd'rous, plain murd'rous."

"Don't say that word!"

She stood over him, her bosom heaving, a pitiful frightened helplessness in her eyes; it was as though she recognized her growing inability to struggle against fate.

Jim Baird looked at her with the faint bravado that is the

17

invariable cloak of cowardice; then he sat down at the table and began to eat, after the manner of his kind.

Allie watched him with a strange horror, a cumulative loathing that was as new in its expression as it was old in its origin. He ate like a beast.

It seemed that this week of bad weather was bringing to the surface many of her hidden emotions, her secret opinions, her long-concealed hatreds. The endless drip of the rain had begun to wear upon her calloused spirit; to rasp her nerves. She could not remember when she had been shut up with him, under one roof, for such a long time before. She wished that he had not said it was murderous weather.

After breakfast he went into the front room—a pathetically drooping chamber filled with ornaments that belied their mission of cheer; the chamber in which was gathered the concentrated dreariness of that house.

From a small cabinet he took a bottle, and drank—not recklessly but rather stingily, as though fearful of imbibing more than was strictly necessary to his intoxication, after which he filled his pipe and sat down by the window.

Allie moved slowly about the kitchen, prolonging as far as possible the washing of the dishes. At last she picked up the carving knife, a long, sharp-bladed affair, and began to scour it with trembling hands. There was an appalling tumult in her heart. The frightened look had returned to her eyes.

Suddenly she lifted her head. The knife fell clattering to the floor. With an air of grim determination she walked into the front room and sat down at her husband's side.

"Jim—I—want—to talk to you."

The peaceful vacuity of Jim Baird's countenance gave place to an uncontrollable peevishness; but he managed an artificial smile.

"All right, Allie, talk ahead. I guess you're lonesome—is that it?"

"That's it, Jim. I'm lonesome. And it doesn't seem right, somehow. It doesn't seem natural. We're husband and wife, Jim, and—we ought—to—talk—more. We ought to talk about—"

"The weather?"

"God—no!"

"Then what, Allie?"

She shook her head hopelessly.

"What do other husbands and wives talk about, when they're shut in together? Are they all like this? If they are, then they're nothing but *prisoners!*"

"Now, Allie—"

"You've got to talk to me, Jim. You've got to find something we can share, something we can take an interest in. All our lives we've gone along like this. We're strangers, after eighteen years, and it's—killing me! Oh, Jim, if you'd only try to be a man! If you'd only quit drinking, and go to work again. I mean *real work*, work that *means* something. I'll help you, Jim! I'll work with you—"

"Why, Allie, what's come over you? Ain't you got three meals a day, and a good bed to sleep in?"

"Yes, but that's not living. That's just keeping your body warm. I want something else, something I can look forward to—a trip to Portland maybe, or a new dress, or one of those little autos that don't cost so much, that I could run myself—"

"An automobile! *An automobile!* Ha! Ha! Ha! Allie Baird wants an automobile. That's what it's all about, eh? I knew there was somethin' on your mind besides the weather. An automobile! God A'mighty, ain't I got troubles enough, without havin' a spendthrift wife?"

He had risen from his chair, and was facing her in a sullen fury. She drew back slowly, her arm half lifted as though to ward off a blow. But still she clung to the hopeless dream of making him see, of making him understand.

"It isn't that, Jim! I swear it isn't that! I don't care about having an auto. I only want something that we could take pleasure in—and—and—"

"You lie, Allie Baird! Git back into that kitchen, and be thankful you ain't walkin' the streets in the rain—"

Her arms fell to her sides; a dry sob escaped her lips. She turned and went wearily from the room.

In the kitchen she sank down by the window, and put her head on her arms.

It seemed as though the rain had stopped at last. In the orchard behind the rambling old farmhouse, a young girl walked with her lover. The air was sweet with the fragrance of apple blossoms. The twilight established about them a kingdom of shadows, and infinite solitudes, where they might wander in peace and safety.

The man was fair-haired, blue-eyed, with the proud carriage of a young Viking. He was sailing at daybreak for Georges Banks. It was to be his last trip before they were married.

"You'll be standin' at the window," he said, tightening his arm about her waist, "and you'll see the *Swallow* roundin' the Point—you can tell her by the canvas she carries! And you'll put on the ring I gave you, for you'll know it's Hartley Taylor comin' home for his sweetheart—"

"If you shouldn't come!" she whispered, and swayed against him. He took her in his arms and kissed her.

"I'll come one way or another," he said. "One way or another. Wait for me always."

He went at dawn in the *Swallow* schooner. She stood at the window, his ring against her lips, watching his sails until they showed no more.

A week later the remnants of the fishing fleet came driving home in the teeth of the gale; but Hartley Taylor did not come, though she watched the Point night and day, all the long winter through. And when the spring came again, and her heart was dead in her breast, she went down to the edge of the great water, and gave his ring to the sea.

The following June, at the urgent request of both her father and mother, she married Jim Baird, who wanted a wife, and was willing to trade for one upon a purely business basis.

Allie awoke with a sigh; her glance involuntarily sought the distant headland, thrust like a welcoming hand into the sea. Was it a sail that she saw, or was it another illusion of her mind?

The ceaseless patter of rain at the window stirred her to full consciousness. Her relaxed nerves tightened. Her brain throbbed with the endless reiteration of the thought that she had been fighting against ever since the dawn.

She cooked dinner, and sat in her chair by the window while Jim Baird ate. She herself did not taste food. The carving knife still lay on the floor between them. The man picked it up, muttering something about her carelessness, and placed it on the table beside her. She did not speak nor turn her head.

He returned to the front room, renewed his miserly dissipations; but now he drank more boldly, with a false courage born of hate. Allie's plea had shaken him from that numbing lethargy, that sensual refuge into which he had crept for shelter against the very thing she demanded so passionately—*life!* And he raged inwardly at her who had pricked him.

By night he was thoroughly drunk. When she called him to his supper he came reeling, and fell into his chair with a loud laugh that echoed mockingly through the silent house. For some moments he essayed a ghastly humor, making jests about the rain, which he likened to the Flood, vowing that it presaged the end of the world. Allie sat with her back toward him, her body rigid, her hands gripping the chair.

Finally he rose and approached her.

"You told me t' git drunk—and beat you," he snarled; and struck her on the cheek with his open hand. "Come t' th' table," he added, breathing hard. "'Tain't right t' turn your back on your husband. 'Tain't—natural."

To his own maudlin amazement she did exactly as he commanded. She sat down opposite him, leaned her elbows on the table, and looked at him with a smile. It was a smile that lighted her whole countenance, a strange radiance caused by some burning within her breast. It was as though in striking her he had kindled a slumbering spark to flame. Her eyes gleamed. Her cheeks were flushed as with a fever.

That night, for the first time in eighteen years, Allie Baird did not wash the supper dishes. As soon as he had gone, she went upstairs and put on her white dress—the only one she owned beside her monotonous gingham. Then she returned to the kitchen, blew out the lamp, and waited for Jim Baird to go to bed.

The lighthouse on the Point had begun to glow. She kept her gaze upon that distant flame. It steadied her.

The rain fell steadily, monotonously, as it had fallen for days—as it had fallen for ages! She heard Jim's stumbling progress up the stairs, his heavy breathing, his low-voiced growl as he cursed the dark. Still she waited, in her white dress, her hair down her back. Time, that had seemed so interminable to her that morning, was now but an inconsequential trifle.

A clock in the front room struck three, with muffled tones. She rose from her chair, picked up the long-bladed knife, and slowly mounted the stairs.

As she entered the bedroom, a reek of whiskey assailed her nostrils. She felt, rather than saw, her husband's huge bulk upon the bed. He was sleeping the deep sleep of drunkenness, and he whimpered a little as he breathed. She crept close, leaned down and kissed him.

"Poor Jim!" she whispered; then lifting the knife high in air, she drove it home.

She had reached the open window—somehow—and was kneeling before it, her arms across the sill.

A ship was coming for her through the rain, a schooner with all canvas set, plunging through the grey sea of the mist; a white shape afloat upon the air.

The woman at the window smiled, and reached into her bosom for the ring her lover had given her; but the ring was not there.

Then she glanced once more at the oncoming ship, and saw Hartley Taylor standing at the lee-rail, with the ring in his hand, and the light of its single stone filling the world with glory!

"I'll come—one way or another!"

She felt the light upon her face, upon her hair, and held out her hands to him in greeting, crying his name across the shriveled waters!

Jim Baird awoke with a start; groaned ponderously and fell back upon his pillow.

"Still rainin', Allie?"

There was no reply. He glanced toward the window, and saw her kneeling at the sill in a brilliant flood of sunshine— her head upon her arms and her yellow hair falling about her shoulders like so much spun gold. He began to scold her querulously.

"Now, Allie, you'll catch your death—"

Something in her stillness checked the words on his lips. He got awkwardly out of bed, his face a mottled grey, and walked slowly toward the kneeling figure.

Suddenly he halted, and stared panic-stricken at a dark stain on the floor. His legs gave way beneath him. He sank into a chair, a growing horror in his eyes.

"Just like you, Allie," he moaned. "Couldn't stand a little bad weather—If you'd just waited another day—Sun's out now!"

He looked once more at that still figure by the window; saw the light on her hair, felt the immeasurable distance between them.

Then he began to sob weakly.

Born in Ohio in 1888, Dana Burnet had several careers: lawyer, reporter for the New York Evening Sun, *and playwright. His fiction was often included in O'Brien's* Best Short Stories of the Year *selections. Known for his supernatural, often mystical and religiously oriented stories, Burnet's work included "Fog" and "The Question." He died in 1962.*

Sandy knew Wayne only listened to the music of the 1960s, but she never expected him to become obsessed with the music of the dead.

THREE

On 202

Jeff Hecht

The leaves skittered across the road as the cold November wind blew out of the western Massachusetts hills. They were a familiar sight to Sandy, but the first time the headlights of the old Volvo caught them, Wayne started to brake the car and stalled the engine. He muttered an obscenity.

"Why did you do that? You're going to get us stuck out here," Sandy grumbled. "I told you we should have stayed the night in Amherst." Even though they were both tired and it was nearly midnight before they'd left Sandy's friends' apartment, Wayne had insisted on making the two-hour trip to her parents' home in Lowell that night.

"There were animals running across the road," Wayne replied as he shifted into neutral and steered the slowing car toward the side of the road. The engine caught, and he shifted back into drive. "Didn't you see them? They were little dark things, rats I think." He accelerated and pulled the car back toward the middle of the empty road.

"They were just leaves, blown by the wind. It's something you never see in California."

"Then I'm glad I missed them. California's always had everything I wanted."

"Except me."

"Sometimes I wonder about that."

It was an old line of banter that, like many other things, was souring on them both, but Wayne's twisting of it hurt Sandy. The trip had been her idea—she'd wanted to visit family and friends back East, and hoped that the trip would help bring her and Wayne back together. But nothing had gone right; even the old car she'd brought West with her years ago was dying. "Come on, Wayne. You agreed to come back with me. You said you wanted to see the East, remember?"

"Yeah, I guess I did. There was nothing better to do. But it's so damn alien here."

Sandy stared out the windshield, trying to find a way to snap Wayne out of his foul mood. The wind was picking up, bringing with it some snowflakes which were settling on the empty road that would take them to Pelham, where they would pick up Route 202 and drive north for miles to Route 2, then to Route 495, and finally into Lowell. She knew the route well from her college years, but she'd never taken it so late at night.

In the silence, Wayne reached over and turned on the radio. He punched two buttons and got only static, but the third brought Jimi Hendrix's voice into the car: "Two riders were approaching, and the wind began to howl . . ." The last word echoed down the road with them and the wind, then faded back into static as they went down a hill.

Sandy shuddered. "Turn it off, Wayne, please."

"Why? I like it; I haven't heard it in ages."

"It bothers me. Hendrix has been dead for ten years now. To hear him now is like—like a ghost singing."

Wayne laughed. "Don't be silly. It's just electronics, just music. It's grooves on a record being translated electromechanically into signals that can make a speaker move. There's nothing supernatural about it." He stared out into the thickening snow. "The only thing that's spooky around here is the country."

"What do you mean?"

"It's strange, that's all. Ancient and foreboding and now—" he pointed to the bare trees beside the road, "—barren."

"You call this barren after living around Los Angeles?" Sandy thought of the scraggly shrubs that failed to cover the dry soil of the Angeles National Forest, and of the sandy desert east of San Bernardino.

"No, I mean empty, menacing. You remember that book we read by Lovecraft? He lived in New England, and this is his kind of country. Even the names match. I remember the name of one of his characters—Whateley, Wilbur Whateley.

25

There's a town named after him. We drove through it, remember?"

"The town spells it differently—W-h-a-t-e-l-y. Lovecraft had an extra *e* in it. I checked."

Wayne shrugged. "It doesn't matter. It's still a horror-story kind of place, a dark and sleepy town that time and the highway passed by."

Sandy watched the snowflakes as she tried to sort through her thoughts. "I don't understand." She saw a single light on the hillside; outside of their headlights it seemed to be the only light in the world. "Why does it bother you?"

"It's empty, it's—" he groped for words. "Well, I can't really find the words, but it's just not right."

"For God's sake, Wayne, it sounds like you're taking those old horror stories seriously!"

He turned from the road and looked at her. "So how many horror stories have they written about Los Angeles?" They came up over a hill and saw a handful of lights among the snowflakes and the dark houses of Pelham. "Look, Sandy," he stated, but was interrupted by John Lennon singing from the radio: "All we are saying, is give peace a chance."

Sandy shivered. "Please turn it off."

"But it's good music—great music. It takes me back to the good years, back when the Movement was alive."

"Lennon is dead," she said, realizing as the words came from her mouth that they would have no more impact than reminding Wayne that the Movement had died, too. He had never been able to cope with that reality, and music had become his way of tuning out the world. At times—often when she was out working—he would sit for hours listening over headphones. "Just listening," he would say when she came home and asked. He insisted that the only reason he used the headphones was that they sounded better than the speakers, but she suspected that he really was trying to keep his beloved old music to himself. Perhaps he wanted to slip back a decade to when the music was being made, and to when he wasn't the only one drifting aimlessly through life.

Wayne shifted into neutral and kept his foot on the gas while braking for the flashing red light at the end of the road. It wasn't the best treatment for an automatic transmission, but it was the only way they'd found to keep the car from stalling when they slowed it. This time it worked.

"We don't have to worry about that again for a while," Sandy said as they coasted through the left turn and Wayne began accelerating on Route 202. "It's probably twenty miles before the next stop light."

"That far?"

"There's not much out this way. We're going through the watershed of the Quabbin Reservoir—Boston's water supply. There aren't any houses for miles." They were out of the village of Pelham before they realized it. The snow was coming down heavily now, and Wayne eased off the gas. With the snow blowing outside and the speedometer light out, Sandy couldn't estimate their speed. The trees seemed to meet overhead at places, and it looked as if they were driving through an endless tunnel defined by their headlights.

Wayne stared out into the snow, trying to see the road. "The snow's early, isn't it?"

"A little. But it does this sometimes." The sad, flabby voice of Elvis Presley sang meaningless words in the background. Sandy tuned them out automatically.

"It's a desolate land, Sandy, and these are desolate times." Wayne's voice seemed remote, as if he was speaking from the other end of a tunnel rather than from the other side of the car. "The music helps me hold off the worst of it, lets me try to recapture the magic that's gone. Sometimes it seems like I'm the only one left who remembers it all, you know, like everybody else had forgotten peace and love and copped out and voted for Ronnie Reagan."

"What do you mean?" Sandy kept her question short, hoping it would keep Wayne from drifting back into the silent brooding that she dreaded the most.

"Even the music has become a big business. Take Elvis— or Lennon. What did they say Lennon was worth when that guy shot him—two hundred million? What did he do to deserve all of that? And how many people could he have fed with his money?"

It was a familiar tirade. Wayne had always been jealous of people who had money because he wished he had some, and Sandy told him so once again. She didn't expect him to become a businessman, but there were times that she did get tired of supporting him.

"It's not the money, dammit, it's the waste. Lennon and Yoko rode around in chauffeured Rolls Royces while people starved to death. And look at your friends out there in that little town with all that land. They have a great big lawn, some pasture for a couple of horses, and forty acres of woods. That land could be feeding people like it used to. Now it's covered by the darkness of the forest because the rich think it's pretty."

The tone of the words scared Sandy. "That soil is awfully rocky, Wayne; you can't farm it very well."

"But people did a hundred years ago. That quaint little house used to be a farmhouse that housed real working people, and those woods used to be a farm that gave them a living. Your friends seemed so proud of that. Why waste land that could be used? Why hand it over to the darkness of the forest?"

"What's the matter with the forest? We need trees; they can be lovely."

"They cut out the sun and hide the light. The forest breeds bugs and decay and disease."

"That's where you had your bad trip, wasn't it. Out in the woods in Oregon somewhere? You're not getting a flashback now, are you? Not after all these years?"

Wayne stared through the windshield at the tunnel of snow illuminated by the cold light of the headlamps. "No." He seemed to be switching his attention back to the road. The wind had died down, and enough of the heavy snow had accumulated to make the surface slippery.

The distorted voice of a disk jockey cut through the static, a strange voice that Sandy felt sure she'd heard years before. "In Enfield this is WEND, 666 on your AM dial. That's the number of the beast, folks, you come to it and it comes to you, via the miracle of Mr. Marconi and others long dead. And you're listening to the voices of the dead tonight—"

Sandy leaned forward and punched another button on the radio. There was only static.

"Turn it back. I want to hear it."

"It fits your mood tonight, doesn't it? Voices of the dead from the dead past."

"Come on, dammit. I'm driving; I can pick what I want to listen to. I need it to keep awake—you're not going to find anything else on the air out here at this hour, are you?"

"I thought you wanted to talk."

"I did, for a while." He reached over to the radio and pushed the button that brought the music back. Jim Morrison's voice was singing: "Break . . . break . . . break on through . . . to the other side." Wayne turned the volume up.

"What's the matter?" Sandy asked, but Wayne didn't seem to hear her. She forced her voice to shout, trying to make herself heard over the music. "Turn it down!" When there was no response, she did. Wayne appeared to frown at her, but it was hard to be sure. With the dashboard lights out, the only light inside the car was the reflection of the headlights from the snow, and the feeble blue glow of the high-beam indicator. While she was looking at him, Wayne switched to low beams.

"Damn snow freaks me out," he muttered. "I can't see much out there, just the snowflakes and the darkness. The trees look like claws reaching into the night. I wish I was back in California."

Sandy turned her eyes to the heavy snow. The latticework of flakes drifting to the ground, dancing in front of the windshield, drew her attention. After she strained for a while, she could focus her eyes on the road. The car seemed to be crawling, probably going only about ten miles an hour. "Do you want me to drive? I can see in this—"

"No," Wayne snapped. "You said you were tired, and I told you I'd get you there."

"What about stopping?"

"We'd freeze out here."

"Maybe in Orange or Athol. There's got to be a motel somewhere around there. You're not going to make it this way, you know."

Wayne said nothing as the song drew to its crescendo and closed. He was being drawn into the music as Sandy had seen a hundred times before. He was nodding his head to it; she couldn't see his face, but she saw his head silhouetted against the snow. Jim Croce began singing "Bad, Bad Leroy Brown."

Wayne settled down for a moment. "It's the newest one they've played all night."

"It's not that new. Croce died years ago." Sandy couldn't remember when Croce's plane had crashed; it had faded into the haze that she identified as the middle seventies. "All the disco bands picked it up and turned it into mush."

Wayne was looking out into the snow, still bobbing his head faintly to the music. "It's good music, Sandy. Croce was one of the greats. I'd like to hear him now, you know, him and the others. But so many of them are gone— Hendrix and Elvis and Lennon and Morrison and—"

"Can you see where you're going, Wayne?"

"Of course not, not in this snow."

"Then let me drive. You're too tired, too far spaced out on something. You were smoking grass before we left, weren't you?"

"I'm okay," Wayne replied without taking his eyes from the falling snow. "You couldn't do any better in this mess. I'll make it—I always have."

Sandy didn't see how Wayne could see the road through the snow. They seemed to be alone in a world of whiteness, drifting through the space defined by their headlights. She hadn't seen another car moving since they'd left Amherst, but she wasn't surprised by that. The natives knew better than to drive on a country road in a nighttime snowstorm. And even if Route 202 was a U.S. highway, it was still a country road. "I'm scared," she said.

"So am I. I see the dark out there, I see the cold. I see things lurking in the trees, waiting for us. I see snow that would trap us here and freeze us to death. I see time, I see emptiness. I've never sensed an emptiness like this before. Even when we drove across the desert, it was on an interstate highway full of trucks and cars and at night there were at least other headlights. But this . . ."

Wayne's voice drifted away as the disk jockey returned. ". . . not the Grateful Dead, this night or ever here on Enfield Radio WEND, just the ungrateful dead . . ."

"Snap out of it, please, Wayne!" Sandy tried to shout, but the car seemed to muffle the words.

". . . Janis Joplin," were the disk jockey's words, tumbling out of the speaker. "You remember how she overdosed and they found her and we were all so scared that death had come to our beautiful world. . . ."

"Wayne!"

"I can see the road now, Sandy. Don't worry, don't worry. I can steer across the trackless waste between the vampire trees."

Sandy closed her eyes, bowed her head, and made the sign of the cross on her breast. It was the first time in years, since her grandmother had dragged her to church a few days after her seventeenth birthday. She tried to recapture the strand of faith that she'd let slip from her hands years before, tried to shut her eyes and ears to the outside and to pray.

Joplin's words drifted her into awareness—"Me and Bobby McGee," a song that had always reminded Sandy of people that once had been precious to her but now were gone. When the familiar voice of the dead woman she had never met came to the words "I let him slip away," Sandy broke into sobs. She thought of losing Wayne, and before him of losing Michael and Barney and Andy. She thought of her grandmother and her uncle Bill, both alive when she'd left Massachusetts, now both dead. She thought of the 4 A.M. phone call from her mother, begging her to come back home and see her grandmother before she died and how, standing naked in the tiny apartment in the cool California morning, she had begged off, trying to avoid telling her mother or admitting to herself how shaken she was.

As her tears began to subside, the music drifted back into her awareness. It was Morrison's voice again, louder than before and badly distorted: "This is the end, my only friend, the end . . ."

She looked at Wayne. He seemed rigid, hypnotized by the snow, but his arms still moved just enough to steer the car around curves. The flakes were coming at them faster— the car seemed to be speeding up. "Wayne, turn it off!" she demanded. He said nothing; Morrison's ghost voice sang of "a desperate land."

She reached to push a button, but couldn't make the dial move. When she moved her hand toward the volume control, Wayne's hand pushed hers away.

31

Sandy shivered. "Please, Wayne, please let me turn it off. It's scaring me, it's terrifying me, it's trying to kill me."

"I need it on." His voice was flat, almost calm except for its rigidity. "I can't see where I'm going without it." He steered the car around a curve and up a hill.

Sandy couldn't make herself believe that he knew what he was doing. In front of the car, she saw only snowflakes; to the side she knew there must be trees. She crossed herself, not recognizing the motion until she'd completed it. She tried to pray, to force the music out of her awareness, to push away Morrison's dead plea: "Ride the snake, he's old and his skin is cold. . . ."

The song evoked the fears that had haunted Sandy in the lonely, desolate years a decade earlier. It made her remember her last night with Barney, of lying sleeplessly beside him with the song haunting her long after the record had ended and the turntable shut itself off, leaving her alone with the silence and the certainty that she never wanted to see Barney again.

She prayed, trying to hold herself away from tears and the music. The words reached again for her attention after the long instrumental passage ended. A phrase touched her: "It hurts to set you free, but you'll never follow me." She would follow Wayne no more; she'd stay in Massachusetts and have someone send her things back from California.

"This . . ." the refrain repeated in the last line seemed to drag on forever and ". . . is . . ." tried to seize her, although ". . . the . . ." words were deceptively soft. The last of them ". . . ennnnnd . . ." stretched on to the end of the world as she tried to flee from it.

The force of the impact threw her against the seat and shoulder belts and knocked her unconscious.

She woke as two men in hunting jackets bundled her into a blanket. One was big and paunchy, an awkward man trying to handle her gently. The other was thinner and looked about twenty years older. "Does it hurt anywhere?" the older man asked when he saw her eyes were open.

She ignored the pain in her chest. "Wayne—what about Wayne?"

"The man in the car?" he asked, then realized that he didn't have to ask. "I'm afraid—afraid he's dead, ma'am."

"He's messed up real bad—stuck in there," the younger man said as they eased her into the back seat of their big old car.

Sandy cried then, cried as the older man laid something more over her, and cried as they started the car and drove on in the night. Much later, when she got control of herself, she asked them where Enfield was.

"Nothing there anymore, ma'am," the older man replied. "They drowned it more than forty years ago; it's under the Quabbin."

"There's an Enfield in Connecticut, Dad, down by Hartford," the younger man added.

Sandy heard him, but it didn't matter anymore.

Born in Connecticut in 1947, Jeff Hecht attended schools all over the United States before getting a degree in electronic engineering from the California Institute of Technology, followed by two years of graduate study at the University of Massachusetts at Amherst. After editing a trade magazine, Laser Focus, *for seven years, he became a full time writer in 1981. Co-author of* Laser: Super Tool for the '80s, *he has now turned to fiction such as "On 202."*

They say the devil never comes to New Hampshire, not after his last argument with Daniel Webster.

FOUR

The Devil and Daniel Webster
Stephen Vincent Benét

It's a story they tell in the border country, where Massachusetts joins Vermont and New Hampshire.

Yes, Dan'l Webster's dead—or, at least, they buried him. But every time there's a thunderstorm around Marshfield, they say you can hear his rolling voice in the hollows of the sky. And they say that if you go to his grave and speak loud and clear, "Dan'l Webster—Dan'l Webster!" the ground'll begin to shiver and the trees begin to shake. And after a while you'll hear a deep voice saying, "Neighbor, how stands the Union?" Then you better answer the Union stands as she stood, rock-bottomed and copper-sheathed, one and indivisible, or he's liable to rear right out of the ground. At least, that's what I was told when I was a youngster.

You see, for a while, he was the biggest man in the country. He never got to be President, but he was the biggest man. There were thousands that trusted in him right next to God Almighty, and they told stories about him that were like the stories of patriarchs and such. They said, when he stood up to speak, stars and stripes came right out in the sky, and once he spoke against a river and made it sink into the ground. They said, when he walked the woods with his fishing rod, Killall, the trout would jump out of the streams right into his pockets, for they knew it was no use putting up a fight against him; and, when he argued a case, he could turn on the harps of the blessed and the shaking of the earth

34

underground. That was the kind of man he was, and his big farm up at Marshfield was suitable to him. The chickens he raised were all white meat down through the drumsticks, the cows were tended like children, and the big ram he called Goliath had horns with a curl like a morning-glory vine and could butt through an iron door. But Dan'l wasn't one of your gentlemen famers; he knew all the ways of the land, and he'd be up by candlelight to see that the chores got done. A man with a mouth like a mastiff, a brow like a mountain and eyes like burning anthracite—that was Dan'l Webster in his prime. And the biggest case he argued never got written down in the books, for he argued it against the devil, nip and tuck and no holds barred. And this is the way I used to hear it told.

There was a man named Jabez Stone, lived at Cross Corners, New Hampshire. He wasn't a bad man to start with, but he was an unlucky man. If he planted corn, he got borers; if he planted potatoes, he got blight. He had good-enough land, but it didn't prosper him; he had a decent wife and children, but the more children he had, the less there was to feed them. If stones cropped up in his neighbor's field, boulders boiled up in his; if he had a horse with the spavins, he'd trade it for one with the staggers and give something extra. There's some folks bound to be like that, apparently. But one day Jabez Stone got sick of the whole business.

He'd been plowing that morning and he'd just broke the plowshare on a rock that he could have sworn hadn't been there yesterday. And, as he stood looking at the plowshare, the off horse began to cough—that ropy kind of cough that means sickness and horse doctors. There were two children down with the measles, his wife was ailing, and he had a whitlow on his thumb. It was about the last straw for Jabez Stone. "I vow," he said, and he looked around him kind of desperate—"I vow it's enough to make a man want to sell his soul to the devil! And I would, too, for two cents!"

Then he felt a kind of queerness come over him at having said what he'd said; though, naturally, being a New Hampshireman, he wouldn't take it back. But, all the same, when it got to be evening and, as far as he could see, no notice had been taken, he felt relieved in his mind, for he was a

35

religious man. But notice is always taken, sooner or later, just like the Good Book says. And, sure enough, next day, about suppertime, a soft-spoken, dark-dressed stranger drove up in a handsome buggy and asked for Jabez Stone.

Well, Jabez told his family it was a lawyer, come to see him about a legacy. But he knew who it was. He didn't like the looks of the stranger, nor the way he smiled with his teeth. They were white teeth, and plentiful—some say they were filed to a point, but I wouldn't vouch for that. And he didn't like it when the dog took one look at the stranger and ran away howling, with his tail between his legs. But having passed his word, more or less, he stuck to it, and they went out behind the barn and made their bargain. Jabez Stone had to prick his finger to sign, and the stranger lent him a silver pin. The wound healed clean, but it left a little white scar.

After that, all of a sudden, things began to pick up and prosper for Jabez Stone. His cows got fat and his horses sleek, his crops were the envy of the neighborhood, and lightning might strike all over the valley, but it wouldn't strike his barn. Pretty soon, he was one of the prosperous people of the county; they asked him to stand for se-lectman, and he stood for it; there began to be talk of run-ning him for state senate. All in all, you might say the Stone family was as happy and contented as cats in a dairy. And so they were, except for Jabez Stone.

He'd been contented enough, the first few years. It's a great thing when bad luck turns; it drives most other things out of your head. True, every now and then, especially in rainy weather, the little white scar on his finger would give him a twinge. And once a year, punctual as clockwork, the stranger with the handsome buggy would come driving by. But the sixth year, the stranger lighted, and, after that, his peace was over for Jabez Stone.

The stranger came up through the lower field, switching his boots with a cane—they were handsome black boots, but Jabez Stone never liked the look of them, particularly the toes. And, after he'd passed the time of day, he said, "Well, Mr. Stone, you're a hummer! It's a very pretty prop-erty you've got here, Mr. Stone."

"Well, some might favor it and others might not," said Jabez Stone, for he was a New Hampshireman.

"Oh, no need to decry your industry!" said the stranger, very easy, showing his teeth in a smile. "After all, we know what's been done, and it's been according to contract and specifications. So when—ahem— the mortgage falls due next year, you shouldn't have any regrets."

"Speaking of that mortgage, mister," said Jabez Stone, and he looked around for help to the earth and the sky, "I'm beginning to have one or two doubts about it."

"Doubts?" said the stranger, not quite so pleasantly.

"Why, yes," said Jabez Stone. "This being the U.S.A. and me always having been a religious man." He cleared his throat and got bolder. "Yes, sir," he said, "I'm beginning to have considerable doubts as to that mortgage holding in court."

"There's courts and courts," said the stranger, clicking his teeth. "Still, we might as well have a look at the original document." And he hauled out a big black pocketbook, full of papers. "Sherwin, Slater, Stevens, Stone," he muttered. "I, Jabez Stone, for a term of seven years—Oh, it's quite in order, I think."

But Jabez Stone wasn't listening, for he saw something else flutter out of the black pocketbook. It was something that looked like a moth, but it wasn't a moth. And as Jabez Stone stared at it, it seemed to speak to him in a small sort of piping voice, terrible small and thin, but terrible human. "Neighbor Stone!" it squeaked. "Neighbor Stone! Help me! For God's sake, help me!"

But before Jabez Stone could stir hand or foot, the stranger whipped out a big bandanna handkerchief, caught the creature in it, just like a butterfly, and started tying up the ends of the bandanna.

"Sorry for the interruption," he said. "As I was saying—"

But Jabez Stone was shaking all over like a scared horse.

"That's Miser Stevens' voice!" he said, in a croak. "And you've got him in your handkerchief!"

The stranger looked a little embarrassed.

"Yes, I really should have transferred him to the collecting box," he said with a simper, "but there were some rather unusual specimens there and I didn't want them crowded. Well, well, these little contretemps will occur."

"I don't know what you mean by contertan," said Jabez Stone, "but that was Miser Stevens' voice! And he ain't dead! You can't tell me he is! He was just as spry and mean as a woodchuck, Tuesday!"

"In the midst of life—" said the stranger, kind of pious. "Listen!" Then a bell began to toll in the valley and Jabez Stone listened, with the sweat running down his face. For he knew it was tolled for Miser Stevens and that he was dead.

"These long-standing accounts," said the stranger with a sigh; "one really hates to close them. But business is business."

He still had the bandanna in his hand, and Jabez Stone felt sick as he saw the cloth struggle and flutter.

"Are they all as small as that?" he asked hoarsely.

"Small?" said the stranger. "Oh, I see what you mean. Why, they vary." He measured Jabez Stone with his eyes, and his teeth showed. "Don't worry, Mr. Stone," he said. "You'll go with a very good grade. I wouldn't trust you outside the collecting box. Now, a man like Dan'l Webster, of course—well, we'd have to build a special box for him, and even at that, I imagine the wing spread would astonish you. But, in your case, as I was saying—"

"Put that handkerchief away!" said Jabez Stone, and he began to beg and to pray. But the best he could get at the end was a three years' extension, with conditions.

But till you make a bargain like that, you've got no idea of how fast four years can run. By the last months of those years, Jabez Stone's known all over the state and there's talk of running him for governor—and it's dust and ashes in his mouth. For every day when he gets up, he thinks, "There's one more night gone," and every night when he lies down, he thinks of the black pocketbook and the soul of Miser Stevens, and it makes him sick at heart. Till, finally, he can't bear it any longer, and, in the last days of the last year, he hitches up his horse and drives off to seek Dan'l Webster. For Dan'l was born in New Hampshire, only a few miles from Cross Corners, and it's well known that he has a particular soft spot for old neighbors.

It was early in the morning when he got to Marshfield, but

Dan'l was up already, talking Latin to the farm hands and wrestling with the ram, Goliath, and trying out a new trotter and working up speeches to make against John C. Calhoun. But when he heard a New Hampshireman had come to see him, he dropped everything else he was doing, for that was Dan'l's way. He gave Jabez Stone a breakfast that five men couldn't eat, went into the living history of every man and woman in Cross Corners, and finally asked him how he could serve him.

Jabez Stone allowed that it was a kind of mortgage case.

"Well, I haven't pleaded a mortgage case in a long time, and I don't generally plead now, except before the Supreme Court," said Dan'l, "but if I can, I'll help you."

"Then I've got hope for the first time in ten years," said Jabez Stone, and told him the details.

Dan'l walked up and down as he listened, hands behind his back, now and then asking a question, now and then plunging his eyes at the floor, as if they'd bore through it like gimlets. When Jabez Stone had finished, Dan'l puffed out his cheeks and blew. Then he turned to Jabez Stone and a smile broke over his face like the sunrise over Monadnock.

"You've certainly given yourself the devil's own row to hoe, Neighbor Stone," he said, "but I'll take your case."

"You'll take it?" said Jabez Stone, hardly daring to believe.

"Yes," said Dan'l Webster. "I've got about seventy-five other things to do and the Missouri Compromise to straighten out, but I'll take your case. For if two New Hampshiremen aren't a match for the devil, we might as well give the country back to the Indians."

Then he shook Jabez Stone by the hand and said, "Did you come down here in a hurry?"

"Well, I admit I made time," said Jabez Stone.

"You'll go back faster," said Dan'l Webster, and he told 'em to hitch up Constitution and Constellation to the carriage. They were matched grays with one white forefoot, and they stepped like greased lightning.

Well, I won't describe how excited and pleased the whole Stone family was to have the great Dan'l Webster for a guest, when they finally got there. Jabez Stone had lost his hat on the way, blown off when they overtook a wind, but he didn't take much account of that. But after supper he sent the family off to bed, for he had most particular business with Mr. Webster. Mrs. Stone wanted them to sit in the front parlor, but Dan'l Webster knew front parlors and said he preferred the kitchen. So it was there they sat, waiting for the stranger, with a jug on the table between them and a bright fire on the hearth—the stranger being scheduled to show up on the stroke of midnight, according to specifications.

Well, most men wouldn't have asked for better company than Dan'l Webster and a jug. But with every tick of the clock Jabez Stone got sadder and sadder. His eyes roved round, and though he sampled the jug you could see he couldn't taste it. Finally, on the stroke of 11:30 he reached over and grabbed Dan'l Webster by the arm.

"Mr. Webster, Mr. Webster!" he said, and his voice was shaking with fear and a desperate courage. "For God's sake, Mr. Webster, harness your horses and get away from this place while you can!"

"You've brought me a long way, neighbor, to tell me you don't like my company," said Dan'l Webster, quite peaceable, pulling at the jug.

"Miserable wretch that I am!" groaned Jabez Stone. "I've brought you a devilish way, and now I see my folly. Let him take me if he wills. I don't hanker after it, I must say, but I can stand it. But you're the Union's stay and New Hampshire's pride! He mustn't get you, Mr. Webster! He mustn't get you!"

Dan'l Webster looked at the distracted man, all gray and shaking in the firelight, and laid a hand on his shoulder.

"I'm obliged to you, Neighbor Stone," he said gently. "It's kindly thought of. But there's a jug on the table and a case in hand. And I never left a jug or a case half finished in my life."

And just at that moment there was a sharp rap on the door.

"Ah," said Dan'l Webster, very coolly, "I thought your clock was a trifle slow, Neighbor Stone." He stepped to the door and opened it. "Come in!" he said.

The stranger came in—very dark and tall he looked in the firelight. He was carrying a box under his arm—a black, japanned box with little air holes in the lid. At the sight of the box, Jabez Stone gave a low cry and shrank into a corner of the room.

"Mr. Webster, I presume," said the stranger, very polite, but with his eyes glowing like a fox's deep in the woods.

"Attorney of record for Jabez Stone," said Dan'l Webster, but his eyes were glowing too. "Might I ask your name?"

"I've gone by a good many," said the stranger carelessly. "Perhaps Scratch will do for the evening. I'm often called that in these regions."

Then he sat down at the table and poured himself a drink from the jug. The liquor was cold in the jug, but it came steaming into the glass.

"And now," said the stranger, smiling and showing his teeth, "I shall call upon you, as a law-abiding citizen, to assist me in taking possession of my property."

Well, with that the argument began—and it went hot and heavy. At first, Jabez Stone had a flicker of hope, but when he saw Dan'l Webster being forced back at point after point, he just scrunched in his corner, with his eyes on that japanned box. For there wasn't any doubt as to the deed or the signature—that was the worst of it. Dan'l Webster twisted and turned and thumped his fist on the table, but he couldn't get away from that. He offered to compromise the case; the stranger wouldn't hear of it. He pointed out the property had increased in value, and state senators ought to be worth more; the stranger stuck to the letter of the law. He was a great lawyer, Dan'l Webster, but we know who's the King of Lawyers, as the Good Book tells us, and it seemed as if, for the first time, Dan'l Webster had met his match.

Finally, the stranger yawned a little. "Your spirited efforts on behalf of your client do you credit, Mr. Webster," he said, "but if you have no more arguments to adduce, I'm rather pressed for time"—and Jabez Stone shuddered.

Dan'l Webster's brow looked dark as a thundercloud.

"Pressed or not, you shall not have this man!" he thundered. "Mr. Stone is an American citizen, and no American citizen may be forced into the service of a foreign prince. We fought England for that in '12 and we'll fight all hell for it again!"

"Foreign?" said the stranger. "And who calls me a foreigner?"

"Well, I never yet heard of the dev—of your claiming American citizenship," said Dan'l Webster with surprise.

"And who with better right?" said the stranger, with one of his terrible smiles. "When the first wrong was done to the first Indian, I was there. When the first slaver put out for the Congo, I stood on her deck. Am I not in your books and stories and beliefs, from the first settlements on? Am I not spoken of, still, in every church in New England? 'Tis true the North claims me for a Southerner and the South for a Northerner, but I am neither. I am merely an honest American like yourself—and of the best descent—for, to tell the truth, Mr. Webster, though I don't like to boast of it, my name is older in this country than yours."

"Aha!" said Dan'l Webster, with the veins standing out in his forehead. "Then I stand on the Constitution! I demand a trial for my client!"

"The case is hardly one for an ordinary court," said the stranger, his eyes flickering. "And, indeed, the lateness of the hour—"

"Let it be any court you choose, so it is an American judge and an American jury!" said Dan't Webster in his pride. "Let it be the quick or the dead; I'll abide the issue!"

"You have said it," said the stranger, and pointed his finger at the door. And with that, and all of a sudden, there was a rushing of wind outside and a noise of footsteps. They came, clear and distinct, through the night. And yet, they were not like the footsteps of living men.

"In God's name, who comes by so late?" cried Jabez Stone, in an ague of fear.

"The jury Mr. Webster demands," said the stranger, sipping at his boiling glass. "You must pardon the rough appearance of one or two; they will have come a long way."

And with that the fire burned blue and the door blew open and twelve men entered, one by one.

If Jabez Stone had been sick with terror before, he was blind with terror now. For there was Walter Butler, the loyalist, who spread fire and horror through the Mohawk Valley in the times of the Revolution; and there was Simon Girty, the renegade, who saw white men burned at the stake and whooped with the Indians to see them burn. His eyes were green, like a catamount's, and the stains on his hunting shirt did not come from the blood of the deer. King Philip was there, wild and proud as he had been in life, with the great gash in his head that gave him his death wound, and cruel Governor Dale, who broke men on the wheel. There was Morton of Merry Mount, who so vexed the Plymouth Colony, with his flushed, loose, handsome face and his hate of the godly. There was Teach, the bloody pirate, with his black beard curling on his breast. The Reverend John Smeet, with his strangler's hands and his Geneva gown, walked as daintily as he had to the gallows. The red print of the rope was still around his neck, but he carried a perfumed handkerchief in one hand. One and all, they came into the room with the fires of hell still upon them, and the stranger named their names and their deeds as they came, till the tale of twelve was told. Yet the stranger had told the truth—they had all played a part in America.

"Are you satisfied with the jury, Mr. Webster?" said the stranger mockingly, when they had taken their places.

The sweat stood upon Dan'l Webster's brow, but his voice was clear.

"Quite satisfied," he said. "Though I miss General Arnold from the company."

"Benedict Arnold is engaged upon other business," said the stranger, with glower. "Ah, you asked for a justice, I believe."

He pointed his finger once more, and a tall man, soberly clad in Puritan garb, with the burning gaze of the fanatic, stalked into the room and took his judge's place.

"Justice Hathorne is a jurist of experience," said the stranger. "He presided at certain witch trials once held in Salem. There were others who repented of the business later, but not he."

"Repent of such notable wonders and undertakings?" said the stern old justice. "Nay, hang them—hang them all!" And he muttered to himself in a way that struck ice into the soul of Jabez Stone.

Then the trial began, and, as you might expect, it didn't look anyways good for the defense. And Jabez Stone didn't make much of a witness in his own behalf. He took one look at Simon Girty and screeched, and they had to put him back in his corner in a kind of swoon.

It didn't halt the trial, though; the trial went on, as trials do. Dan'l Webster had faced some hard juries and hanging judges in his time, but this was the hardest he'd ever faced, and he knew it. They sat there with a kind of glitter in their eyes, and the stranger's smooth voice went on and on. Every time he'd raise an objection, it'd be "Objection sustained," but whenever Dan'l objected, it'd be "Objection denied." Well, you couldn't expect fair play from a fellow like this Mr. Scratch.

It got to Dan'l in the end, and he began to heat, like iron in the forge. When he got up to speak he was going to flay that stranger with every trick known to the law, and the judge and jury too. He didn't care if it was contempt of court or what would happen to him for it. He didn't care any more what happened to Jabez Stone. He just got madder and madder, thinking of what he'd say. And yet, curiously enough, the more he thought about it, the less he was able to arrange his speech in his mind.

Till, finally, it was time for him to get up on his feet, and he did so, all ready to bust out with lightnings and denunciations. But before he started he looked over the judge and jury for a moment, such being his custom. And he noticed the glitter in their eyes was twice as strong as before, and they all leaned forward. Like hounds just before they get the fox, they looked, and the blue mist of evil in the room thickened as he watched them. Then he saw what he'd been about to do, and he wiped his forehead, as a man might who's just escaped falling into a pit in the dark.

For it was him they'd come for, not only Jabez Stone. He read it in the glitter of their eyes and in the way the stranger hid his mouth with one hand. And if he fought them with their own weapons, he'd fall into their power; he knew that, though he couldn't have told you how. It was his own anger and horror that burned in their eyes; and he'd have to wipe that out or the case was lost. He stood there for a moment, his black eyes burning like anthracite. And then he began to speak.

He started off in a low voice, though you could hear every word. They say he could call on the harps of the blessed when he chose. And this was just as simple and easy as a man could talk. But he didn't start out by condemning or reviling. He was talking about the things that make a country a country, and a man a man.

And he began with the simple things that everybody's known and felt—the freshness of a fine morning when you're young, and the taste of food when you're hungry, and the new day that's every day when you're a child. He took them up and he turned them in his hands. They were good things for any man. But without freedom, they sickened. And when he talked of those enslaved, and the sorrows of slavery, his voice got like a big bell. He talked of the early days of America and the men who had made those days. It wasn't a spread-eagle speech, but he made you see it. He admitted all the wrong that had ever been done. But he showed how, out of the wrong and the right, the suffering and the starvations, something new had come. And everybody had played a part in it, even the traitors.

Then he turned to Jabez Stone and showed him as he was—an ordinary man who'd had hard luck and wanted to change it. And, because he'd wanted to change it, now he was going to be punished for all eternity. And yet there was good in Jabez Stone, and he showed that good. He was hard and mean, in some ways, but he was a man. There was sadness in being a man, but it was a proud thing too. And he showed what the pride of it was till you couldn't help feeling it. Yes, even in hell, if a man was a man, you'd know it. And he wasn't pleading for any one person any more, though his voice rang like an organ. He was telling the story and the failures and the endless journey of mankind. They got tricked and trapped and bamboozled, but it was a great journey. And no demon that was ever foaled could know the inwardness of it—it took a man to do that.

The fire began to die on the hearth and the wind before morning to blow. The light was getting gray in the room when Dan'l Webster finished. And his words came back at the end to New Hampshire ground, and the one spot of land that each man loves and clings to. He painted a picture of that, and to each one of that jury he spoke of things long forgotten. For his voice could search the heart, and that was his gift and his strength. And to one, his voice was like the forest and its secrecy, and to another like the sea and the storms of the sea; and one heard the cry of his lost nation in it, and another saw a little harmless scene he hadn't remembered for years. But each saw something. And when Dan'l Webster finished he didn't know whether or not he'd saved Jabez Stone. But he knew he'd done a miracle. For the glitter was gone from the eyes of judge and jury, and, for the moment, they were men again, and knew they were men.

"The defense rests," said Dan'l Webster, and stood there like a mountain. His ears were still ringing with his speech, and he didn't hear anything else till he heard Judge Hathorne say, "The jury will retire to consider its verdict."

Walter Butler rose in his place and his face had a dark, gay pride on it.

"The jury has considered its verdict," he said, and looked the stranger full in the eye. "We find for the defendant, Jabez Stone."

With that, the smile left the stranger's face, but Walter Butler did not flinch.

"Perhaps 'tis not strictly in accordance with the evidence," he said, "but even the damned may salute the eloquence of Mr. Webster."

With that, the long crow of a rooster split the gray morning sky, and judge and jury were gone from the room like a puff of smoke and as if they had never been there. The stranger turned to Dan'l Webster, smiling wryly.

"Major Butler was always a bold man," he said. "I had not thought him quite so bold. Nevertheless, my congratulations, as between two gentlemen."

"I'll have that paper first, if you please," said Dan'l Webster, and he took it and tore it into four pieces. It was queerly warm to the touch. "And now," he said, "I'll have you!" and his hand came down like a bear trap on the stranger's arm. For he knew that once you bested anybody like Mr. Scratch in fair fight, his power on you was gone. And he could see that Mr. Scratch knew it too.

The stranger twisted and wriggled, but he couldn't get out of that grip. "Come, come, Mr. Webster," he said, smiling palely. "This sort of thing is ridic—ouch!—is ridiculous. If you're worried about the costs of the case, naturally, I'd be glad to pay—"

"And so you shall!" said Dan'l Webster, shaking him till his teeth rattled. "For you'll sit right down at that table and draw up a document, promising never to bother Jabez Stone nor his heirs or assigns nor any other New Hampshireman till doomsday! For any hades we want to raise in this state, we can raise ourselves, without assistance from strangers."

"Ouch!" said the stranger. "Ouch! Well, they never did run very big to the barrel, but—ouch!—I agree!"

So he sat down and drew up the document. But Dan'l Webster kept his hand on his coat collar all the time.

"And, now, may I go?" said the stranger, quiet humble, when Dan'l'd seen the document was in proper and legal form.

"Go?" said Dan'l, giving him another shake. "I'm still trying to figure out what I'll do with you. For you've settled the costs of the case, but you haven't settled with me. I think I'll take you back to Marshfield," he said, kind of reflective. "I've got a ram there named Goliath that can butt through an iron door. I'd kind of like to turn you loose in his field and see what he'd do."

Well, with that the stranger began to beg and to plead. And he begged and he pled so humble that finally Dan'l, who was naturally kindhearted, agreed to let him go. The stranger seemed terrible grateful for that and said, just to show they were friends, he'd tell Dan'l's fortune before leaving. So Dan'l agreed to that, though he didn't take much stock in fortune-tellers ordinarily. But, naturally, the stranger was a little different.

Well, he pried and he peered at the lines in Dan'l's hands. And he told him one thing and another that was quite remarkable. But they were all in the past.

"Yes, all that's true, and it happened," said Dan'l Webster. "But what's to come in the future?"

The stranger grinned, kind of happily, and shook his head.

"The future's not as you think it," he said. "It's dark. You have a great ambition, Mr. Webster."

"I have," said Dan'l firmly, for everybody knew he wanted to be President.

"It seems almost within your grasp," said the stranger,

"but you will not attain it. Lesser men will be made president and you will be passed over."

"And, if I am, I'll still be Daniel Webster," said Dan'l. "Say on."

"And have two strong sons," said the stranger, shaking his head. "You look to found a line. But each will die in war and neither reach greatness."

"Live or die, they are still my sons," said Dan'l Webster. "Say on."

"You have made great speeches," said the stranger. "You will make more."

"Ah," said Dan'l Webster.

"But the last great speech you make will turn many of your own against you," said the stranger. "They will call you Ichabod; they will call you by other names. Even in New England, some will say you have turned your coat and sold your country, and their voices will be loud against you till you die."

"So it is an honest speech, it does not matter what men say," said Dan'l Webster. Then he looked at the stranger and their glances locked.

"One question," he said. "I have fought for the Union all my life. Will I see that fight won against those who would tear it apart?"

"Not while you live," said the stranger, grimly, "but it will be won. And after you are dead, there are thousands who will fight for your cause, because of words that you spoke."

"Why, then, you long-barreled, slab-sided, lantern-jawed, fortune-telling note shaver!" said Dan'l Webster, with a great roar of laughter, "be off with you to your own place before I put my mark on you! For, by the thirteen original colonies, I'd go to the Pit itself to save the Union!"

And with that he drew back his foot for a kick that would have stunned a horse. It was only the tip of his shoe that caught the stranger, but he went flying out the door with his collecting box under his arm.

"And now," said Dan'l Webster, seeing Jabez Stone beginning to rouse from his swoon, "let's see what's left in the jug, for it's dry work talking all night. I hope there's pie for breakfast, Neighbor Stone."

But they say that whenever the devil comes near Marshfield, even now, he gives it a wide berth. And he hasn't been seen in the state of New Hampshire from that day to this. I'm not talking about Massachusetts or Vermont.

Stephen Vincent Benét was born in 1898 in Pennsylvania, and his first book was published when he was only seventeen. Educated at Yale, Benét won a Guggenheim Fellowship grant in 1926, and began work on John Brown's Body, *which won the Pulitzer Prize in 1929. He wrote a series of short stories featuring legendary Americans in larger-than-life roles, including "The Devil and Daniel Webster." Benét's last works included the script for President Franklin Roosevelt's 1942 Flag Day broadcast and radio dramas supporting the American effort in World War II. He died in 1943.*

Everyone knows cats have nine lives, but what if each one is a little bigger and meaner than the one before?

FIVE

Emmett
Dahlov Ipcar

Some of the things that happen in this world can be so crazy that you hate even to think about them. That's the way I feel about this business I've just been through with Artie. I'm just an ordinary guy with a wife and three kids and a nice quiet desk job, and I'm the last person in the world you'd expect to get mixed up in anything really weird.

But there I was in as deep as all hell, right up to my ears— and all I'd wanted was a nice quiet week of hunting in the Maine woods, same as I've had every year since I went to work for Eastern Bio Supplies. You see, I'm willing to stick around in August, when everyone else wants out of the city, so they give me this extra week in November or whenever the deer season opens up there in Sagadahoc County. Artie had this little old rundown farm way off in the woods, and he throws me a standing invitation. So every November that's where I'd head for. I just liked to get in a week away from the wife and kids, beating the brush, and boozing a little, and yacking with my old pal. Usually I'd come back with a whitetail tied to my fender—the Great Maine Hunter bit—playing it to the hilt for the kids. But it's not really the Call of the Wild with me, not really the Old Blood Lust and all that, I just like the chance to get out of the city and tramp around in the woods where it's nice and peaceful and smells good.

Artie always gave me a big welcome. I'd tell him all the off-color stories I'd picked up during the year, and he'd come up with a few good ones he'd collected, mostly from the vet who doctored his cows; because, believe it or not,

50

Artie really farmed. He had about twelve of these cows and a few hens and this little ol' beagle called Lady Anne, and he lived there in his old house by himself as happy as a clam at high water. I won't swear he lived a virtuous life. He boozed some, and he entertained lady friends; but he never let any of them move in on him. He'd always been a queer egg, sort of an odd-ball, a real hermit type. Didn't want to get tied down to a woman's apron strings, he said; though he sure was tied to those cows tails, and that's a helluva lot worse. He couldn't go anywhere, even for a day. He always had to be back to milk those four-legged bosses of his— now I know why they call all cows "boss."

But old Artie, he thrived on the life; always looked healthy as an ox, made me feel like I was pale and flabby and going to pot sitting at a desk, though I jog eight blocks to work every morning. I guess it's a good thing I get that much exercise or a week in the woods would kill me. Sometimes I envied Artie; sometimes I thought he was nuts—the way he lived. But he had a good thing going for him there. Not that those twelve cows brought in much income, but they gave Artie something to write about. He wrote a lot of articles for magazines on "How to Be Happy with a Manure Pile and a Fly Swatter" and stuff like that, and it sold like hot cakes. So it seems he was doing okay. He sure always seemed brimming over with health and good spirits—that is until this November.

We'd been bosom pals ever since we were kids. We'd both been sent to this Manumassett School in New Jersey, a progressive-type boarding school. They had this beat-up farm set up—lots of lambkins sporting on the green, cocks treading hens, and cows producing milk and calves and manure like mad. The idea was to take us city kids and introduce us to Nature, elevate our minds by rubbing our noses in the dirt, teach us about the flowers and the bees so we wouldn't get stung, and all that hokum.

Most of it went over with me like a ton of lead, but Artie just ate it up, especially the farm bit. He was the kind of kid who'd follow around behind a cow and admire the beautiful plops she made. He used to tell me all kinds of weird stuff about what the animals were thinking, how they felt about us humans and all. He told me once when he was about

51

nine that everything had a soul and feelings, even trees and vegetables. He claimed it hurt a tree to get chopped down, and that the sap that flowed out of it was just like tears. He had quite an imagination, that kid. I didn't put much stock in the crying vegetables, but sometimes it made kitchen duty a lot pleasanter if I just *pretended* that the carrots and potatoes were suffering as much as I was suffering at having to peel them. Because we all had to pitch in and work as well as keep up on our studies; that was part of the big deal.

But some of the Nature gimmick I really liked, and that was the times we took to the woods on biology walks, collecting specimens. There was this real mucky swamp nearby, where we used to go wading around, coming home with jars full of salamanders and centipedes as long as your arm, and snakes and tree toads and the worst cases of poison ivy on record. I guess that's where I learned to like tramping around in the woods, same as Artie got the rage to go live on a farm for the rest of his life. I know some of that stuff was supposed to rub off on us kids, but I kind of doubt if they expected us to apply it as literally as Artie did. I think they expected us to *sublimate our experience,* like me sitting here writing out orders for frogs in formaldehyde.

Artie and I roomed together for all of six years, and we got so damn close, we could just about read one another's minds. But the most important thing that happened to us there, I never even thought was important at all—until this business came up.

You see, there was this one teacher, Old Hoyle, who used to entertain us with stories on Friday nights. He'd hold a real session around the big fireplace in the main hall. All the lights would be out, just the fire flickering away, and he'd usually tell these real spooky ghost stories. We really ate it up, though sometimes he just about scared the pants off us. I never forgot one night when he got going on a series of tales about cats. One of them was Edgar Allan Poe's story "The Black Cat"—that one where the cat gets walled up in the cellar with the corpse and wails like crazy. That story really gave me the willies, and Artie got the willies worse than I did. He was so shook up he wouldn't let me turn out the light in our room that night. And for a whole month at least, he made me keep the light burning, though I'd got over the effects long before that.

We were just little kids about ten; but while I got over it, like I said—Artie never did get over it. He never went back to listen to any more storytelling—and he developed this real thing about cats. He never could stand to have a cat near him again. When he got older he told people he was allergic to them, but I knew better; I knew he was plain scared to death of them. I admit that black-cat story got me too, but it didn't make me hate cats. It just made me avoid reading any more Poe for about ten years.

After he grew up, Artie bummed around a while. He never could stick at any city job for long. Finally he bought this little farm in Maine. And then the guy was happy, just living there with his cows and his chickens and his beagle— and *no cats*. I guess he encouraged that beagle to be a cat-killer, because no stray cats ever moved in on him, that is—I never heard of any—before this November when I showed up for the opening of deer season.

The first thing that struck me as I got out of my car was how lousy Artie looked. He really looked sick, sort of nervous and haggard and run-down, his hands shaking and his eyes kind of haunted-looking. I really felt worried about him, but he swore he was in the best of health. He seemed awful glad to see me. We broke open a bottle of the bourbon I'd brought, and I told him a couple of my best stories that I'd been saving, and he seemed to cheer up.

But at four in the afternoon he got up to go milk his cows. This struck me as peculiar; because always, ever since I could remember, he'd milked the cows after supper— sometimes as late as ten or eleven at night. That way he didn't have to get up early to milk them again in the morning. That's the kind of farmer he was—casual.

"What's the idea?" I asked. "We going somewhere tonight or something?"

"No," he said. "No. I'm not going anywhere. *Not at night!*" He said this with such emphasis that it took me kind of aback. "I've just started milking the cows early lately, that's all," he said, sort of irritable. "I've reformed."

I didn't quite buy it, but anyhow, he had the cows all

53

milked by five-thirty. We ate supper and sat around and jawed and drank more bourbon, and then around nine o'clock I decided I'd turn in. I wanted to get an early start on the opening day of the season.

I'd left my gear in the car, so I went out to get it. I was standing alongside the car, just getting out the rifle and the shells, when I heard this peculiar noise, sort of a long hiss with a snarl in it. It seemed to come from the darkness not too far off, so I reached in and flicked on the headlights. And there in the lights was the biggest damn Canada lynx—a great big white long-legged bastard—sort of snarling at me. He seemed blinded by the headlights and just stood there for a full minute, and I stood there too, just as stupified. Then, suddenly I realized I had the rifle in my hand, and I slammed back the bolt and rammed in a shell. The cat seemed to recover himself too. He turned and leapt off into the darkness; but I could see him plain, a white shape bounding away, and I blasted him. He tumbled head over heels and lay there a while kicking.

Boy! I had never felt so excited in my life! I yelled for Artie, but he didn't come out. So I walked up on the cat cautiously, and when I was sure he was really dead, I dragged him back into the headlights and laid him out to admire. He was sure a helluva big one, all white and sort of freckled brownish all over—with long, tufted ears. As handsome an animal as I ever saw.

I ran back in the house, all excited. Artie was sitting there, his head in his hands. He looked up at me real wild-eyed. "You didn't kill him?" he asked. "Oh, God, you didn't, did you?"

"If you mean that lynx, I sure as hell did. Come look at him!" I tried to drag him up on his feet, but he was sort of shaking all over and moaning something about cats and a bigger one coming—none of which made any sense to me.

"Was that what had you so worried?" I asked, kind of beginning to catch on. "You mean that cat's been hanging around, and you've been scared to go out at night?" Hell, I didn't blame him, for a guy that was scared of cats this one was just the ticket. But what baffled me was why he seemed so upset that I had shot the damn thing. You'd think he'd be tickled pink.

But no, he kept moaning, "You shouldn't have shot him. You shouldn't have killed him." Sometimes he'd say something like, "I can't stay here. I've got to get away before the next one comes—" and he'd start shaking like a leaf again.

I got some more bourbon into him and calmed him down some, and he began to make sense after a fashion. Finally he told me the whole story about what was bothering him. It came out sort of bit by bit, but it seemed it had all started about a month before.

He'd been delivering milk to this house on his route, when this little boy had come out holding a little fuzzy white kitten. He shoved it right in Artie's face and said, "This is my kitten. His name is Emmett."

Well, Artie had been upset as hell and yelled at the kid to get the damn thing away from him, and the kid had cried, and he'd had to apologize to the kid's mother, and all that had really gotten him stirred up. Then just as he was ready to drive off, there was the damn kitten sitting right in the driveway. He said he could have blown his horn or waited until it ran off, but he was sore and he hated cats anyhow. So he just stepped on the gas and ran the kitten over, squashed it flat. He didn't even feel guilty doing it, he said. But the kid screamed and carried on, and he had to apologize some more. He said he remembered the little kid yelling at him, "You're a murderer! You murdered Emmett!" That had bothered him, because he may have hated cats, but he kind of liked kids.

Anyhow, that was the beginning. The next thing that happened was a small gray kitten showed up in his barn a few days later, and he didn't hesitate to bait it with milk and poison it. Then about three days after that another kitten appeared, a half-grown one. This one was more wary, but Artie laid for it and got it with his shotgun. Then another cat turned up. He heard this commotion among his hens, and there was this yellow cat running off with a half-grown chick in its mouth. He sicked the beagle on it, and the dog caught up with it halfway to the woods and broke its back.

That was four cats down, but it seems there were more to come. Artie had never been so plagued with cats before, but he didn't really put two and two together yet. He was beginning to get the feeling though, and he wasn't too surprised when a big black-and-white tom cat started hanging around his hen yard. This one was big enough to have a real scrap with the beagle and come out alive. But Artie and his shotgun caught up with him too.

There was about a week, Artie said, when everything seemed to be back to normal. And then one night he put Lady Anne out before he went to bed, and he heard this terrific row out in the yard, the dog yelping like mad and howling, and a snarling and spitting like all the cats of hell. He got out there with his shotgun as fast as he could, and there was this big brown bobcat tangling with old Lady Anne and getting much the best of it. Artie let him have it with both barrels. He killed the bobcat all right; but he wounded the beagle, who was pretty torn up anyhow, and she died at the vet's that night.

Artie was pretty shook up. He felt bad at losing his dog, and he was just beginning to think the thing through— about all those cats coming, one after the other, and each one bigger than the last. The real clincher was when he got back from the vet's that same night. As he pulled up in front of his house, there, sitting by the side of the road in the full glare of the headlights, was this big white Canada lynx—the same one I had killed.

That had really got through to him. He said he sat in his car all night with that animal prowling around in the darkness, letting out earsplitting yells. He didn't dare leave the car until morning when the big cat had gone. That had been two weeks ago, he told me, and that damn lynx had hung around all the time. He didn't dare step out of his door at night. It had raided his hen house and cleaned out all his hens, and he didn't dare let his cows out of the barn. Even in the daytime he walked around looking over his shoulder and getting back under cover as fast as he could.

"But why in hell didn't you try to shoot it?" I asked.

He looked at me pretty funny. "Don't you get it?" he asked. "Don't you understand? That damn cat has nine lives. There's always a bigger cat comes back! I didn't *want* to kill the lynx. I was scared to death of what would show up next. But now you've gone and done it. I've got to get out of here, that's all. I've got to get away—far away—before the next *bigger* cat comes. It may be out there now," he said, shivering as he stared at the black night outside the window.

I tried to reason with him. I thought it all sounded pretty damn silly. I told him it was probably just a coincidence, the lynx following the bobcat like that. "Maybe there's some condition up in the North woods," I told hm. "Something that's making the big cats move down this way." But that wasn't exactly the right thing to say.

"Oh, there's a *condition,* all right," he said; and he started giggling hysterically, sort of choking and shivering all over. It really got me to see him in such a state.

"Look," I said, as reasonably as I could. "There just isn't any bigger cat that can come now. You know damn well there isn't anything bigger than a Canada lynx around here. You know that!"

"It's got to come," he said. "It's got to come. I've counted them all up; there were only seven—there are still two more lives—still two more bigger cats."

"Oh for chrissake!" I said. I was getting kind of fed up with all the argument. "What you need is a real rest. Maybe you ought to see a doctor, get away from this place. You've been alone here too damn much."

"You bet your sweet life I'm getting away," he said. "The first thing in the morning!"

"Well, let's get some sleep," I said, "so we can get an early start."

An early start deer hunting, I meant. I wasn't going along with any of this midnight raving. So he turned in. And so did I, but first I went out and hung my big lynx up in the shed. It was the biggest and handsomest trophy I'd ever shot, and I wasn't going to let it get messed up no matter how nuts Artie was on the subject of cats.

I set the alarm for five to give me plenty of time to get dressed and out in the woods before sunup. But around 3:00 A.M. I woke up and remembered something I'd completely forgotten—one of those spooky cat tales that Old Hoyle had told us kids the night Artie got so bugged on the subject of cats. Before this I'd always thought it was that tale of Poe's that had got to him, same as it got me; but now I remembered another tale Hoyle had told that same night.

As a matter of fact, it wasn't much of a story. It was kind of a foolish thing without even much point. But, of course, Hoyle was a darn good storyteller, and to even a half-baked yarn, he'd given a lot of atmosphere and built up the suspense. As near as I can remember the story went something like this:

There was this young fellow walking alone through the hills at night, and it gets real dark, and a storm comes up, blowing a gale, and the boy starts looking for some shelter. Up on a high hill he sees this big old house, all dark and deserted-looking. He goes up there and knocks on the door, and nobody answers. But the door isn't locked, so he goes inside, and here is this big spooky old mansion, all full of cobwebs and stuff, and one big room with a huge fireplace in it. He's cold and wet, so he gathers some wood together and builds himself a fire. He's sitting there warming up and enjoying the blaze, when he hears a door creak on its hinges, and in walks this black cat. It walks up to the fire and sits down and looks at him. Then it yawns and sort of blinks its eyes and licks its chops, and it says, "Well, I'll just wait 'til Emmett comes."

He gets up and he says to the cat, "Good evening. I hope you don't mind me warming myself a little here by the fire."

But the cat just looks at him poisonous-like and sits there watching him. The boy sits down again and is sort of dozing off, when he hears the door creak again, and another bigger black cat walks in and sits down alongside the first one. And it too yawns and kind of licks its chops hungry-like, and it says, "Well, I'll just wait 'til Emmett comes."

Then one cat after another comes in and sits down alongside the others, and each one is bigger and blacker than the one before. And each one says in the same kind of ominous way, "Well, I'll just wait 'til Emmett comes."

Finally, a cat walks in, and even sitting down, it's all of six feet tall. It just sits there looking down at him with big green ferocious eyes, with a hungry look in them; and when that cat yawns at him, it's like looking into the mouth of a cave, and it, too, says, "Well, I'll just wait 'til Emmett comes."

But at this, the boy gets up, and he bows with great dignity, and he says to all the cats lined up there watching him, "When Emmett comes, will you all please tell him that I done set, and I done rested myself, and I done left!" And he grabs his hat and lights out of there at a dead run.

Well, that's all there was to the story, and you can see it was pretty damn silly, not even real spooky. Heck, you'd think whoever made it up could've come up with a real spooky name instead of something as common-sounding as "Emmett."

But I figured, lying there half awake, that it was that little kid calling his kitten "Emmett" that had started poor old Artie off on this whole crazy bat. I figured I'd tell him in the morning, show him what had made him flip, and maybe he'd see there was nothing supernatural about it all. I was determined I was going to get in a week of deer hunting or else. So I turned over and went to sleep.

I slept so sound that I never heard the alarm; what woke me up was a whole barrage of rifle fire that sounded like it was right under my window. I jumped out of bed with the daylights scared out of me. The first thing that crossed my mind was that Artie had really gone berserk and was starting the day with some kind of crazy mayhem. But when I barged out into the hall in my pajamas, there was Artie coming out of his room looking as startled as I was.

"They've got their damn nerve," he said right off. It's not even sunup. If they've shot any of *my* deer on *my* place, I'll have the game warden on the whole lot of them!"

I was relieved, I'll tell you. He sounded like his old self. We looked out all the windows, but the shots must have come from the nearby woods, because no hunters were in sight. We neither of us mentioned cats, but got dressed and were just heating up some coffee, when there comes this knock at the door, and these two hunters are standing there all excited.

"Can we use your phone?" one of them asks. "You guys won't believe it, but we just shot the biggest damn mountain lion—right out here in your woods!"

And then Artie really went all to pieces. He started screaming at them, and at me, and practically frothing at the mouth.

I rushed those two guys outside as fast as I could. They must have thought he was nuts, and I'm not sure he wasn't.

But anyway, I went with these two guys, and they showed

me this cat they had killed. It was a mountain lion all right, big and gray with a black tip on his tail, and these two sad black stripes running down his muzzle. There'd always been rumors of mountain lions in Maine; but it was like UFOs, only nuts believed in them. Even standing there, looking down at that big cat, I didn't believe it.

"Listen," I said to those two guys, "I don't care what you do with this cat—take him off and get your pictures in the paper, or bury him right here, but for chrissake get him out of sight, and don't bring him around where my friend is!"

They really thought I was crazy. They tried to argue with me. Their car was parked four miles down the road, they said; all they wanted was to phone and have someone pick them up. They tried to persuade me to drive them down to their car, but I was in a hurry to get back to Artie.

"You get that cat out of here, if you have to drag it all the way!"

"Have a heart, Mac," they begged. "It must weigh three hundred pounds. We had a helluva time lugging it this far."

I didn't waste any more time with them; I just beat it back to the house. I found Artie busy packing, tearing open drawers and grabbing stuff and tossing it in suitcases.

He looked up real wild-eyed when I came in. "Don't try to talk me out of leaving!" he said. "I'm not waiting for any bigger cats!"

"Oh," I said. "You remember that story too."

"What story?" he said and went on throwing stuff around.

But I didn't think it would do any good to go over all that business about the story, not now. I made one last attempt. "You can't just walk out like this, Artie. What about your cows?"

"To hell with the cows," he said. Then he picked up the phone.

He really got pretty efficient there for a while. First he phoned a cattle dealer. "Come pick up the whole herd," he said. "Today. It's got to be today. Sixteen head, counting calves. No, I haven't got time to tell you about them! I'm getting out of here right now. I haven't fed or milked them this morning, so you better get down here today. You can send me a check, whatever the market price is. I'm not going to argue."

He hung up and phoned a real estate agent. "I want to sell my place," he said. "Sell or rent, I don't care. Yeh, lock, stock, and barrel, the works. I'll mail you the keys." That was that.

He phoned the power company and the phone company. Then he went back to packing, gathering up papers and stuff. He may have left something undone, but I don't know what. He even had me down in the cellar with a pipe wrench, draining the water system. It was the fastest house-closing I ever saw. Then we piled all our bags into my car—I wasn't trusting him to drive his own—and we got off, well inside of an hour.

We were tooling down the road, and damned if we didn't pass those two guys, sweating and staggering along, carrying that big lion slung on a pole between them. Here I'd wanted to keep Artie from seeing that cat, but it was too late now. He stared at it, his eyes bugging out, as we sailed by. And those two guys stared back, all grins until they saw who it was, then they looked like they really hated our guts.

Artie started shaking like a leaf. "You see the size of that thing?" he asked me in this queer dead voice. He turned and looked at me, just about as hateful as those two hunters. "You're the guy said there wasn't any bigger cat than that lynx!" He sucked in his breath, and I could hear his teeth chattering. The tears started running down his cheeks.

"Take it easy," I said. "Take it easy, Artie. We're getting out of here. You'll be all right." I went on talking to him like you talk to a kid that's had a nightmare, and after a while, he began to calm down again. I sure felt sorry for him, but I wasn't feeling any too good about it all myself. Things had been happening too fast. I'd even forgotten all about my own trophy I'd left hanging in the shed, but somehow, it didn't seem as wonderful as it had—I wished I'd never shot the damn thing.

We went along okay for about three hours, and I thought Artie was starting to relax at last. Then just outside Boston on the by-pass this cat dashes across the road in front of us.

It was just an ordinary cat. Hell, it wasn't even *black*—

and we missed it by a mile. But right away Artie goes all to pieces again. I mean he threw a real fit: he moaned and thrashed around, and spit ran out of his mouth, and he started breathing in this ghastly kind of way, and scared the living daylights out of me.

I pulled up alongside the road and tried to get some bourbon down him—he looked as gray as a corpse—but he just seemed to get more excited when I stopped the car. "Keep going," he managed to gasp. "Just keep going! Please—please keep going!"

So then I figured he was more than I could handle, and I decided to get him to a doctor as fast as I could. I left the turnpike at the next exit and stopped at the first house I came to. By then Artie had passed out on me.

"Where's the nearest doctor?" I asked this dame.

"Well," she says, real slow, and I could have booted her, "the *nearest* doctor is Dr. Vorbrichten, but he's retired."

"I don't want no doctors of divinity or doctors of philosophy," I said. "If he's a medical doctor just tell me where he is."

"Oh, he's a *medical* doctor. He lives about three miles down the road. But he doesn't *practice*. He's *retired*."

"I don't care how retired he is," I said, feeling real desperate. "This is an emergency!"

I finally got the directions out of her and went on down that road like a bat out of hell, with old Artie all slumped over and passed out beside me.

I found the house and ran up the steps and pounded on the door. This old lady answers it.

"I've got an awful sick friend out in the car," I tell her. "Please, I've got to have the doctor look at him. It's a matter of life or death!" Boy, was I right!

"Come in," she says. "The doctor is in his study. I'll ask him."

Well, she sounded so doubtful that as soon as she opened this study door, I barged right on in determined to convince this guy to get out there and help Artie. I stopped dead in my tracks.

There, standing in the middle of the Persian rug, was the biggest damn African lion I'd ever seen!

I dropped. I dropped like I was sandbagged, keeled right over, passed out cold.

When I came to, I was on this couch; and the doctor, a red-faced, white-haired old guy, was waving smelling salts under my nose and feeling my pulse and all.

"The lion!" I gasped. I tried to sit up. He pushed me back down.

"The lion is nothing to be afraid of, young man," he said. "It's an old, old pet, as gentle as a lamb. There's nothing to be afraid of."

And the damn lion was still there, sitting on his haunches now, looking at me with these mild, gold-colored eyes, very sad-like. But the end of his tail with that big black tassel on it kept sort of twitching, and then he opened his mouth and yawned—and brother!—you never saw such teeth. You could have made a powder horn out of any one of them.

I kind of grabbed onto the doctor and begged him please to take care of Artie out in the car. "But don't let him see that lion!" I almost screamed this. "For chrissake, Doc, I don't care how tame he is. Just don't let Artie see him!"

"Please calm yourself," the doctor said, like I was being unreasonable. "I will put the lion away in his den. You understand, I don't practice medicine any more, otherwise, I would not have such a pet. But there is really nothing, absolutely nothing, to fear."

"Just don't let my friend see him!" I begged, still clutching at his arm.

He managed to pry my fingers loose; and then, holding that lion by a hunk of his shaggy mane, he led him out of the room.

He was back in a few seconds with a pill and a glass of water, which he made me swallow. "That will calm you down," he said. "I'm sorry to have to tell you this, but your friend was beyond my help. I'm afraid he died of heart failure. Of course, it will be just as well to have him examined thoroughly—I have already phoned the hospital—but I'm sure you will find my diagnosis is correct."

"That lion!" I cried sitting up. "He saw that damn lion!"

"No," said the doctor. "No, that is impossible. It was not

the lion. I'm afraid he was dead *before* you ever reached my house."

"You mean he died *without* seeing the lion?" I couldn't believe it.

"Please," the doctor protested. "Why do you keep concerning yourself about the lion? I keep telling you: he is a family pet, as gentle as a kitten—Old Emmett wouldn't hurt a fly."

I wasn't so sure about that. There had been a kind of look in those dreamy gold eyes, and I didn't like that yawn—it was kind of a warning.

But the thing that really struck me then—the thing that really got me—was that like the guy in the story—Artie had gone *without waiting until Emmett came.*

Of course, I feel bad about Artie, but otherwise I'm not too sure how I feel about the whole crazy business. I kept thinking about all those cats until I began to get almost as psyched out as Artie. Finally, a couple of days after I got back, I phoned this Curator of Mammals up at the Museum of Natural History, and I asked him if there'd ever been any real proof that there were mountain lions in Maine. He said yes there had been, which made me feel a little better. But I didn't much like the evidence he cited. He said that as a matter of fact just ten days before, two men in southwest Maine had shot a big two hundred and twenty pound male lion *felis concolor.*

As far as I'm concerned that doesn't prove a damn thing!

Author and self-taught illustrator of children's books, Dahlov Ipcar was born in Vermont in 1917. Her parents gave her no training, hoping to keep her style free and fresh. She had the first of many one-woman shows in 1939 at the Museum of Modern Arts. Later shows were at the Cocoran Gallery and the Carnegie Institute. She specializes in children's books, mostly self-illustrated, such as The Marvelous Merry-Go-Round. *She also writes adult fiction for such magazines as* Argosy *and* Yankee, *and adult fantasy novels like* A Dark Wind Blowing.

Lorilla had disappeared years ago. So who was the little girl Connie saw in the barn?

SIX

The Little Silver Heart
Josephine Daskam Bacon

The trouble is that ever since it happened Connie hasn't been able to remember so well about the strange things at Aunt Betsy's. It all seems to slip away from her, and more and more all the time. It is a very good thing she told Ben and me about it as soon as she got here, because now she will even ask Ben questions, like, "What was it I said when they asked me whether she talked to me?" or, "Where was I sitting when I saw her?"

The reason why Connie went out to Aunt Betsy's was because she had too many dreams at night and recited poetry all the time. It was the doctor himself that sent her there. She used to be his nurse, and he used to spend the summer with her when he was a little boy. It only took an hour on the train and then a long drive, but when you got there it was 'way back in the country.

Aunt Betsy was quite old, and her niece Mrs. Annie took care of her. There was another niece, Mrs. Edward, that took care of Gran'ma Biggs, down in the cottage, and there was Ann Ellen, that was the maid. That is, she was the maid in one way, because she did the washing and other things, but she ate at the table with them and she called Mrs. Annie, "Annie." She had a bad temper, but she sang nice songs, and when she wasn't busy she told Connie stories of the Indian massacres.

You might think it would be lonely there, with nobody to play with, but for a long time, almost a week, Connie didn't think so. To begin with, it was a very interesting house indeed. There was a bookcase in the sitting room with all kinds of queer books in it; there was a music-box, square, that played four tunes, with a looking glass in it; and a big tall screen made of white cloth like sheets and pillowcases. This cloth was entirely covered up with pictures, plain and colored, and little bits of poetry and jokes and photographs and colored birds of all kinds, pasted on to exactly fit each other, so that not a speck of cloth showed except where some had been torn off. It was made by Dr. Welles and his brothers when they were boys, and Connie spent hours reading it: both sides were covered.

There were some queer-looking photographs in there, and a melodeon that Connie used to go in and play on whenever she got the chance, but that wasn't often, because they made her stay outdoors all the time. She was sorry for that, because the melodeon sounded so sad and loud, and it made her think about things long ago that she had nearly forgotten, she said.

She used to hear about Gran'ma Biggs, but for some time she didn't see her, because, though she often went down to the cottage on errands, Mrs. Edward was always in the kitchen, and there didn't seem to be anybody about but Mr. Biggs, her husband, and he never said a word. For two months that she was there Connie never heard him open his mouth but once, and then he only said two words.

Well, one day when Connie went down to get some pickled pears, Mrs. Edward wasn't in the kitchen, and Connie went through into the next room, and it was a bedroom, strange to say. In it was a big high bed with long ruffles like skirts around the bottom, and a great big bureau with glass knobs, and Connie said she didn't believe the windows had been opened for a year. There was a little thin old woman in the bed in a queer white nightcap, just as in old-fashioned pictures. She was very old indeed, with only a few teeth, and she was brown and wrinkled and had very bright eyes. She was staring straight at Connie, so Connie felt she ought to say something, and she said: "How do you do? I hope you're feeling better, Gran'ma Biggs," for she knew who it must be.

"Why," said Gran'ma Biggs, "if it ain't little Lorilla! How air ye, Lorilla, child? I ain't seen ye for weeks. Why ain't ye been down?"

"I'm Constantia Van Cott," said Connie, "and you've never met me before, but I'm glad to know you." Con is always very polite.

Then Gran'ma Biggs began to laugh, such a queer laugh—like a squeaky door, Connie told us.

"Allus up to your monkey tricks," she said. "I never see such a child for games. Seem's if you had to play sump'n different every time you come. Well, come an' shake hands with old gran'ma, anyway."

So Connie went up to the bed, and she says that unless a parrot ever climbed up on your fingers you never will know what it felt like to shake hands with Gran'ma Biggs.

"Ain't you brought Spot?" said gran'ma. "I thought you allers brought her. Didn't I hear her bark?"

"That's old Joe that came up with me," Connie told her. "He has a good many spots, but that's not his name."

Just then Mrs. Edward came running in, all out of breath.

"What are you doing in here?" she asked Connie, quite crossly, and then she said to Gran'ma Biggs, "Mother, I hope you haven't been talking any nonsense."

"Well, I guess not," said gran'ma. "I'm too glad to see Lorilla to talk nonsense. Why ain't you let her down before? Here I've been a-beggin' an' a-prayin' for her, an' you puttin' me off for weeks—or months, for aught I know. But the dear child's come fin'lly to see her gran'ma, all by herself, ain't you, lovely?"

"This ain't Lorilla, Mother; it's the little girl Fred sent down—don't you remember I told you?" said Mrs. Edward, very quick and shaking her head at Gran'ma Biggs.

"An' Spot, too—I ain't seen old Spotty for a long time," gran'ma went on.

Mrs. Edward took hold of Connie's arm and just dragged her out of the room.

"That's not Spot, Mother; you remember when she died; 'twas ten years ago, an' the pup's thirteen now. You remember little Joe that upset the milk, don't you?" she asked gran'ma, and she tried to shut the door. But Gran'ma Biggs sat right up in bed and shook her fist at her; and Connie said it was dreadful to see her, with her arm all brown and thin and her old hooked nose.

"Then you bring me Lorilla right off," she called out,

"and no shenannegin about it! I'll speak to Edward tonight, mind you that."

But by that time the door was shut, and Mrs. Edward walked home with Connie.

"You mustn't mind Mother," she told her; "her mind sort o' wanders; you see she's 'most ninety years old. Spot's been dead these ten years."

"And Lorilla," says Connie. "Is she dead, too?"

"I don't see how you ever got in there," said Mrs. Edward. "It beats all how things will go wrong some days. Sick people are a great care."

You see she never answered Connie's question at all. As soon as they got back she sent Connie out to play, and then she called Mrs. Annie and Aunt Betsy, and Connie knew perfectly well that she was telling them about it, from the way they looked out of the window at her.

Well, just about then Connie began to get lonely. She thought how all the girls at Springfield had somebody to play with, and there she was with only an old spotted dog for a companion. There wasn't any house but the cottage for a long distance, and she began to feel how all alone and deserted everything was—anything might happen to them there, with no telephone. And just then it clouded over and thundered and some drops fell, and Connie thought she might as well begin to cry then and there, she felt so sad and lonesome.

She went into the house by the side door and up the back stairs, and started to go into the little hall that led to her room; but when she pushed in the door it wasn't that little hall at all, but some attic stairs. Connie was so surprised she stopped crying and went on up the stairs. The ceiling sloped down to the floor at each end and it was quite dim, because there were only a few little windows and they were very cobwebby; besides, the rain made things dark. There were one or two old trunks there and some queer bandboxes and a little tin bathtub, all painted with flowers. There were several broken chairs with painted backs and seats made of that stuff that looks like straw, and a wooden crib that shut up like a camp chair in the middle. There was a dusty old wire cage for a squirrel, and a whole lot of dried catnip tied up in bunches, and other smelly things.

Connie poked along, to see how small she would have to bow down as the roof got lower and lower, and just as she was going to get on her hands and knees she stumbled over a little trunk. It was so small that she knew it must have been a doll's trunk, and she sat right down and opened it, because, though she never would touch any of the other trunks and boxes for the world, of course she felt that she had a right to see the little-girl things.

The first thing in the trunk was a pile of doll's clothes; they weren't very nice, but they were made just as well as if the cloth had been better, but very old-fashioned. And it must have been a grown-up doll, too, because there were hats for it, with strings like Aunt Betsy's. And there were nightcaps like Gran'ma Biggs's.

Under the clothes were some other playthings—a long string all covered with buttons of many different sorts, a little box with the top all made of shells pasted on close together, and a little cup made of striped shiny wood that had printed on it, "Made of wood from Mt. Tom, Massachusetts." In the shell box there was a lock of black curly hair tied with blue ribbon in an envelope, and on it was written, "My dear Spotty's hair when she was six months old." In another envelope was some yellow hair, not real, and that said, "A lock of Estella's old hair that was burned when Fred sent the new wig." You see, that was the doll. There was one more with brown hair, but the writing was all scratched out, so that Connie couldn't read it.

Under the box was a book, in a cover made of brown cloth like what is behind furniture sometimes; it was called *The Third Reader.* They used to learn to read in books like that, but Connie says we'd better be thankful that we don't now, for the stories in this one were silly. They were babyish, and the poetry especially. There was no name in the front, but instead it said, "If my name you wish to see, look on page one hundred and three." She turned to that page, and then it said, "If my name you still would find, look on page marked fifty-nine." So she looked there, and there was the name: "Lorilla Biggs. If on this name you chance to look, think of me and close the book."

And that is just what Connie did. She would have been so glad if Lorilla had been there; it was all she needed to make

69

her contented—somebody to play with, you see. She said it almost seemed as if Lorilla *was* there, because there were her things and the locks of hair and the writing that said to think of her. It was almost dark, and Connie played that Lorilla was over behind one of the trunks, and that the noise the rain made on the roof was her feet running around. She said afterwards she wouldn't have been surprised if Lorilla had come out any minute. But of course she didn't, and Connie knew well enough that she must either be dead or grown up by this time.

The sound of the rain made her feel sleepy, it was so quiet in there, and the catnip and things smelled so strong, too—such things always made Con sleepy. So she fell asleep, and the water leaked in right over her shoulder, and when she woke up she was quite wet, and the doll's things, too. It was awfully dark and she was scared to death, so she just tumbled the things under the trunk and felt her way down-stairs, and changed her dress quickly so that Mrs. Annie shouldn't be worried, for her throat felt sore.

Well, they were so delighted to see her, they never scolded her a bit, for they'd been out hunting all over for her; they thought she was lost somewhere. And Aunt Betsy kissed her, and they all cried, and Mrs. Edward's husband said, "Well, well!" That's every word she ever heard him say.

Of course she told them where she had been, and then she said, "Was Lorilla your sister, Mrs. Annie?"

Connie says they looked at her and then at each other and never said a word. Then they all began to say something, and all stopped together. Finally Aunt Betsy said: "Well, Annie, there's no need to make a bad matter worse by fightin' the truth. Nobody knows what mother's said, so we might's well out with it."

"All right," said Mrs. Annie; "you're in charge, and what you say goes. I guess the truth's the best myself."

So then she told Connie about little Lorilla. She was their sister Etta's little girl, and her father died when she was a baby, so she was all her mother had, and her mother was dreadful choice of her, Mrs. Annie said. She was pretty and good and a real comfort, and Gran'ma Biggs just worshipped the ground she walked on. She had to play most of the time by herself, because she was the only child, but she was real contented, and she set great store by Spot; they'd play by the hour together, "just like you and old Joe," Mrs. Annie said. She was eleven years old, like Connie, and she had dreadful old-fashioned ways and sewed patchwork just like a woman. She made the quilt in Connie's room.

Well, one morning Spot went off to the river to take a swim, and while she was gone Lorilla said she guessed she'd go out and try to find some closed gentians for her mother, because they were her mother's favorite flower, and September was the month to find them. So they said all right, and her mother said to kiss her goodbye. And Lorilla laughed and said she wouldn't be gone long enough for that; but then she changed her mind and came back and kissed her. "I'll kiss you, too, Aunt Annie," she said; and then Aunt Betsy pretended to cry and said, "No kiss for poor old Aunt Betsy?" Then Lorilla nearly cried herself, because she thought Aunt Betsy was in earnest, and she was too tender hearted to hurt a fly. She went out after she gave her a kiss, too, and shut the door after her very carefully, the way she always did. And they never saw her again.

They hunted and they hunted for weeks and weeks, and poor old Spot used to run around the barn where they used to play together, howling and crying till they had to chain her up, but they never found any sign of her. Dr. Welles's father sent three detectives up there, and everybody for miles around helped them hunt, and they arrested a band of gipsies that was roaming about, a mile away, and thought they had her once, but they couldn't prove that the gipsies had seen her, and they had to let them go. After the gipsies had got away they found out that three or four of them had escaped before the rest were caught, and gone away on a train, and people always thought they were the ones that had little Lorilla.

Her mother only lived a year after that; she just pined off, Mrs. Annie said. But she always said Lorilla was dead, and she was the only one that thought that, for everybody else was sure she was living with the gipsies or carried away into another country.

Of course that was very exciting and interesting, and Connie asked so many questions that she didn't have time

71

to tell about her throat, and it got sorer all the time. She dreamed about Lorilla all night, and the next morning she went out with old Joe and walked along by the river and pretended that she was going to meet her there, after Lorilla got the gentians, and that they were going to play. Finally she got tired pretending to wait, and she thought all of a sudden that she might just as well pretend Lorilla *had* come. So she did. She said she felt rather silly when she first said, "Why, here you are at last, Lorilla! I'd about given you up," but after that it was just as easy as anything, and before long she was talking away, first for herself and then for Lorilla, and having quite a nice time. It wasn't nearly so lonely, of course, and it was fun to plan out what Lorilla would have said. At first she used to stop and think, but after a while she answered back very quickly, not stopping at all, and sometimes she would speak so fast that she really didn't know what she was going to say, and it surprised her when she'd said it—if you see what I mean. If you knew Con, you wouldn't be surprised that she got so excited doing this that her head ached, and she never went home till they came to get her for dinner. She wouldn't tell about her throat then, for she wanted to get right back to Lorilla, and she was afraid Mrs. Annie would make her go to bed. So she went directly there and sat down by the river and began to play again.

While she was playing she happened to look behind her and saw somebody walking through the trees. Of course she stopped talking and felt ashamed of herself to be making so much noise all alone, and she was afraid whoever it was would laugh, because she was talking with two voices, one for Lorilla and one for herself. She waited for them to get by, and then she began again. But when she looked around to make sure, she saw somebody step behind a bush, and she could see that it was a woman, for she saw her dress and her sunbonnet. She supposed it was Mrs. Annie coming to see what she was doing, and got up to catch her, but she hid behind some of the bushes and kept so still that Con got very cross and nearly cried, she felt so tired and her head ached so. Finally she called out, "You can hide there all day if you want to; I sha'n't hunt!" and went back to her place. But she only whispered then, partly to tease Mrs. Annie and partly because she hated to have any-body hear her. But she knew that nobody had gone away, for she listened carefully, and suddenly she turned around, and it wasn't Mrs. Annie, after all, but a little girl not much bigger than Connie herself. Connie stared at her for a min-ute, but she looked very scared, and jumped behind a big tree that was there, and all of a sudden Con got frightened herself, it was so still there, and called Joe and ran home. She looked around once or twice, but she didn't see the little girl, which she was sorry for, because she looked nice, though scared. When she got to the house she asked what little girl lived around there, and Mrs. Annie said, not any.

"Did you see one?" she asked her, and when Connie told her about it she laughed and said that it must be Henry Barber's little girl from Millers Falls. "Henry comes once a week to see if we want any pot-cheese or buttermilk and get the rags for his wife to make her rugs of," she said, "and I told him last week to bring Josie with him to visit with you. She's dreadful shy, and I guess when she saw you she couldn't come up to the scratch. You oughtn't to 'a' run, though."

Pretty soon Mrs. Edward came over and Mrs. Annie told her about Josie, but Mrs. Edward said that Henry Barber had just driven by and Josie wasn't with him.

"Well, then, he's left her in the woods there, and Con-nie'd better run right back and hunt her up," said Mrs. An-nie; so Connie went back and hunted and called, but for a long time she couldn't find anybody. Once or twice, though, she saw her just ahead, and then she'd call out: "Oh, please wait! Please stay till I catch up, Josie!" One time the little girl waited till Con was quite near, and turned and smiled, but then she looked scared again, and slipped off to one side, where the bushes were thick. Finally Connie thought she'd sit down and pretend not to notice, and see if she'd come up; so she sat down on a big stone and shut her eyes and waited, and when she opened them softly there was the little girl standing quite near, looking at her. Connie kept on sitting still, and by and by the little girl sat down near her and watched her. So then Connie smiled and she smiled, and they smiled back and forth, and at last Connie asked her if she knew that her father had started home without her, and she shook her head.

"We'd better start on and see if we can catch him," Connie said. "Come on!" and she jumped up, but that frightened the little girl, and she was up like lightning and running away. She ran so quick and so soft that the leaves rustling covered up the footsteps, and once Connie lost track of her she couldn't get her again. By this time poor Con was pretty tired, and she was so disappointed she began to cry; and when she got back they had to get her some cookies and milk before she could stop. Mrs. Annie was awfully cross with Josie for being so silly, and told Connie never to mind; she'd take her up to the Barbers' and teach Josie manners if her own mother couldn't.

"She'll come round all right," she said; "those black eyes o' hers'll snap when she sees what I've brought her—I know what she likes."

"Her eyes aren't black—they're gray," said Connie; "and if she doesn't like me, she needn't, so there!"

"What you talkin' about, child? Her eyes are black as ink," said Mrs. Edward.

Then Connie lost her temper and pushed away the cookie, which didn't taste very good, anyway, and contradicted dreadfully.

"Her eyes are not black—they are as gray as mine," she said, very crossly.

"There, there!" Mrs. Annie said. "Don't mind the child; she's tired to death, and she looks to me as if she's caught a chill besides."

She made Connie change her stockings and gave her some milk toast for supper; but it didn't taste good, but bitter, like the cookie, and Connie was glad to go to bed. But she woke up in the middle of the night, and couldn't get to sleep again for a long time. She thought about little Lorilla, and how nice it would have been if she had been at Aunt Betsy's, and how they would have played together and told stories and slept in the same room, and it seemed to her she simply couldn't bear it to stay there alone much longer. She thought maybe she'd go to sleep if she could count a few stars, which she'd heard makes you sleepy, and she got up and sat on the windowsill and looked out. It was so still she could hear the leaves rustle on trees a long way off, and Gran'ma Biggs's cottage and the barn at the end of the lane behind it looked like pictures of houses, all flat. Just as she started to count the stars on top of the barn she saw something move beside it, and when she looked down near the ground she saw it was a person, stealing quietly around the corner of the barn, and she knew by the sunbonnet and the apron that it was the little girl. At first she couldn't believe it, but the more she looked the more she was sure, and then she leaned out of the window and waved her hand, hoping to get her attention and then go down and let her in. The little girl didn't seem to dare to go very far from the barn, because as soon as she had taken a few steps she'd turn around and run behind it again, just the way she did by the river. But Connie kept on waving—of course she didn't dare call out loud—and pretty soon she thought the little girl saw her, for she tipped her bonnet high as though she was looking up, and started along toward the cottage. In a moment she was by it, and then she came into the lane, and pretty soon she was quite near Aunt Betsy's house. Then Connie was sure she saw her, for she waved her hand and hurried faster, when all of a sudden, just as she reached the well, Joe began to bark and howl. It was a dreadful noise, coming when everything was so still, and it frightened Connie so that she screamed and nearly fell out of the window. It frightened the little girl still more, for she turned right around and ran back to the barn, and disappeared behind it.

Of course that woke up Mrs. Annie, and she came running to Connie's room, and when Connie told her that the little girl hadn't found her father, after all, but was hiding behind the barn and too afraid to come out, Mrs. Annie stared at her in the strangest way and said: "Child, you're dreaming. There's no little girl there. You've been walking in your sleep."

"I think I know a person when I see one," said Connie, half crying, "and she waved her hand to me, too. You go down behind the barn and you'll see."

"Oh, nonsense!" said Mrs. Edward. "Look here, child; Josie Barber's down with the measles, and how could she be here? Henry told me so himself; he stopped in after you went to bed."

"Then it's some other little girl," said Connie, "and she's out all alone behind the barn," but they put her back into bed and said that there wasn't any little girl that it could be, and made her go to sleep.

So Connie went to sleep, and she dreamed that she and little Lorilla were playing in the barn, and the hay got into her nose and choked her, and she was dying, and Lorilla shook her and said, "Wake up! wake up!" and she woke up with a jump, all hot and stuffy and choking.

Well, I suppose you'll think she was crazy, but she got up out of bed and put on her wrapper and her shoes and stockings, and opened the door softly and started downstairs. She said she had to go and find that little girl. She just had to. And she was so hot besides, she thought it would be cooler outdoors. Her head felt very big, and she says that she skipped down the stairs just like dancing, as you do in dreams. She went out by the kitchen door very softly, and it was beautiful in the yard, almost light, with only one big star and the sky a kind of white. You could see everything very plainly, and she wasn't a bit afraid. It smelled so good that she felt very happy, and she ran along the path to the barn, in that dancing kind of way, so quickly that she got there in a moment, though it was really quite a long way.

And there was the little girl waiting for her, just as she knew she would be. She wasn't a bit shy by that time, and they began to play directly. Connie meant to ask her why she didn't go home to bed, and where she lived, but she forgot all about it somehow, and her head felt so big and queer that she couldn't remember much of anything. We've often asked Connie what they played, but it made her very cross after a while, because at first she used to say, "Oh, we just played, that's all," and finally she had to own up that she couldn't remember, but they had a beautiful time. We asked her what the little girl talked about, and at first she used to say, "Oh, everything, you know—just different things"; but when Ben asked her to tell one thing—just some one thing that the little girl said—she thought very hard and finally said that she couldn't remember one word, really; but of course she must have talked, or they couldn't have played, could they?

After a while Con got sleepy and wanted the little girl to come in and go to bed, but she wouldn't go so far from the barn: she'd run behind it if she heard a noise, and once when the black rooster, that always woke up first, began to crow, she ran in and made Connie hunt a long time before she found her. That made Connie cross and her head ached terribly, and she felt dizzy, too, so she said she was going back to the house unless the little girl told her the secret place she hid in. Then the little girl put her fingers on her lips and looked very wise, and beckoned to Connie to come and see something, and not make any noise; and Con went softly after her. She knelt down and swept away some hay from the back of the floor and caught her finger nail into a little kind of crack in the board and lifted the board up and pointed down. And there was a lovely little place under the floor, just big enough to hide in, and the board would drop back, and nobody would ever in the world guess you were there. Then Con was ashamed for being so cross and begged the little girl's pardon, the place was so fine; and she smiled very kindly, and took off her neck a blue ribbon with a silver heart strung on it and held it out to Connie. Connie put out her hand for it, but before she touched it the little girl let go of it and it dropped into the secret place and the board fell back, and there it was—gone.

"Look out! Look out!" Connie called, very loud, and the little girl gave a jump and Connie fell down, and when she got up the little girl was gone. Connie said she felt as if she'd been asleep and just waked up, and she knew she was sick or something, her head was so queer and her legs shook. She ran out of the barn and stumbled along to the house and fell asleep right on the kitchen floor, and Mrs. Annie found her there when she came down.

Now, what do you think? When Connie told them where she went and about the little girl, they just looked at each other and told her she dreamed it. They said she had walked in her sleep to the kitchen door and never gone any farther.

And Aunt Betsy said: "Annie, I'm going to write for Fred this minute. You get the quinine now. It's chills 'n' fever."

Well, that was too much for poor Con to bear, and she burst out crying and couldn't stop.

"Go out to the barn, then, if you don't believe me, and get into the secret place and find the silver heart she gave me—then you'll see!" she told them, sobbing and crying.

Hardly had she said that, when Aunt Betsy put her hand up to her belt and tumbled over in her chair, and Mrs. Annie and Mrs. Edward stared at Connie and swallowed in their throats; and Mrs. Annie whispered:

"The heart? The silver heart? Which one? Tell me, deary; tell Aunt Annie."

So Connie told them, and Mrs. Edward got up and said: "The Lord help poor Etta, girls—she's seen Lorilla's locket! I'm going for Mr. Weed, an' you look after Betsy."

Connie said that after that nobody seemed to pay any attention to her, and when they did they stared at her and didn't pet her at all, and she felt bad, too. Aunt Betsy cried and cried, and the coffee boiled all over the stove and smelled dreadful, and Connie took a great big cup, and they never said a word. It made her feel very well and her head got small again. She had to sit in the room with Aunt Betsy, and nobody did a thing till Mr. Weed came, and then she had to tell him the whole thing over again. And he shook his head and asked her to describe the locket; and when she said it was on a blue ribbon, Aunt Betsy cried harder than ever.

"Come out with me to the barn, my child," said Mr. Weed, and they went, and some other people that Connie had never seen before, and Mr. Barber and the hired man and Ann Ellen. And Connie went right to the place and pushed away the hay, and the board wasn't there at all, but smaller ones, all nailed down tight. It had been changed, and now she knew they wouldn't believe her, and she began to cry.

"You see, my child," said Mr. Weed, and he looked very sadly at her, "you have made a great deal of pain for these poor sisters, and to no purpose. There is no board here such as you describe."

"But there was, there was!" Connie cried out. "It was as

wide as three of these boards and loose at the end, and dark brown. And now some one has covered it up, and I can't get my locket, and the little girl gave it to me."

Just then Henry, the hired man, stepped out and coughed and said: "This here floor ain't only been laid but eight years, Mis' Edward, since I come, and the old boards was like she says. It was laid right on top o' the other."

Then Mr. Weed looked very sharply at Henry, and Mrs. Annie gave a scream and ran to the place and began to pick at the nails.

"Oh, Mr. Weed! Oh, poor Etta!" she cried out. "I remember now. That's what Lorilla meant. She told me one day that if ever the Indians sh'd come again they'd never get her, for she knew a place they'd never find in a hundred years. 'I'll be safe there, Aunt Annie,' says she, 'you'll see;' but she never'd tell me. It was under there—my poor baby, 'twas under there!"

Connie couldn't move a step, her legs shook so, and Mr. Weed held her hand so tight.

"My friends," he said, "out of the mouths of babes and sucklings a strange matter has been disclosed to us. Let some one bring a chisel and a hammer!"

Henry went away, and suddenly Aunt Betsy sat right down on the floor and made motions to Mrs. Annie.

"Annie," she said, very hoarse, just as if she had caught cold,—"Annie. 'Twas the day she went away that we had the hay in!"

When Henry came back there were more people with him, and it was so still you could hear the long nails squeak when he knocked the boards up. When he had got them off—he broke them at the other end—Connie pulled her hand away and ran. "There's my board," she said, "and here's where you put your finger nail," and she fitted her nail in and pulled the board back a little way. "I told you somebody had covered it up," she said. "Now I'll find my locket," and she started to look in, but Mr. Weed pulled her back.

"Hush, my child!" he said, and Connie says his hand was cold as ice. "Go back with the women. I will look."

He looked down and jumped back, and then he looked again, with his hand out behind him so nobody could come.

79

Everybody was crying but Connie, and she was feeling queerer and queerer.

"My friends," he said, very gentle and still, "let us pray."

Then he made a prayer and everybody knelt down, and Connie can't remember what he said except the end: "who in Thine own good time revealest everything so that we may be at peace. Amen."

"And now please give me my locket," says Connie, who tried to be polite while he was praying, "for my throat is so sore."

And he leaned down over the secret place and put down his hand a moment, and then he held it out, and there, tied to an old grayish kind of string, was a little silver heart.

Mrs. Annie gave a long sigh, like when you hold your breath, and then Connie says, the floor sank down under her and left her standing in the air, and she seemed to forget everything after that, but somebody carried her away. And when she got well she was at home, and Ben and I came to see her.

She has never seen them again, Mrs. Annie and Mrs. Edward and Gran'ma Biggs, and nobody would tell her anything about them, so she has nearly forgotten, now; but Ben thinks that nothing in any book is more wonderful than this story of little Lorilla.

A feminist forerunner whose fiction focused on the problems of women trying to make a living in a man's world, Josephine Daskam Bacon was born in Connecticut in 1879. Educated at Smith College, she began writing for such magazines as Collier's *and* Saturday Evening Post. *Her books* Smith College Stories *and* Memoir of a Baby *were instant hits. She also wrote award-winning lyrics, was a member of the Girl Scout Executive Board (1914-24), was a public health worker, and did radio work for the government during World War II. She died in 1961.*

Professor Ellis Fowler thought his life of teaching poetry had been a waste until some of his former students held a special assembly just for him.

SEVEN

The Changing of the Guard

Rod Serling
adapted by Anne Serling

What you are about to read is not just the story of the end of a semester. It happens to be the end of an era. Professor Ellis Fowler, a teacher of literature, a gentle, bookish guide to the young, is about to find a package under his Christmas tree . . . and not a pleasant one. He doesn't realize it yet, but after half a century of planting seeds of wisdom, and then watching the fruits of his harvest, he is to discover that he has come to the end of the field and is about to be discarded. And that the campus of Rock Hill School for Boys lies on a direct path to another institution commonly referred to as . . . The Twilight Zone.

The Rock Hill School for Boys was located in a small town in Connecticut. There was nothing particularly unique about the school, nothing to differentiate it from any other boys' school of the time. The ivy clung to the brick walls, its thick carpet broken only in a few places where dusty, diamond-shaped panes of glass could be seen. The boys looked the same. The classrooms contained the same, wooden desks, lined up in rows, with names and thoughts of the time carved deep into the wood. The long, dark corridors retained the same musty smells that never dissipated, even on sunny days. The halls echoed with the same laughter, the same angers, the same disappointments that one might find in any other school. No, there was nothing really distinctive, nothing except Professor Ellis Fowler.

Professor Fowler was seventy-seven, with a great gray mop of hair and a beard the same color that moved up and down as he spoke. He had a kindly, tremendously intelligent old face with sparkling blue eyes that still questioned. His glasses constantly slipped down over the bridge of his nose and he intermittently, though fruitlessly, tried to push them back where they should be. He was thin and angular, not unlike a deflated Santa Claus.

His classroom was filled, on this the last day of the term. His students, a handful of young teenagers, sat in various postures of semi-bored lethargy before him. Professor Fowler peered at the book in his hand and, looking like a kindly old owl, began the morning.

"You'll remember that we've talked of the work of Alfred Edward Housman, born—what year, Mr. Graham?"

Graham, a sixteen-year-old linebacker, whose body had grown without him, blinked and suddenly came to attention. "What year, sir?"

There was a thin trickle of laughter. Graham shifted in his seat, looked out of the window, and fingered his varsity letter. "Ah, sometime this century. I think."

Professor Fowler smiled and nodded. "Close, Mr. Graham. Closer than usual. Sometime this century." He looked off thoughtfully, scratched his beard, and addressed the class. "Mr. Graham's career is laid out for him. He will be a second assistant in the Information Booth at Kennedy Airport."

The class laughed and, anticipating a bit of fun, sat up and centered their attention on Fowler. The professor peered at Graham over his glasses. "The date of Alfred Housman's birth, Mr. Graham, and for the benefit of the rest of the class, was eighteen fifty-nine. His death occurred—what year, Mr. Butler?"

An exuberant, runty little enthusiast, who had the kind of head that looked like it would spend the rest of its life wearing a beanie, jumped to his feet with alacrity. "Sir, around nineteen hundred."

Professor Fowler straightened his glasses and again scratched his beard. "'Pon my word, young Mr. Butler, you and Mr. Graham are kindred spirits. Alfred Housman died in nineteen thirty-six. Now, with yours and Mr. Graham's permission, this is somewhat less moving than a screen pass or

82

what a T-formation quarterback tells his line in a huddle, but I hope you'll bear with me for a moment of truth. All of you will recall, no doubt, 'A Shropshire Lad,' a little of which I will now read to you:

> When I was one-and twenty
> I heard a wise man say,
> 'Give crowns and pounds and guineas
> But not your heart away.'

He continued to recite but his eyes left the book, moved over the heads of the students, and fastened on some far distant corner of the universe.

> "'Give pearls away and rubies
> But keep your fancy free.'
> But I was one-and-twenty,
> No use to talk to me."

The book slowly lowered in his hand and he continued:

> "'The heart out of the bosom
> Was never given in vain;
> 'Tis paid with sighs a-plenty
> And sold for endless rue.'
> And I am two-and-twenty,
> And oh, 'tis true, 'tis true."

Professor Fowler smiled and nodded and was lost for a protracted moment in which he was several thousand miles away, responding to a truth. He was suddenly aware of the boys looking at him and closed the book. He took off his glasses, checked them, blew on them, wiped them off, and smiled from face to face. Clearing his throat, he said, "It is quite an odd phenomenon, really, how you react to that poem much as your fathers did. It is a fact that I've been reading it for fifty-one years to various classes who failed to get its meaning at all. Said meaning, is, simply: Give sparingly of your youth. Embrace it for the precious thing it is. It's the most fleeting chapter in the book of your lives." He leaned over his desk and peered at the students. "You will, I am sure, at some future moment of your lives, understand precisely what I'm getting at."

Then, smiling, he said, "Now, gentlemen, this being the last day of the semester, and this being just three days before the Christmas holidays, I thought it might behoove me to show at least a minute degree of compassion and let you out early. I might add, here, that while your final exam papers are not ready to be returned to you, you have all— amazingly enough—passed. My delight is surpassed only by my sense of shock. It is rare, young men, that in some fifty-one years of teaching I have ever encountered such a class of dunderheads." He looked down, then up over his glasses, and his eyes were twinkling. "But nice dunderheads, and potentially fine young men who will make their marks, and leave their marks. God bless you all. And a Merry Christmas!"

The boys rose and Professor Fowler started down the aisle nodding, smiling, and shaking on occasional hand as the students filed out into the hall. Their voices lifted in youthful laughter, as thoughts of Christmas and holiday and going home sent spirit through the halls. Locker doors were slammed shut. Books and papers were stashed away with great haste and exuberant shouts of "freedom" echoed through the building.

Professor Fowler walked through the hall, exchanging nods and hellos with the boys. He was about to pass the Headmaster's Office when the door opened and the Headmaster called out. He was a tweedy young man still rather new to the job and somewhat smug about it. He pointed an overlarge briar pipe at the Professor. "I say, Fowler, could you step in for a moment?"

Fowler nodded. "Why, of course."

The Headmaster walked over to his desk and sat down, lighting his pipe. "Sit down, Fowler. Be comfortable."

Professor Fowler sat down in the overstuffed chair, looked around the office and at the Headmaster's desk—neat and tidy and altogether unused appearing. He took his pocket watch out and peered at it.

The Headmaster, watching him closely, asked, "Am I keeping you?"

Professor Fowler replied, "No, no, no. There is going to

be a broadcast of *Messiah* at five o'clock, but I have plenty of time. It's a lovely thing. Very Yule-like."

The Headmaster, his pomposity oozing out of him, replied, "I agree. I agree." He then arranged the papers on his desk, straightened them again, lined them up, and laid them back down. "This won't take long."

There was a long silence. Fowler sat quietly, expectantly. The Headmaster ran a long finger down the wooden desk, sucked up his pipe, moved some more paper, and then, finally, reluctantly, looked up. "You—aaah—you did not respond to the letter that the Trustees sent you last week."

The Professor pushed his glasses further up his nose and with a thoughtful pause said, "Letter? I'm terribly sorry, Headmaster. It suddenly occurs to me that I haven't opened my mail for the last few weeks. Final exams, grading, preparation for the holiday—that sort of thing." He smiled and continued. "Though I'm rather certain I know the contents of that letter."

The Headmaster looked away. "And—aaah—your reactions, Professor?"

The Professor took off his glasses and went through the ritual of checking and cleaning them. "Well, I'll naturally go along."

The Headmaster beamed and rubbed his hands. "Well, I think that's very perspicacious of you, Professor. Then I'll tell the Trustees that you received the communication and agreed to it. Now, as to your replacement—"

Professor Fowler was not listening to the Headmaster now. He was smiling a little vacantly and interrupted without being aware he was interrupting. "I told my housekeeper, not a week ago, that I should very likely teach in this place until I'm a hundred years old. Two years ago I actually taught the grandson of one of my earlier students. I venture to say that I'll live to teach a great-grandson one of these days. It was the Reynolds boy. You know him. His father was Damon Reynolds and his grandfather—a regular rascal of a boy who persisted in calling me 'weird beard.'" He chuckled and wiped his glasses. "'Weird beard' didn't know that I knew that that's what he was calling me. Oh, a regular rascal of a boy. Went into the stock market. Made himself a fortune. Came back for his twentieth reunion. Shook my hand and said, 'Professor Fowler, please forgive me for calling you 'weird beard.'" Fowler looked up at the ceiling and shook his head and smiled.

The Headmaster coughed slightly. His voice was very low and tentative. "Professor Fowler. You'll forgive me, sir, but—I think you should best read the communication that the Trustees sent."

Fowler looked at him and nodded, "Oh, indeed I will. Though it's really an odd formality, this contract signing year after year. You can tell them for me, Headmaster, that old Fowler won't depart the ship. Oh, no, indeed. He'll stand at the wheel through fair weather and foul, and he'll watch the crews come aboard and then depart, come aboard and then depart. And he'll see that the ship will stay on course."

The Headmaster cut in. His voice was very quiet and not without some pity. "Professor Fowler, please hear me out, sir." He rose, walked behind the desk over to a window, and stared at the snow-filled day. "The communication that the Trustees sent you was not a contract." He turned away very slowly from the window. "As a matter of fact—it was a notice of termination. You've been on the faculty here for over fifty years. You've passed the normal retirement age several years ago. We decided at our winter meeting that perhaps a younger man—" He stopped and looked across the room to Fowler, who had risen to his feet. "If you could have been at the meeting, sir, you would have been very proud at the things said about you and your work. A teacher of incalculable value to all of us. But—" He turned and retraced his steps back to the desk and stood there with his head down. He did not want to look at the old man's face, but finally had to.

Professor Fowler's voice was almost a whisper, "Mr. Headmaster, am I to understand that my contract is not to be renewed? I'm discharged?"

The Headmaster began pacing the room. "Discharged? Please! Don't call it that. Retirement. *And* at half salary for the rest of your life."

Fowler very softly said, "For—the—rest—of—my—life?" Suddenly, he looked very old. He walked toward the door, then stopped, his back to the Headmaster. "Well, it—it certainly proves one thing, 'pon my word it does. A man should read his mail. He most certainly should read his mail." He walked out the door and down the corridor.

Two boys passed and smiled at him, "Merry Christmas, Professor. Have a happy holiday, sir."

Professor Fowler studied their faces. "Mr. Hallidy and Mr. McTavish." His voice was shaking, perceptibly. "I wish you a safe and happy journey and a happy reunion with your families. And I trust you will not eat too much turkey—and too much—too much stuffing. I've, I've known it to happen Christmas after Christmas, you young rascals go home and eat yourselves into insensi—insensibility."

The boys looked at one another as tears appeared in Professor Fowler's eyes.

With trembling fingers, the Professor touched each boy's face in turn. "You're both fine men. Have a Merry Christmas, both of you. Have a—" His voice broke. He turned and walked away from them a few feet, and leaned against a bulletin board, struggling for composure.

He heard the boys' voices behind him. "What's the matter with old 'weird beard'? He was crying. Did you see that? He was crying."

Fowler turned away from the bulletin board and started a slow walk down the corridor. He ran his hand along the wall, feeling the carved molding that had been worn smooth through the years. He stopped and looked around for a moment, taking in the sights and sounds of this building he had virtually lived in for half a century. Finally, pushing open the heavy oak door, he walked outside and, oblivious to the bitter chill, started home. Once, he stopped to gaze behind him at the building that he had cherished so many years. It was dark in the evening twilight and the building was almost hidden by the falling snow.

With difficulty he climbed the steps to his house and stamped the snow off his feet, more from habit than conscious concern at that moment. He walked directly to the hall table. A little Christmas tree sat on it, laden with ornaments and growing more top-heavy each year. Each ornament had a history—a special meaning—because all were gifts from his "boys." After the Christmas season was over, each treasure was wrapped and stored on a high shelf with great ceremony. But Professor Fowler wasn't looking at the tree that night. He was looking at the letters lying beside the tree. Still in his hat and coat, he fumbled through them, the front door behind him still open to the winter chill.

From the dark recesses of the house, Mrs. Landers, the Professor's housekeeper, materialized. After twenty-odd years of living with and caring for the Professor she had grown very fond of him and was used to his absentminded-ness—almost expected it. She closed the door and straight-ened her hair that had been blown loose by a gust of wind, and turned to the Professor. "I didn't hear you come in. It's certainly snowing and blowing to beat the band, isn't it?"

But Fowler, having finally found the letter that he had been searching for, absentmindedly responded. "Well, I guess it is. I hadn't noticed."

Mrs. Landers studied the Professor's face, and, noting his stooped shoulders and ashen color with growing concern, asked him if anything was wrong.

The Professor shook his head and looked down at the letter. "I guess that would depend on the point of view. If you're a Trustee of this institution, anxious to inject new young blood into the faculty, I'm sure you'd think there was nothing wrong at all." He very slowly picked up the letter and stared at it. "But if you're an old man who has spent the better part of his life inside those halls, those classrooms—then you might be forgiven a degree of consternation."

He suddenly chuckled a long, low chuckle. "As a matter of fact, everything is *not* all right. Everything happens to be very wrong."

Mrs. Landers pointed to the letter in his hand. "What is it, Professor? What's happened?"

Professor Fowler looked down at the letter and read aloud from it. "'And since it is the policy of the school to ensure our students the most up-to-date educational con-cepts, we think it advisable that you consider this retirement to be a mutually beneficial thing. Please understand the spirit in which this request is made and understand further that your contributions to Rock Hill School for Boys are a matter of record, as is our appreciation."

The housekeeper bit her lower lip, "Oh, my word, Pro-fessor, that means—"

The Professor finished her thought. "That means, Mrs.

Landers, stripped of some of its sophistry, its subtlety, its back-breaking effort to break it gently—that I'm canned." He walked towards his study and asked Mrs. Landers, "Were any of my boys here?"

Mrs. Landers, confused and somewhat shaken, looked at him, "Your boys, sir?"

"The students, Mrs. Landers. They had a wonderful tradition that went on for many years. On the last afternoon of the winter term, they would gather outside there and sing Christmas carols. I got to expecting it after a while."

Mrs. Landers very softly said, "They haven't done that in years, Professor. Not since before the war, as I recall."

Fowler nodded and turned away from her again. "Of course. I should have remembered." He removed his glasses, peered through them, started to clean them, then suddenly stopped, gripped them tightly, stared at them, and threw them on the table. "Mrs. Landers, I've become a worshipper of tradition and a fervent follower of ritual. I know it now. I know it and I can admit it. I guess that's why this whole thing has hit me so hard."

He walked across the worn oriental rug and sat down at his desk. "I'm an antique guarding antiques. I am the curator of a museum that houses nothing but some very fragile memories."

Mrs. Landers shook her head. She was close to tears. "Professor, you're the finest man. You're absolutely the finest man."

Professor Fowler smiled at her gratefully. "And you, Mrs. Landers, are the most loyal woman. Now, would you do me a favor? Would you brew me up some tea? Handel's *Messiah* is on the radio in a few minutes. I'd like to listen to it."

Fowler closed his eyes, rested on his elbows for a moment, and then sat back. His eyes scanned the desk and he very slowly took a key off his key chain, unlocked the lower right-hand drawer, rummaged through it, and took out a revolver. He stared at it for a long moment, placed it inside his sweater, and moved to the old rocking chair.

The gentle snow still falling from the night sky was visible through the windows behind the desk. Professor Fowler finished the tea Mrs. Landers had brought him and the empty cup sat on the table as he listened to *The Messiah*.

89

The music ended on a triumphant sweeping note just as Mrs. Landers entered the room. Almost on tiptoe, she walked around to the other side of the chair and peered into Fowler's face. He opened his eyes.

"Yes, Mrs. Landers?"

Mrs. Landers, somewhat startled, said, "Oh, I thought you were asleep, Professor. Would you care for some more tea?"

Fowler shook his head, his mind a million miles away. "Thank you, no."

"I'll have dinner ready in half an hour. Why don't you take a little nap?"

Fowler reached over and turned off the radio. "I know I'm being very difficult, but could we put off dinner this evening? I haven't much of an appetite."

"Professor, you've got to eat something. I could keep it warm for you. Perhaps after your nap?"

Fowler looked at her kind, aging, lovely face and smiled a little. "Perhaps later."

He rose from the chair and walked across the room, over to the bookcase. Three of the shelves were devoted to the Rock Hill School yearbooks; the wood that supported them sagged from their weight. The books dated back many years. Fowler went through his daily ritual of lightly dusting them, and touching them, as if through osmosis he could transform himself back through the years. He took one book out and carried it over to the desk. He very carefully opened it, thumbed through the pages, and studied the faces and names.

Mrs. Landers sat in the chair across from him. She watched him adoringly, yet sadly, feeling his loss.

Fowler mused aloud. "Timothy Arnold. Never thought that one would pass. Had an incorrigible habit of chewing bubble gum and popping it. Sounded like a howitzer. 'Pon my word, it sounded like a howitzer. William Hood. Little Bill Hood—smallest boy ever to play varsity football here, and had a penchant for Shelley." He turned the page again and a smile lit up on his face. "Artie Beachcroft. Now there was a lad. There was a staunch lad. Full of heart, that one." He looked off thoughtfully. "Was he the one? Yes, yes—I recall now. His father sent me a letter. He was killed on Iwo Jima. Frecklefaced little fellow, always grinning. Never stopped grinning; most infectious grin. He'd walk into a classroom and you had to smile."

He continued turning the pages, and then finally closed the book. He looked down at it for a long moment. "They come and go like ghosts. Faces, names, smiles, the funny things they did—or sad things, or poignant ones. I gave them nothing at all. I realize that now. Poetry that left their minds as soon as they themselves left. Aged slogans that were already out of date when I taught them. Quotations that were so dear to me that were meaningless to them."

Fowler shook his head. "Mrs. Landers, I am a failure. I am an old relic that walks from class to class. Speaking by rote to unhearing ears, unwilling heads. I am an abject, dismal failure. I moved no one. I left no imprint on anyone. Now where do you suppose I got the idea that I was accomplishing anything?"

Tears began to brim in Mrs. Landers' eyes. She shook her head as if trying to protest, but no words came out. Fowler smiled at her, excusing her for her silence and understanding it. He left the desk and walked to the door. "I will take that nap now. And I hope I haven't inconvenienced you, putting off dinner like this." He walked out of the room with slow, measured footsteps.

Mrs. Landers touched his yearbook, almost fondling it, and carried it over to the bookcase. She went back to the desk and started to put things in order. She touched the pipe, the book, the glasses—all with a very special touch, indicative of love. Seeing some papers sticking out of one of the drawers she reached down, opened the drawer, and suddenly stopped, transfixed in horror. There, under the papers, she saw the empty gun holster. She picked it up, held it at arm's length, made a motion as if to run through the room, stopped, looked at the holster again, and then carefully put it back in the drawer. With a growing feeling of panic and desperation, she screamed, "Professor Fowler" and ran into the hall. The front door was wide open. She quickly picked up the telephone and dialed the Headmaster.

Fowler walked slowly across the campus, his footsteps echoing in the silence and his breath coming in short, quick gasps in the cold night air. His overcoat was awry and misbuttoned. He was hatless and looked lost and forlorn. Halfway across the campus he stopped in front of a full-sized bronze statue. Wiping some of the snow off the base so that the legend carved there was readable, he softly spoke the words: "Horace Mann, Educator. Seventeen-ninety-six to eighteen-fifty-nine." Fowler knelt down in the snow and very thoughtfully said, "I was just wondering if you had any self-doubts." He smiled and shook his head. "I'm sure not." He brushed some more snow off until he could see the rest of the quotation beneath Mann's name.

"'Be ashamed to die until you have won some victory for humanity.'" He looked away, his face emotionless, and said, "I have won no victory—No victory at all." He looked down at his coat pocket, his voice very low. "And now I am ashamed to die." Very slowly, he took out the revolver, clicked off the safety catch, and was about to raise it when his motion was stopped by the sound of distant, ringing bells that pealed a melodious, and strangely urgent, call.

Fowler turned abruptly and looked off in the direction of the bells. He musingly said, "Class bells? Now that's odd. Why would they ring now? There's no special assembly now. There's nothing of that sort."

In the distance, the bells began to ring again. Fowler started to walk toward the school, unconsciously putting the gun back into his pocket. He reached the main buiding, where the door stood curiously open. Inside, he looked into each empty classroom and then up toward the ceiling, as the bells continued ringing. He was completely alone. He stopped at the door to his classroom and then walked inside and started up the aisle between the desks. Halfway up, he stopped again and listened. There was a strange echoing hollow sound of boys talking and laughing, as if coming from some far distant place. He continued on to the front of the room, bewildered and perplexed and then, gradually, amazed. In each seat a figure began to emerge—first from a kind of ghostlike transparency and then into the flesh-and-blood figure of a boy, until each seat was filled, and a dozen boys were looking expectantly toward him.

Professor Fowler unbuttoned his coat, and his lips moved in soundless questions. "I—I don't understand. Forgive me, boys, but I'm not at all sure—what I mean is, I don't re-collect how—"

The boys smiled at him and finally one rose. "Artie Beachcroft, sir. Second form. Class of forty-one. How have you been, Professor?"

Fowler looked at him and shook his head from side to side quizzically. "How's that? How's that again? You say you're Artie Beachcroft?" He began to nod slowly. "Of course you are. I'd recognize you anywhere." He walked over to the boy, held out his hands, and grabbed the boy's hand. He sniffled and wiped away a tear. "I'm delighted to see you. I'm truly delighted to see you. I've missed you, Artie." He then stared at the boy and began shaking his head again. "But—but what are you doing here? Forgive me, but you shouldn't be here. You were—"

The boy smiled and finished the Professor's thought. "I was killed on Iwo Jima, sir. That's right, Professor." He reached into his pocket, took out a small case, opened it and displayed a medal. "I wanted to show this to you, sir. It's the Congressional Medal of Honor. It was given to me posthumously."

Fowler looked at it and then up into the boy's face. "A very prideful thing, Mr. Beachcroft, a very prideful thing, and I am indeed proud of you. You were always a fine young man. A *fine* young man." He stared at the boy, closed his eyes, shook his head, and then blinked his eyes open. "I—I don't understand."

A boy from across the room called out, "Professor?"

Fowler turned toward him.

"I'm Bartlett. Third form. Class of twenty-eight. I died in Roanoke, Virginia. I was doing research on X-ray treatment for cancer. I was exposed to radioactivity. I contacted leukemia."

Fowler said softly, "I remember, Bartlett. I *do* remember. That was an incredibly brave thing you did, an incredibly brave thing."

The boy continued. "I kept remembering, Professor, something you'd said to me. A quote. A poet named Walter."

Fowler nodded knowingly. "Howard Arnold Walter. I remember."

Bartlett, in a strong voice, began quoting.

93

"I would be true, for there are those who trust me; I would be pure, for there are those who care; I would be strong, for there is much to suffer. I would be brave, for there is much to dare."

He looked at the Professor. "I never forgot that, Professor. It was something you left me. I never forgot."

Fowler's lips began to tremble. "How—how very decent of you, Bartlett, to say that."

Artie Beachcroft shared the sentiment. "That's why I brought the medal to show you, Professor Fowler, because it's partly yours. You taught me about courage. You taught me what it meant."

Fowler said, very, very softly, "Why—why, how incredible." His eyes scanned the room and stopped on a very small boy. He walked over to him and touched the boy's face. "Why, it's—it's Weiss, isn't it? Dickie Weiss? You were the first one, Dick—"

The boy got to his feet. "The first one to die, Professor. I was at Pearl Harbor on the *Arizona*. I was an ensign."

Fighting building emotion, Fowler said, "I remember, Dick. You saved a dozen men. You got them out of the boiler room after they were trapped, and lost your life doing it."

The boy smiled and nodded. "You were at my elbow that day, Professor. You may not have known it, but there you were. It was a poem you had taught me.

". . . . any man's death diminishes me, because I am involved in mankind; and therefore never send to know for whom the bell tolls; it tolls for thee."

Fowler smiled and looked at the boys, who were all looking up at him. His smile grew broader, his eyes brighter in the silence that ensued. The bell rang again, but this time very softly. He walked by the boys and they each in turn rose.

"I'm Thompson, sir; second form, class of thirty-nine. I died in New Guinea, but you taught me about patriotism."

"Rice, sir. Third form, class of nineteen-seventeen. I died of wounds at Château-Thierry. You taught me about courage."

"Hudson, sir. Second form, class of nineteen twenty-two. You taught me about loyalty."

"Whiting, sir. Fourth form, class of fifty-one. You taught me about ethics and honesty."

Fowler blinked back his tears, surveyed the class, sniffled, coughed, wiped his eyes, then took off his glasses, peered through them, cleaned them, and then put them back on.

Each boy watched this and smiled. They remembered this ritual fondly; none of them had ever forgotten it. For a moment there was a still silence.

Finally Beachcroft said, "We have to go back now, Professor, but we wanted to let you know that we were grateful—that we were forever grateful, that each of us has, in turn, carried with him something that you gave him. We wanted to thank you, Professor."

Once again, the figures of the boys took on a transparency and finally disappeared altogether. And once more, the bells began to ring.

Fowler walked down the aisle, looked at the desks, touching that one, pausing by another, and finally went out the door and into the snow. He pulled his coat closer in the chill and walked across the campus toward home.

When he arrived, Mrs. Landers was on the telephone. When she saw him, she broke into a relieved smile. She said into the telephone, "Yes, Headmaster, he's home now. He's all right. Yes, he's just fine. Thank you." She put the phone down, and Fowler smiled at her. They both suddenly looked up as they heard the sound of Christmas caroling from outside.

Fowler turned, and framed in the window, he saw the boys outside knee deep in snow and heard their voices lifted in the last refrain of a Christmas carol. They finished and one boy stepped in front of the group. "Merry Christmas, Professor! Merry Christmas to you!"

Fowler opened the window and called out, "And a merry Christmas to you, young men, a very merry Christmas, indeed. And may I add how—how grateful I am to all of you. I've always thought that Christmas caroling is—is a wonderfully special tradition. Merry Christmas, boys, and God bless you!"

95

The boys smiled and waved as they walked off, beginning another song.

Fowler lowered the window and turned to Mrs. Landers. "I've had a chance to think it over, Mrs. Landers, I think I *will* retire. I do believe that I've taught all that I can teach. And I wouldn't want the returns to diminish."

He turned, once again, and stared out the window. He took off his glasses, went through the ritual of peering through them, then cleaning them, and then putting them back on. There was the sound of chimes from a distant tower and then a soft Christmas carol from beyond.

"Mrs. Landers, I do believe—I do believe that I may *have* left my mark. A few gauntlets of knowledge that I've thrown down—they've been picked up."

He smiled. "'Be ashamed to die until you have won some victory for humanity.' Mrs. Landers, I didn't win them, but I helped others to win them. I believe that now. So in that way—even in a small measure—they are victories that I can share."

He turned back and looked out the window, smiling and nodding. "I've had a very good life, Mrs. Landers. A very rich life. A very fruitful life. This particular changing of the guard—I wouldn't have it any other way."

EPILOGUE

Professor Ellis Fowler, teacher. Who discovered, rather belatedly, something of his own value. A very small scholastic lesson from the campus of . . . The Twilight Zone.

Rod Serling was born in New York in 1924 and educated at Antioch College. His success in radio and television came almost overnight with "Patterns," about the competitive world of big business, followed by a series of dramas about social problems, including "The Comedian" and "Requiem for a Heavyweight." He won six Emmys, two Christopher Awards, the George Foster Peabody Award, two Sylvania Awards, and others. Serling also wrote filmscripts, including Seven Days in May, *but he enjoyed success with his half-hour television dramas featuring "a fifth dimension, beyond that known to man . . . an area that might be called "The Twilight Zone," which ran from 1959 to 1964. Serling died in 1975.*

The story included in this volume, co-written with his daughter Anne, is an adaptation of an episode of The Twilight Zone.

Herbert West knew he could bring the dead back to life, but where was he going to get fresh bodies?

EIGHT

Herbert West—
Reanimator
H. P. Lovecraft

From the Dark

Of Herbert West, who was my friend in college and in after life, I can speak only with extreme terror. This terror is not due altogether to the sinister manner of his recent disappearance, but was engendered by the whole nature of his life-work, and first gained its acute form more than seventeen years ago, when we were in the third year of our course at the Miskatonic University Medical School in Arkham. While he was with me, the wonder and diabolism of his experiments fascinated me utterly, and I was his closest companion. Now that he is gone and the spell is broken, the actual fear is greater. Memories and possibilities are ever more hideous than realities.

The first horrible incident of our acquaintance was the greatest shock I ever experienced, and it is only with reluctance that I repeat it. As I have said, it happened when we were in the medical school, where West had already made himself notorious through his wild theories on the nature of death and the possibility of overcoming it artificially. His views, which were widely ridiculed by the faculty and by his fellow students, hinged on the essentially mechanistic nature of life; and concerned means for operating the organic machinery of mankind by calculated chemical action after the failure of natural processes. In his experiments with various animating solutions he had killed and treated immense numbers of rabbits, guinea pigs, cats, dogs, and monkeys, till he had become the prime nuisance of the college. Several times he had actually obtained signs of life in animals supposedly dead; in many cases violent signs; but he soon saw that the perfection of his process, if indeed possible, would necessarily involve a lifetime of research. It likewise became clear that, since the same solution never worked alike on different organic species, he would require human subjects for further and more specialized progress. It was here that he first came into conflict with the college authorities, and was debarred for future experiments by no less a dignitary than the dean of the medical school himself—the learned and benevolent Dr. Allan Halsey, whose work in behalf of the stricken is recalled by every old resident of Arkham.

I had always been exceptionally tolerant of West's pursuits, and we frequently discussed his theories, whose ramifications and corollaries were almost infinite. Holding with Haeckel that all life is a chemical and physical process, and that the so-called "soul" is a myth, my friend believed that artificial reanimation of the dead can depend only on the condition of the tissues; and that unless actual decomposition has set in, a corpse fully equipped with organs may with suitable measures be set going again in the peculiar fashion known as life. That the psychic or intellectual life might be impaired by the slight deterioration of sensitive brain cells which even a short period of death would be apt to cause, West fully realized. It had at first been his hope to find a reagent which would restore vitality before the actual advent of death, and only repeated failures on animals had shown him that the natural and artificial life-motions were incompatible. He then sought extreme freshness in his specimens, injecting his solutions into the blood immediately after the extinction of life. It was this circumstance which made the professors so carelessly skeptical, for they felt that true death had not occurred in any case. They did not stop to view the matter closely and reasoningly.

It was not long after the faculty had interdicted his work that West confided to me his resolution to get fresh human bodies in some manner, and continue in secret the experiments he could no longer perform openly. To hear him discussing ways and means was rather ghastly, for at the college we had never procured anatomical specimens ourselves. Whenever the morgue proved inadequate, two local Negroes attended to this matter, and they were seldom questioned. West was then a small, slender, spectacled youth with delicate features, yellow hair, pale blue eyes, and a soft voice, and it was uncanny to hear him dwelling on the relative merits of Christchurch Cemetery and the potter's field. We finally decided on the potter's field, because practically every body in Christchurch was embalmed; a thing of course ruinous to West's researches.

I was by this time his active and enthralled assistant, and helped him make all his decisions, not only concerning the source of bodies but concerning a suitable place for our loathsome work. It was I who thought of the deserted Chapman farmhouse beyond Meadow Hill, where we fitted up on the ground floor an operating room and a laboratory, each with dark curtains to conceal our midnight doings. The place was far from any road, and in sight of no other house, yet precautions were none the less necessary; since rumors of strange lights, started by chance nocturnal roamers, would soon bring disaster on our enterprise. It was agreed to call the whole thing a chemical laboratory if discovery should occur. Gradually we equipped our sinister haunt of science with materials either purchased in Boston or quietly borrowed from the college—materials carefully made unrecognizable save to expert eyes—and provided spades and picks for the many burials we should have to make in the cellar. At the college we used an incinerator, but the apparatus was too costly for our unauthorized laboratory. Bodies were always a nuisance—even the small guinea pig bodies from the slight clandestine experiments in West's room at the boarding house.

We followed the local death notices like ghouls, for our specimens demanded particular qualities. What we wanted were corpses interred soon after death and without artificial preservation; preferably free from malforming disease, and certainly with all organs present. Accident victims were our best hope. Not for many weeks did we hear of anything suitable; though we talked with morgue and hospital authorities, ostensibly in the college's interest, as often as we could without exciting suspicion. We found that the college had first choice in every case, so that it might be necessary to remain in Arkham during the summer, when only the limited summer school classes were held. In the end, though, luck favored us; for one day we heard of an almost ideal case in the potter's field: a brawny young workman drowned only the morning before in Sumner's Pond, and buried at the town's expense without delay or embalming. That afternoon we found the new grave, and determined to begin work soon after midnight.

It was a repulsive task that we undertook in the black small hours, even though we lacked at the time the special horror of graveyards which later experiences brought to us. We carried spades and oil dark lanterns, for although electric torches were then manufactured, they were not as satisfactory as the tungsten contrivances of today. The process of unearthing was slow and sordid—it might have been gruesomely poetical if we had been artists instead of scientists—and we were glad when our spades struck wood. When the pine box was fully uncovered West scrambled down and removed the lid, dragging out and propping up the contents. I reached down and hauled the contents out of the grave, and then both toiled hard to restore the spot to its former appearance. The affair made us rather nervous, especially the stiff form and vacant face of our first trophy, but we managed to remove all traces of our visit. When we had patted down the last shovelful of earth we put the specimen in a canvas sack and set out for the old Chapman place beyond Meadow Hill.

On an improvised dissecting-table in the old farmhouse, by the light of a powerful acetylene lamp, the specimen was not very spectral looking. It had been a sturdy and apparently unimaginative youth of wholesome plebeian type—large-framed, grey-eyed, and brown-haired—a sound animal without psychological subtleties, and probably having vital processes of the simplest and healthiest sort. Now, with the eyes closed, it looked more asleep than dead; though the expert test of my friend soon left no doubt on that score. We had at last what West had always longed for—a real dead man of the ideal kind, ready for the solution as prepared according to the most careful calculations and theories for human use. The tension on our part became very great. We knew that there was scarcely a chance for anything like complete success, and could not avoid hideous fears at possible grotesque results of partial animation. Especially were we apprehensive concerning the mind and impulses of the creature, since in the space following death some of the more delicate cerebral cells might well have suffered deterioration. I, myself, still held some curious notions about the traditional "soul" of man, and felt an awe at the secrets that might be told by one returning from the dead. I wondered what sights this placid youth might have seen in inaccessible spheres, and what he could relate if fully restored to life. But my wonder was not overwhelming, since for the most part I shared the materialism of my friend. He was calmer than I as he forced a large quantity of his fluid into a vein of the body's arm, immediately binding the incision securely.

The waiting was gruesome, but West never faltered. Every now and then he applied his stethoscope to the specimen, and bore the negative results philosophically. After about three-quarters of an hour without the least sign of life he disappointedly pronounced the solution inadequate, but determined to make the most of his opportunity and try one change in the formula before disposing of his ghastly prize. We had that afternoon dug a grave in the cellar, and would have to fill it by dawn—for although we had fixed a lock on the house we wished to shun even the remotest risk of a ghoulish discovery. Besides, the body would not be even approximately fresh the next night. So taking the solitary acetylene lamp into the adjacent laboratory, we left our silent guest on the slab in the dark, and bent every energy to the mixing of a new solution; the weighing and measuring supervised by West with an almost fanatical care.

The awful event was very sudden, and wholly unexpected. I was pouring something from one test tube to another, and West was busy over the alcohol blast lamp which had to answer for a Bunsen burner in this gasless edifice, when from the pitch black room we had left there burst the most appalling and demoniac succession of cries that either of us had ever heard. Not more unutterable could have

101

been the chaos of hellish sound if the pit itself had opened to release the agony of the damned, for in one inconceivable cacophony was centered all the supernal terror and unnatural despair of animate nature. Human it could not have been—it is not in man to make such sounds—and without a thought of our late employment or its possible discovery both West and I leaped to the nearest window like stricken animals; overturning tubes, lamp, and retorts, and vaulting madly into the starred abyss of the rural night. I think we screamed ourselves as we stumbled frantically toward the town, though as we reached the outskirts we put on a semblance of restraint—just enough to seem like belated revelers staggering home from a debauch.

We did not separate, but managed to get to West's room, where we whispered with the gas up until dawn. By then we had calmed ourselves a little with rational theories and plans for investigation, so that we could sleep through the day— classes being disregarded. But that evening two items in the paper, wholly unrelated, made it again impossible for us to sleep. The old deserted Chapman house had inexplicably burned to an amorphous heap of ashes; that we could understand because of the upset lamp. Also, an attempt had been made to disturb a new grave in the potter's field, as if by futile and spadeless clawing at the earth. That we could not understand, for we had patted down the mold very carefully.

And for seventeen years after that West would look frequently over his shoulder, and complain of fancied footsteps behind him. Now he had disappeared.

The Plague Demon

I shall never forget that hideous summer sixteen years ago, when like a noxious afrite from the halls of Eblis typhoid stalked leeringly through Arkham. It is by the satanic scourge that most recall the year, for truly terror brooded with bat-wings over the piles of coffins in the tombs of Christchurch Cemetery; yet for me there is a greater horror in that time—a horror known to me alone now that Herbert West has disappeared.

West and I were doing post-graduate work in summer

classes at the medical school of Miskatonic University, and my friend had attained a wide notoriety because of his experiments leading toward the revivification of the dead. After the scientific slaughter of uncounted small animals the freakish work had ostensibly stopped by order of our skeptical dean, Dr. Allan Halsey; though West had continued to perform certain secret tests in his dingy boarding-house room, and had on one terrible and unforgettable occasion taken a human body from its grave in the potter's field to a deserted farmhouse beyond Meadow Hill.

I was with him on that odious occasion, and saw him inject into the still veins the elixir which he thought would to some extent restore life's chemical and physical processes. It had ended horribly—in a delirium of fear which we gradually came to attribute to our own overwrought nerves—and West had never afterward been able to shake off a maddening sensation of being haunted and hunted. The body had not been quite fresh enough; it is obvious that to restore normal mental attributes a body must be very fresh indeed; and the burning of the old house had prevented us from burying the thing. It would have been better if we could have known it was underground.

After that experience West had dropped his researches for some time; but as the zeal of the born scientist slowly returned, he again became importunate with the college faculty, pleading for the use of the dissecting-room and of fresh human specimens for the work he regarded as so overwhelmingly important. His pleas, however, were wholly in vain; for the decision of Dr. Halsey was inflexible, and the other professors all endorsed the verdict of their leader. In the radical theory of reanimation they saw nothing but the immature vagaries of a youthful enthusiast whose slight form, yellow hair, spectacled blue eyes, and soft voice gave no hint of the super-normal—almost diabolical—power of the cold brain within. I can see him now as he was then—and I shiver. He grew sterner of face, but never elderly. And now Sefton Asylum has had the mishap and West has vanished.

West clashed disagreeably with Dr. Halsey near the end of our last undergraduate term in a wordy dispute that did less credit to him than to the kindly dean in point of courtesy. He felt that he was needlessly and irrationally retarded in a supremely great work; a work which he could of course conduct to suit himself in later years, but which he wished to begin while still possessed of the exceptional facilities of the university. That the tradition-bound elders should ignore his singular results on animals, and persist in their denial of the possibility of reanimation, was inexpressibly disgusting and almost incomprehensible to a youth of West's logical temperament. Only greater maturity could help him understand the chronic mental limitations of the "professor doctor" type—the product of generations of pathetic Puritanism; kindly, conscientious, and sometimes gentle and amiable, yet always narrow, intolerant, custom-ridden, and lacking in perspective. Age has more charity for these incomplete yet high-souled characters, whose worst real vice is timidity, and who are ultimately punished by general ridicule for their intellectual sins—sins like Ptolemaism, Calvinism, anti-Darwinism, anti-Nietzscheism, and every sort of Sabbatarianism and sumptuary legislation. West, young despite his marvelous scientific acquirements, had scant patience with good Dr. Halsey and his erudite colleagues; and nursed an increasing resentment, coupled with a desire to prove his theories to these obtuse worthies in some striking and dramatic fashion. Like most youths, he indulged in elaborate daydreams of revenge, triumph, and final magnanimous forgiveness.

And then had come the scourge, grinning and lethal, from the nightmare caverns of Tartarus. West and I had graduated about the time of its beginning, but had remained for additional work at the summer school, so that we were in Arkham when it broke with full daemoniac fury upon the town. Though not as yet licensed physicians, we now had our degrees, and were pressed frantically into public service as the numbers of the stricken grew. The situation was almost past management, and deaths ensued too frequently for the local undertakers fully to handle. Burials without embalming were made in rapid succession, and even the Christchurch Cemetery receiving tomb was crammed with coffins of the unembalmed dead. This circumstance was not without effect on West, who thought often of the irony of the situation—so many fresh specimens, yet none for his persecuted researches! We were frightfully overworked, and the terrific mental and nervous strain made my friend brood morbidly.

But West's gentle enemies were no less harassed with prostrating duties. College had all but closed, and every doctor of the medical faculty was helping to fight the typhoid plague. Dr. Halsey in particular had distinguished himself in sacrificing service, applying his extreme skill with wholehearted energy to cases which many others shunned because of danger or apparent hopelessness. Before a month was over the fearless dean had become a popular hero, though he seemed unconscious of his fame as he struggled to keep from collapsing with physical fatigue and nervous exhaustion. West could not withhold admiration for the fortitude of his foe, but because of this was even more determined to prove to him the truth of his amazing doctrines. Taking advantage of the disorganization of both college work and municipal health regulations, he managed to get a recently deceased body smuggled into the university dissecting room one night, and in my presence injected a new modification of his solution. The thing actually opened its eyes, but only stared at the ceiling with a look of soul-petrifying horror before collapsing into an inertness from which nothing could rouse it. West said it was not fresh enough—the hot summer air does not favor corpses. That time we were almost caught before we incinerated the thing, and West doubted the advisability of repeating his daring misuse of the college laboratory.

The peak of the epidemic was reached in August. West and I were almost dead, and Dr. Halsey did die on the fourteenth. The students all attended the hasty funeral on the fifteenth, and bought an impressive wreath, though the latter was quite overshadowed by the tributes sent by wealthy Arkham citizens and by the municipality itself. It was almost a public affair, for the dean had surely been a public benefactor. After the entombment we were all somewhat depressed, and spent the afternoon at the bar of the Commercial House; where West, though shaken by the death of his chief opponent, chilled the rest of us with references to his notorious theories. Most of the students went home, or to various duties, as the evening advanced; but

West persuaded me to aid him in "making a night of it." West's landlady saw us arrive at his room about two in the morning, with a third man between us; and told her husband that we had all evidently dined and wined rather well.

Apparently this acidulous matron was right; for about 3:00 A.M. the whole house was aroused by cries coming from West's room, where when they broke down the door they found the two of us unconscious on the bloodstained carpet, beaten, scratched, and mauled, and with the broken remnants of West's bottles and instruments around us. Only an open window told what had become of our assailant, and many wondered how he himself had fared after the terrific leap from the second story to the lawn which he must have made. There were some strange garments in the room, but West upon regaining consciousness said they did not belong to the stranger, but were specimens collected for bacteriological analysis in the course of investigations on the transmission of germ diseases. He ordered them burnt as soon as possible in the capacious fireplace. To the police we both declared ignorance of our late companion's identity. He was, West nervously said, a congenial stranger whom we had met at some downtown bar of uncertain location. We had all been rather jovial, and West and I did not wish to have our pugnacious companion hunted down.

That same night saw the beginning of the second Arkham horror—the horror that to me eclipsed the plague itself. Christchurch Cemetery was the scene of a terrible killing; a watchman having been clawed to death in a manner not only too hideous for description, but raising a doubt as to the human agency of the deed. The victim had been seen alive considerably after midnight—the dawn revealed the unutterable thing. The manager of a circus at the neighboring town of Bolton was questioned, but he swore that no beast had at any time escaped from its cage. Those who found the body noted a trail of blood leading to the receiving tomb, where a small pool of red lay on the concrete just outside the gate. A fainter trail led away toward the woods, but it soon gave out.

The next night devils danced on the roofs of Arkham, and unnatural madness howled in the wind. Through the fevered town had crept a curse which some said was greater than the plague, and which some whispered was the embodied demon-soul of the plague itself. Eight houses were entered by a nameless thing which strewed red death in its wake—in all, seventeen maimed and shapeless remnants of bodies were left behind by the voiceless, sadistic monster that crept abroad. A few persons had half seen it in the dark, and said it was white and like a malformed ape or anthropomorphic fiend. It had not left behind quite all that it had attacked, for sometimes it had been hungry. The number it had killed was fourteen; three of the bodies had been in stricken homes and had not been alive.

On the third night frantic bands of searchers, led by the police, captured it in a house on Crane Street near the Miskatonic campus. They had organized the quest with care, keeping in touch by means of volunteer telephone stations, and when someone in the college district had reported hearing a scratching at a shuttered window, the net was quickly spread. On account of the general alarm and precautions, there were only two more victims, and the capture was effected without major casualties. The thing was finally stopped by a bullet, though not a fatal one, and was rushed to the local hospital amidst universal excitement and loathing.

For it had been a man. This much was clear despite the nauseous eyes, the voiceless simianism, and the demoniac savagery. They dressed its wound and carted it to the asylum at Sefton, where it beat its head against the walls of a padded cell for sixteen years—until the recent mishap, when it escaped under circumstances that few like to mention. What had most disgusted the searchers of Arkham was the thing they noticed when the monster's face was cleaned—the mocking, unbelievable resemblance to a learned and self-sacrificing martyr who had been entombed but three days before—the late Dr. Allan Halsey, public benefactor and dean of the medical school of Miskatonic University.

To the vanished Herbert West and to me the disgust and horror were supreme. I shudder tonight as I think of it; shudder even more than I did that morning when West muttered through his bandages,

"Damn it, it wasn't *quite* fresh enough!"

Six Shots by Moonlight

It is uncommon to fire all six shots of a revolver with great suddenness when one would probably be sufficient, but many things in the life of Herbert West were uncommon. It is, for instance, not often that a young physician leaving college is obliged to conceal the principles which guide his selection of a home and office, yet that was the case with Herbert West. When he and I obtained our degrees at the medical school of Miskatonic University, and sought to relieve our poverty by setting up as general practitioners, we took great care not to say that we chose our house because it was fairly well isolated, and as near as possible to the potter's field.

Reticence such as this is seldom without a cause, nor indeed was ours; for our requirements were those resulting from a life-work distinctly unpopular. Outwardly we were doctors only, but beneath the surface were aims of far greater and more terrible moment—for the essence of Herbert West's existence was a quest amid black and forbidden realms of the unknown, in which he hoped to uncover the secret of life and restore to perpetual animation the graveyard's cold clay. Such a quest demands strange materials, among them fresh human bodies; and in order to keep supplied with these indispensable things one must live quietly and not far from a place of informal interment.

West and I had met in college, and I had been the only one to sympathize with his hideous experiments. Gradually I had come to be his inseparable assistant, and now that we were out of college we had to keep together. It was not easy to find a good opening for two doctors in company, but finally the influence of the university secured us a practice in Bolton—a factory town near Arkham, the seat of the college. The Bolton Worsted Mills are the largest in the Miskatonic Valley, and their polyglot employees are never popular as patients with the local physicians. We chose our house with the greatest care, seizing at last on a rather run-down cottage near the end of Pond Street; five numbers from the closest neighbor, and separated from the local potter's field by only a stretch of meadow land, bisected by a narrow neck of the rather dense forest which lies to the north. The distance was greater than we wished, but we could get no nearer house without going on the other side of the field, wholly out of the factory district. We were not much displeased, however, since there were no people between us and our sinister source of supplies. The walk was a trifle long, but we could haul our silent specimens undisturbed.

Our practice was surprisingly large from the very first—large enough to please most young doctors, and large enough to prove a bore and a burden to students whose real interest lay elsewhere. The mill hands were of somewhat turbulent inclinations; and besides their many natural needs, their frequent clashes and stabbing affrays gave us plenty to do. But what actually absorbed our minds was the secret laboratory we had fitted up in the cellar—the laboratory with the long table under the electric lights, where in the small hours of the morning we often injected West's various solutions into the veins of the things we dragged from the potter's field. West was experimenting madly to find something which would start man's vital motions anew after they had been stopped by the thing we call death, but had encountered the most ghastly obstacles. The solution had to be differently compounded for different types—what would serve for guinea pigs would not serve for human beings, and different human specimens required large modifications.

The bodies had to be exceedingly fresh, or the slight decomposition of brain tissue would render perfect reanimation impossible. Indeed, the greatest problem was to get them fresh enough—West had had horrible experiences during his secret college researches with corpses of doubtful vintage. The results of partial or imperfect animation were much more hideous than were the total failures, and we both held fearsome recollections of such things. Ever since our first demonic session in the deserted farmhouse on Meadow Hill in Arkham, we had felt a brooding menace; and West, though a calm, blond, blue-eyed scientific automaton in most respects, often confessed to a shuddering sensation of stealthy pursuit. He half felt that he was followed—a psychological delusion of shaken nerves, enhanced by the undeniably disturbing fact that at least one of our reanimated specimens was still alive—a frightful carnivorous thing in a padded cell at Sefton. Then there was another— our first—whose exact fate we had never learned.

We had fair luck with specimens in Bolton—much better than in Arkham. We had not been settled a week before we got an accident victim on the very night of burial, and made it open its eyes with an amazingly rational expression before the solution failed. It had lost an arm—if it had been a perfect body we might have succeeded better. Between then and the next January we secured three more; one total failure, one case of marked muscular motion, and one rather shivery thing—it rose of itself and uttered a sound. Then came a period when luck was poor; interments fell off, and those that did occur were of specimens either too diseased or too maimed for use. We kept track of all the deaths and their circumstances with systematic care.

One March night, however, we unexpectedly obtained a specimen which did not come from the potter's field. In Bolton the prevailing spirit of Puritanism had outlawed the sport of boxing—with the usual result. Surreptitious and ill-conducted bouts among the mill workers were common, and occasionally professional talent of low grade was imported. This late winter night there had been such a match; evidently with disastrous results, since two timorous Poles had come to us with incoherently whispered entreaties to attend to a very secret and desperate case. We followed them to an abandoned barn, where the remnants of a crowd of frightened foreigners were watching a silent black form on the floor.

The match had been between Kid O'Brien—a lubberly and now quaking youth with a most un-Hibernian hooked nose—and Buck Robinson, "The Harlem Smoke." The Negro had been knocked out, and a moment's examination showed us that he would permanently remain so. He was a loathsome, gorilla-like thing, with abnormally long arms which I could not help calling fore legs, and a face that conjured up thoughts of unspeakable Congo secrets and tom-tom poundings under an eerie moon. The body must have looked even worse in life—but the world holds many ugly things. Fear was upon the whole pitiful crowd, for they did not know what the law would exact of them if the affair were not hushed up; and they were grateful when West, in spite of my involuntary shudders, offered to get rid of the thing quietly—for a purpose I knew too well.

There was bright moonlight over the snowless landscape, but we dressed the thing and carried it home between us through the deserted streets and meadows, as we had carried a similar thing one horrible night in Arkham. We approached the house from the field in the rear, took the specimen in the back door and down the cellar stairs, and prepared it for the usual experiment. Our fear of the police was absurdly great, though we had timed our trip to avoid the solitary patrolman of that section.

The result was wearily anticlimactic. Ghastly as our prize appeared, it was wholly unresponsive to every solution we injected in its black arm, solutions prepared from experience with white specimens only. So as the hour grew dangerously near to dawn, we did as we had done with the others—dragged the thing across the meadows to the neck of the woods near the potter's field, and buried it there in the best sort of grave the frozen ground would furnish. The grave was not very deep, but fully as good as that of the previous specimen—the thing which had risen of itself and uttered a sound. In the light of our dark lanterns we carefully covered it with leaves and dead vines, fairly certain that the police would never find it in a forest so dim and dense.

The next day I was increasingly apprehensive about the police, for a patient brought rumors of a suspected fight and death. West had still another source of worry, for he had been called in the afternoon to a case which ended very threateningly. An Italian woman had become hysterical over her missing child—a lad of five who had strayed off early in the morning and failed to appear for dinner—and had developed symptoms highly alarming in view of an always weak heart. It was a very foolish hysteria, for the boy had often run away before; but Italian peasants are exceedingly superstitious, and this woman seemed as much harassed by omens as by facts. About seven o'clock in the evening she had died, and her frantic husband had made a frightful scene in his efforts to kill West, whom he wildly blamed for not saving her life. Friends had held him when he drew a stiletto, but West departed amidst his inhuman shrieks, curses, and oaths of vengeance. In his latest affliction the fellow seemed to have forgotten his child, who was still missing as the night advanced. There was some talk of searching the woods, but most of the family's friends were busy with the dead woman and the screaming man. Altogether, the nervous strain upon West must have been tremendous. Thoughts of the police and of the mad Italian both weighed heavily.

We retired about eleven, but I did not sleep well. Bolton had a surprisingly good police force for so small a town, and I could not help fearing the mess which would ensue if the affair of the night before were ever tracked down. It might mean the end of all our local work—and perhaps prison for both West and me. I did not like those rumors of a fight which were floating about. After the clock had struck three the moon shone in my eyes, but I turned over without rising to pull down the shade. Then came the steady rattling at the back door.

I lay still and somewhat dazed, but before long heard West's rap on my door. He was clad in dressing gown and slippers, and had in his hands a revolver and an electric flashlight. From the revolver I knew that he was thinking more of the crazed Italian than of the police.

"We'd better both go," he whispered. "It wouldn't do not to answer it anyway, and it may be a patient—it would be like one of those fools to try the back door."

So we both went down the stairs on tiptoe, with a fear partly justified and partly that which comes only from the soul of the weird small hours. The rattling continued, growing somewhat louder. When we reached the door I cautiously unbolted it and threw it open, and as the moon streamed revealingly down on the form silhouetted there, West did a peculiar thing. Despite the obvious danger of attracting notice and bringing down on our heads the dreaded police investigation—a thing which after all was mercifully averted by the relative isolation of our cottage—my friend suddenly, excitedly, and unnecessarily emptied all six chambers of his revolver into the nocturnal visitor.

For that visitor was neither Italian nor policeman. Looming hideously against the spectral moon was a gigantic misshapen thing not to be imagined save in nightmares—a glass-eyed, ink-black apparition nearly on all fours, covered with bits of mold, leaves, and vines, foul with caked blood, and having between its glistening teeth a snowwhite, terrible, cylindrical object terminating in a tiny hand.

The Scream of the Dead

The scream of a dead man gave to me that acute and added horror of Dr. Herbert West which harassed the latter years of our companionship. It is natural that such a thing as a dead man's scream should give horror, for it is obviously not a pleasing or ordinary occurrence; but I was used to similar experiences, hence suffered on this occasion only because of a particular circumstance. And, as I have implied, it was not of the dead man himself that I became afraid.

Herbert West, whose associate and assistant I was, possessed scientific interests far beyond the usual routine of a village physician. That was why, when establishing his practice in Bolton, he had chosen an isolated house near the potter's field. Briefly and brutally stated, West's sole absorbing interest was a secret study of the phenomena of life and its cessation, leading toward the reanimation of the dead through injections of an excitant solution. For this ghastly experimenting it was necessary to have a constant supply of very fresh human bodies; very fresh because even the least decay hopelessly damaged the brain structure, and human because we found that the solution had to be compounded differently for different types of organisms. Scores of rabbits and guinea pigs had been killed and treated, but their trail was a blind one. West had never fully succeeded because he had never been able to secure a corpse sufficiently fresh. What he wanted were bodies from which vitality had only just departed; bodies with every cell intact and capable of receiving again the impulse toward that mode of motion called life. There was hope that this second and artificial life might be made perpetual by repetitions of the injection, but we had learned that an ordinary natural life would not respond to the action. To establish the artificial motion, natural life must be extinct—the specimens must be very fresh, but genuinely dead.

The awesome quest had begun when West and I were

students at the Miskatonic University Medical School in Arkham, vividly conscious for the first time of the thoroughly mechanical nature of life. That was seven years before, but West looked scarcely a day older now—he was small, blond, clean-shaven, soft-voiced, and spectacled, with only an occasional flash of a cold blue eye to tell of the hardening and growing fanaticism of his character under the pressure of his terrible investigations. Our experiences had often been hideous in the extreme; the results of defective reanimation, when lumps of graveyard clay had been galvanized into morbid, unnatural, and brainless motion by various modifications of the vital solution.

One thing had uttered a nerve shattering scream; another had risen violently, beaten us both to unconsciousness, and run amuck in a shocking way before it could be placed behind asylum bars; still another, a loathsome African monstrosity, had clawed out of its shallow grave and done a deed—West had had to shoot that object. We could not get bodies fresh enough to show any trace of reason when reanimated, so had perforce created nameless horrors. It was disturbing to think that one, perhaps two, of our monsters still lived—that thought haunted us shadowingly, till finally West disappeared under frightful circumstances. But at the time of the scream in the cellar laboratory of the isolated Bolton cottage, our fears were subordinate to our anxiety for extremely fresh specimens. West was more avid than I, so that it almost seemed to me that he looked half-covetously at any very healthy living physique.

It was in July, 1910, that the bad luck regarding specimens began to turn. I had been on a long visit to my parents in Illinois, and upon my return found West in a state of singular elation. He had, he told me excitedly, in all likelihood solved the problem of freshness through an approach from an entirely new angle—that of artificial preservation. I had known that he was working on a new and highly unusual embalming compound, and was not surprised that it had turned out well; but until he explained the details I was rather puzzled as to how such a compound could help in our work, since the objectionable staleness of the specimens was largely due to delay occurring before we secured them. This, I now saw, West had clearly recognized;

creating his embalming compound for future rather than immediate use, and trusting to fate to supply again some very recent and unburied corpse, as it had years before when we obtained the Negro killed in the Bolton prize fight. At last fate had been kind, so that on this occasion there lay in the secret cellar laboratory a corpse whose decay could not by any possibility have begun. What would happen on reanimation, and whether we could hope for a revival of mind and reason, West did not venture to predict. The experiment would be a landmark in our studies, and he had saved the new body for my return, so that both might share the spectacle in accustomed fashion.

West told me how he had obtained the specimen. It had been a vigorous man; a well-dressed stranger just off the train on his way to transact some business with the Bolton Worsted Mills. The walk through the town had been long, and by the time the traveler paused at our cottage to ask the way to the factories his heart had become greatly overtaxed. He had refused a stimulant, and had suddenly dropped dead only a moment later. The body, as might be expected, seemed to West a heaven sent gift. In his brief conversation the stranger had made it clear that he was unknown in Bolton, and a search of his pockets subsequently revealed him to be one Robert Leavitt of St. Louis, apparently without a family to make instant inquiries about his disappearance. If this man could not be restored to life, no one would know of our experiment. We buried our materials in a dense strip of woods between the house and the potter's field. If, on the other hand, he could be restored, our fame would be brilliantly and perpetually established. So without delay West had injected into the body's wrist the compound which would hold it fresh for use after my arrival. The matter of the presumably weak heart, which to my mind imperiled the success of our experiment, did not appear to trouble West extensively. He hoped at last to obtain what he had never obtained before—a rekindled spark of reason and perhaps a normal, living creature.

So on the night of July 18, 1910, Herbert West and I stood in the cellar laboratory and gazed at a white, silent figure beneath the dazzling arc light. The embalming compound had worked uncannily well, for as I stared fascinatedly at the sturdy frame which had lain two weeks without stiffening I was moved to seek West's assurance that the thing was really dead. This assurance he gave readily enough; reminding me that the reanimating solution was never used without careful tests as to life; since it could have no effect if any of the original vitality were present. As West proceeded to take preliminary steps, I was impressed by the vast intricacy of the new experiment; an intricacy so vast that he could trust no hand less delicate than his own. Forbidding me to touch the body, he first injected a drug in the wrist just beside the place his needle had punctured when injecting the embalming compound. This, he said, was to neutralize the compound and release the system to a normal relaxation so that the reanimating solution might freely work when injected. Slightly later, when a change and a gentle tremor seemed to affect the dead limbs, West stuffed a pillow-like object violently over the twitching face, not withdrawing it until the corpse appeared quiet and ready for our attempt at reanimation. The pale enthusiast now applied some last perfunctory tests for absolute lifelessness, withdrew satisfied, and finally injected into the left arm an accurately measured amount of the vital elixir, prepared during the afternoon with a greater care than we had used since college days, when our feats were new and groping. I cannot express the wild, breathless suspense with which we waited for results on this first really fresh specimen—the first we could reasonably expect to open its lips in rational speech, perhaps to tell of what it had seen beyond the unfathomable abyss.

West was a materialist, believing in no soul and attributing all the working of consciousness to bodily phenomena; consequently he looked for no revelation of hideous secrets from gulfs and caverns beyond death's barrier. I did not wholly disagree with him theoretically, yet held vague instinctive remnants of the primitive faith of my forefathers; so that I could not help eyeing the corpse with a certain amount of awe and terrible expectation. Besides—I could not extract from my memory that hideous, inhuman shriek we heard on the night we tried our first experiment in the deserted farmhouse at Arkham.

Very little time had elapsed before I saw the attempt was

not to be a total failure. A touch of color came to cheeks hitherto chalk-white, and spread out under the curiously ample stubble of sandy beard. West, who had his hand on the pulse of the left wrist, suddenly nodded significantly; and almost simultaneously a mist appeared on the mirror inclined above the body's mouth. There followed a few spasmodic muscular motions, and then an audible breathing and visible motion of the chest. I looked at the closed eyelids, and thought I detected a quivering. Then the lids opened, showing eyes which were grey, calm, and alive, but still unintelligent and not even curious.

In a moment of fantastic whim I whispered questions to the reddening ears; questions of other worlds of which the memory might still be present. Subsequent terror drove them from my mind, but I think the last one, which I repeated, was: "Where have you been?" I do not yet know whether I was answered or not, for no sound came from the well-shaped mouth; but I do know that at that moment I firmly thought the thin lips moved silently, forming syllables which I would have vocalized as "only now" if that phrase had possessed any sense or relevancy. At that moment, as I say, I was elated with the conviction that the one great goal had been attained; and that for the first time a reanimated corpse had uttered distinct words impelled by actual reason. In the next moment there was no doubt about the triumph; no doubt that the solution had truly accomplished, at least temporarily, its full mission of restoring rational and articulate life to the dead. But in that triumph there came to me the greatest of all horrors—not horror of the thing that spoke, but of the deed that I had witnessed and of the man with whom my professional fortunes were joined.

For that very fresh body, at last writhing into full and terrifying consciousness with eyes dilated at the memory of its last scene on earth, threw out its frantic hands in a life and death struggle with the air; and suddenly collapsing into a second and final dissolution from which there could be no return, screamed out the cry that will ring eternally in my aching brain:

"Help! Keep off, you cursed little towhead fiend—keep that damned needle away from me!"

The Horror from the Shadows

Many men have related hideous things, not mentioned in print, which happened on the battlefields of the Great War. Some of these things have made me faint, others have convulsed me with devastating nausea, while still others have made me tremble and look behind me in the dark; yet despite the worst of them I believe I can myself relate the most hideous thing of all—the shocking, the unnatural, the unbelievable horror from the shadows.

In 1915 I was a physician with the rank of First Lieutenant in a Canadian regiment in Flanders, one of many Americans to precede the government itself into the gigantic struggle. I had not entered the army on my own initiative, but rather as a natural result of the enlistment of the man whose indispensable assistant I was—the celebrated Boston surgical specialist, Dr. Herbert West. Dr. West had been avid for a chance to serve as surgeon in a great war, and when the chance had come he carried me with him almost against my will. There were reasons why I would have been glad to let the war separate us; reasons why I found the practice of medicine and the companionship of West more and more irritating; but when he had gone to Ottawa and through a colleague's influence secured a medical commission as Major, I could not resist the imperious persuasion of one determined that I should accompany him in my usual capacity.

When I say that Dr. West was avid to serve in battle, I do not mean to imply that he was either naturally warlike or anxious for the safety of civilization. Always an ice-cold intellectual machine; slight, blond, blue-eyed, and spectacled; I think he secretly sneered at my occasional martial enthusiasms and censures of supine neutrality. There was, however, something he wanted in embattled Flanders; and in order to secure it he had to assume a military exterior. What he wanted was not a thing which many persons want, but something connected with the peculiar branch of medical science which he had chosen quite clandestinely to follow, and in which he had achieved amazing and occasionally hideous results. It was, in fact, nothing more or less than an abundant supply of freshly killed men in every stage of dismemberment.

118

Herbert West needed fresh bodies because his life-work was the reanimation of the dead. This work was not known to the fashionable clientele who had so swiftly built up his fame after his arrival in Boston; but was only too well known to me, who had been his closest friend and sole assistant since the old days in Miskatonic University Medical School at Arkham. It was in those college days that he had begun his terrible experiments, first on small animals and then on human bodies shockingly obtained. There was a solution which he injected into the veins of dead things, and if they were fresh enough they responded in strange ways. He had had much trouble in discovering the proper formula, for each type of organism was found to need a stimulus especially adapted to it. Terror stalked him when he reflected on his partial failures; nameless things resulting from imperfect solutions or from bodies insufficiently fresh. A certain number of these failures had remained alive—one was in an asylum while others had vanished—and as he thought of conceivable yet virtually impossible eventualities he often shivered beneath his usual stolidity.

West had soon learned that absolute freshness was the prime requisite for useful specimens, and had accordingly resorted to frightful and unnatural expedients in body-snatching. In college, and during our early practice together in the factory town of Bolton, my attitude toward him had been largely one of fascinated admiration; but as his boldness in methods grew, I began to develop a gnawing fear. I did not like the way he looked at healthy living bodies; and then there came a nightmarish session in the cellar laboratory when I learned that a certain specimen had been a living body when he secured it. That was the first time he had ever been able to revive the quality of rational thought in a corpse; and his success, obtained at such a loathsome cost, had completely hardened him.

Of his methods in the intervening five years I dare not speak. I was held to him by sheer force of fear, and witnessed sights that no human tongue could repeat. Gradually I came to find Herbert West himself more horrible than anything he did—that was when it dawned on me that his once normal scientific zeal for prolonging life had subtly degenerated into a mere morbid and ghoulish curiosity and secret sense of charnel picturesqueness. His interest became a hellish and perverse addiction to the repellently and fiendishly abnormal; he gloated calmly over artificial monstrosities which would make most healthy men drop dead from fright and disgust; he became, behind his pallid intellectuality, a fastidious Baudelaire of physical experiment—a languid Elagabalus of the tombs.

Dangers he met unflinchingly; crimes he committed unmoved. I think the climax came when he had proved his point that rational life can be restored, and had sought new worlds to conquer by experimenting on the reanimation of detached parts of bodies. He had wild and original ideas on the independent vital properties of organic cells and nerve tissue separated from natural physiological systems; and achieved some hideous preliminary results in the form of never-dying, artificially nourished tissue obtained from the nearly hatched eggs of an indescribable tropical reptile. Two biological points he was exceedingly anxious to settle—first, whether any amount of consciousness and rational action be possible without the brain, proceeding from the spinal cord and various nerve-centers; and second, whether any kind of ethereal, intangible relation distinct from the material cells may exist to link the surgically separated parts of what has previously been a single living organism. All this research work required a prodigious supply of freshly slaughtered human flesh—and that was why Herbert West had entered the Great War.

The phantasmal, unmentionable thing occurred one midnight late in March, 1915, in a field hospital behind the lines at St. Eloi. I wonder even now if it could have been other than a daemoniac dream of delirium. West had a private laboratory in an east room of the barn-like temporary edifice, assigned him on his plea that he was devising new and radical methods for the treatment of hitherto hopeless cases of maiming. There he worked like a butcher in the midst of his gory wares—I could never get used to the levity with which he handled and classified certain things. At times he actually did perform marvels of surgery for the soldiers; but his chief delights were of a less public and philanthropic kind, requiring many explanations of sounds which seemed peculiar even amidst that babel of the damned. Among these sounds were frequent revolver shots—surely not uncommon on a battlefield, but distinctly uncommon in a hospital. Dr. West's reanimated specimens were not meant for long existence or a large audience. Besides human tissue, West employed much of the reptile embryo tissue which he had cultivated with such singular results. It was better than human material for maintaining life in organless fragments, and that was now my friend's chief activity. In a dark corner of the laboratory, over a queer incubating burner, he kept a large covered vat full of this reptilian cell matter; which multiplied and grew puffily and hideously.

On the night of which I speak we had a splendid new specimen—a man at once physically powerful and of such high mentality that a sensitive nervous system was assured. It was rather ironic, for he was the officer who had helped West to his commission, and who was now to have been our associate. Moreover, he had in the past secretly studied the theory of reanimation to some extent under West. Major Sir Eric Moreland Clapham-Lee, D.S.O., was the greatest surgeon in our division, and had been hastily assigned to the St. Eloi sector when news of the heavy fighting reached headquarters. He had come in an aëroplane piloted by the intrepid Lieut. Ronald Hill, only to be shot down when directly over his destination. The fall had been spectacular and awful; Hill was unrecognizable afterward, but the wreck yielded up the great surgeon in a nearly decapitated but otherwise intact condition. West had greedily seized the lifeless thing which had once been his friend and fellow scholar; and I shuddered when he finished severing the head, placed it in his hellish vat of pulpy reptile-tissue to preserve it for future experiments, and proceeded to treat the decapitated body on the operating table. He injected new blood, joined certain veins, arteries, and nerves at the headless neck, and closed the ghastly aperture with engrafted skin from an unidentified specimen which had borne an officer's uniform. I knew what he wanted—to see if this highly organized body could exhibit, without its head, any of the signs of mental life which had distinguished Sir Eric Moreland Clapham-Lee. Once a student of reanimation, this silent trunk was now gruesomely called upon to exemplify it.

I can still see Herbert West under the sinister electric light as he injected his reanimating solution into the arm of the headless body. The scene I cannot describe—I should faint if I tried it, for there is madness in a room full of classified charnel things, with blood and lesser human debris almost ankle deep on the slimy floor, and with hideous reptilian abnormalities sprouting, bubbling, and baking over a winking bluish-green specter of dim flame in a far corner of black shadows.

The specimen, as West repeatedly observed, had a splendid nervous system. Much was expected of it; and as a few twitching motions began to appear, I could see the feverish interest on West's face. He was ready, I think, to see proof of his increasingly strong opinion that consciousness, reason, and personality can exist independently of the brain—that man has no central connective spirit, but is merely a machine of nervous matter, each section more or less complete in itself. In one triumphant demonstration West was about to relegate the mystery of life to the category of myth. The body now twitched more vigorously, and beneath our avid eyes commenced to heave in a frightful way. The arms stirred disquietingly, the legs drew up, and various muscles contracted in a repulsive kind of writhing. Then the headless thing threw out its arms in a gesture which was unmistakably one of desperation—an intelligent desperation apparently sufficient to prove every theory of Herbert West. Certainly, the nerves were recalling the man's last act in life; the struggle to get free of the falling aëroplane.

What followed, I shall never positively know. It may have been wholly an hallucination from the shock caused at that instant by the sudden and complete destruction of the building in a cataclysm of German shellfire—who can gainsay it, since West and I were the only proved survivors? West liked to think that before his recent disappearance, but there were times when he could not; for it was queer that we both had the same hallucination. The hideous occurrence itself was very simple, notable only for what it implied.

The body on the table had risen with a blind and terrible groping, and we had heard a sound. I should not call that sound a voice, for it was too awful. And yet its timbre was not the most awful thing about it. Neither was its message—

it had merely screamed, "Jump, Ronald, for God's sake, jump!" The awful thing was its source.

For it had come from the large covered vat in that ghoulish corner of crawling black shadows.

The Tomb-Legions

When Dr. Herbert West disappeared a year ago, the Boston police questioned me closely. They suspected that I was holding something back, and perhaps suspected graver things; but I could not tell them the truth because they would not have believed it. They knew, indeed, that West had been connected with activities beyond the credence of ordinary men; for his hideous experiments in the reanimation of dead bodies had long been too extensive to admit of perfect secrecy; but the final soul-shattering catastrophe held elements of demoniac phantasy which make even me doubt the reality of what I saw.

I was West's closest friend and only confidential assistant. We had met years before, in medical school, and from the first I had shared his terrible researches. He had slowly tried to perfect a solution which, injected into the veins of the newly deceased, would restore life; a labor demanding an abundance of fresh corpses and therefore involving the most unnatural actions. Still more shocking were products of some of the experiments—grisly masses of flesh that had been dead, but that West waked to a blind, brainless, nauseous animation. These were the usual results, for in order to reawaken the mind it was necessary to have specimens so absolutely fresh that no decay could possibly affect the delicate brain cells.

This need for very fresh corpses had been West's moral undoing. They were hard to get, and one awful day he had secured his specimen while it was still alive and vigorous. A struggle, a needle, and a powerful alkaloid had transformed it to a very fresh corpse, and the experiment had succeeded for a brief and memorable moment; but West had emerged with a soul calloused and seared, and a hardened eye which sometimes glanced with a kind of hideous and calculating appraisal at men of especially sensitive brain and especially vigorous physique. Toward the last I became acutely afraid of West, for he began to look at me that way. People did not seem to notice his glances, but they noticed my fear; and after his disappearance used that as a basis for some absurd suspicions.

West, in reality, was more afraid than I; for his abominable pursuits entailed a life of furtiveness and dread of every shadow. Partly it was the police he feared; but sometimes his nervousness was deeper and more nebulous, touching on certain indescribable things into which he had injected a morbid life, and from which he had not seen that life depart. He usually finished his experiments with a revolver, but a few times he had not been quick enough. There was that first specimen on whose rifled grave marks of clawing were later seen. There was also that Arkham professor's body which had done cannibal things before it had been captured and thrust unidentified into a madhouse cell at Sefton, where it beat the walls for sixteen years. Most of the other possibly surviving results were things less easy to speak of— for in later years West's scientific zeal had degenerated to an unhealthy and fantastic mania, and he had spent his chief skill in vitalizing not entire human bodies but isolated parts of bodies, or parts joined to organic matter other than human. It had become fiendishly disgusting by the time he disappeared; many of the experiments could not even be hinted at in print. The Great War, through which both of us served as surgeons, had intensified this side of West.

In saying that West's fear of his specimens was nebulous, I have in mind particularly its complex nature. Part of it came merely from knowing of the existence of such nameless monsters, while another part arose from apprehension of the bodily harm they might under certain circumstances do him. Their disappearance added horror to the situation—of them all West knew the whereabouts of only one, the pitiful asylum thing. Then there was a more subtle fear—a very fantastic sensation resulting from a curious experiment in the Canadian army in 1915. West, in the midst of a severe battle, had reanimated Major Sir Eric Moreland Clapham-Lee, D.S.O., a fellow-physician who knew about his experiments and could have duplicated them. The head had been removed, so that the possibilities of quasi-intelligent life in the trunk might be investigated. Just as the building was wiped out by a German shell, there had been a success. The trunk had moved intelligently; and, unbelievable to relate, we were both sickeningly sure that articulate sounds had come from the detached head as it lay in a shadowy corner of the laboratory. The shell had been merciful, in a way—but West could never feel as certain as he wished, that we two were the only survivors. He used to make shuddering conjectures about the possible actions of a headless physician with the power of reanimating the dead.

West's last quarters were in a venerable house of much elegance, overlooking one of the oldest burying grounds in Boston. He had chosen the place for surely symbolic and fantastically aesthetic reasons, since most of the interments were of the colonial period and therefore of little use to a scientist seeking very fresh bodies. The laboratory was in a subcellar secretly constructed by imported workmen, and contained a huge incinerator for the quiet and complete disposal of such bodies, or fragments and synthetic mockeries of bodies, as might remain from the morbid experiments and unhallowed amusements of the owner. During the excavation of this cellar the workmen had struck some exceedingly ancient masonry; undoubtedly connected with the old burying ground, yet far too deep to correspond with any known sepulchre therein. After a number of calculations West decided that it represented some secret chamber beneath the tomb of the Averills, where the last interment had been made in 1768. I was with him when he studied the nitrous, dripping walls laid bare by the spades and mattocks of the men, and was prepared for the gruesome thrill which would attend the uncovering of centuried grave-secrets; but for the first time West's new timidity conquered his natural curiosity, and he betrayed his degenerating fibre by ordering the masonry left intact and plastered over. Thus it remained till that final hellish night; part of the walls of the secret laboratory. I speak of West's decadence, but must add that it was a purely mental and intangible thing. Outwardly he was the same to the last—calm, cold, slight, and yellow-haired, with spectacled blue eyes and a general aspect of youth which years and fears seemed never to change. He seemed calm even when he thought of that clawed grave and looked over his shoulder; even when he thought of the carnivorous thing that gnawed and pawed at Sefton bars.

The end of Herbert West began one evening in our joint study when he was dividing his curious glance between the newspaper and me. A strange headline item had struck at him from the crumpled pages, and a nameless titan claw had seemed to reach down through sixteen years. Something fearsome and incredible had happened at Sefton Asylum fifty miles away, stunning the neighborhood and baffling the police. In the small hours of the morning a body of silent men had entered the grounds and their leader had aroused the attendants. He was a menacing military figure who talked without moving his lips and whose voice seemed almost ventriloquially connected with an immense black case he carried. His expressionless face was handsome to the point of radiant beauty, but had shocked the superintendent when the hall light fell on it—for it was a wax face with eyes of painted glass. Some nameless accident had befallen this man. A larger man guided his steps; a repellent hulk whose bluish face seemed half eaten away by some unknown malady. The speaker had asked for the custody of the cannibal monster committed from Arkham sixteen years before; and upon being refused, gave a signal which precipitated a shocking riot. The fiends had beaten, trampled, and bitten every attendant who did not flee; killing four and finally succeeding in the liberation of the monster. Those victims who could recall the event without hysteria swore that the creatures had acted less like men than like unthinkable automata guided by the wax-faced leader. By the time help could be summoned, every trace of the men and of their mad charge had vanished.

From the hour of reading this item until midnight, West sat almost paralyzed. At midnight the doorbell rang, startling him fearfully. All the servants were asleep in the attic, so I answered the bell. As I have told the police, there was no wagon in the street; but only a group of strange looking figures bearing a large square box which they deposited in the hallway after one of them had grunted in a highly unnatural voice, "Express—prepaid." They filed out of the house with a jerky tread, and as I watched them go I had an odd idea that they were turning toward the ancient cemetery on which the back of the house abutted. When I slammed the door after them West came downstairs and looked at the box. It was about two feet square, and bore West's correct name and present address. It also bore the inscription, "From Eric Moreland Clapham-Lee, St. Eloi, Flanders." Six years before, in Flanders, a shelled hospital had fallen upon the headless reanimated trunk of Dr. Clapham-Lee, and upon the detached head which—perhaps—had uttered articulate sounds.

West was not even excited now. His condition was more ghastly. Quickly he said, "It's the finish—but let's incinerate—this." We carried the thing down to the laboratory—listening. I do not remember many particulars—you can imagine my state of mind—but it is a vicious lie to say it was Herbert West's body which I put into the incinerator. We both inserted the whole unopened wooden box, closed the door, and started the electricity. Nor did any sound come from the box, after all.

It was West who first noticed the falling plaster on that part of the wall where the ancient tomb masonry had been covered up. I was going to run, but he stopped me. Then I saw a small black aperture, felt a ghoulish wind of ice, and smelled the charnel bowels of a putrescent earth. There was no sound, but just then the electric lights went out and I saw outlined against some phosphorescence of the nether world a horde of silent toiling things which only insanity—or worse—could create. Their outlines were human, semi-human, fractionally human, and not human at all—the horde was grotesquely heterogeneous. They were removing the stones quietly, one by one, from the centuried wall. And then, as the breach became large enough, they came out into the laboratory in single file; led by a stalking thing with a beautiful head made of wax. A sort of mad-eyed monstrosity behind the leader seized on Herbert West. West did not resist or utter a sound. Then they all sprang at him and tore him to pieces before my eyes, bearing the fragments away into that subterranean vault of fabulous abominations. West's head was carried off by the wax-headed leader, who wore a Canadian officer's uniform. As it disappeared I saw that the blue eyes behind the spectacles were hideously blazing with their first touch of frantic, visible emotion.

Servants found me unconscious in the morning. West was gone. The incinerator contained only unidentifiable ashes. Detectives have questioned me, but what can I say? The Sefton tragedy they will not connect with West; not that, nor the men with the box, whose existence they deny. I told them of the vault, and they pointed to the unbroken plaster wall and laughed. So I told them no more. They imply that I am either a madman or a murderer—probably I am mad. But I might not be mad if those accursed tomb-legions had not been so silent.

Called the greatest writer of the supernatural since Poe, H. P. Lovecraft was a gaunt, almost-reclusive writer born in Rhode Island in 1890. Precocious and largely self-educated, Lovecraft was writing a monthly astrology column at sixteen. Patterning his life after that of an English gentleman of the 1800s, Lovecraft became a ghost writer and revisionist to supplement his income as a writer of the macabre. His first professional sale was "Herbert West: Reanimator," and he is noted for his Cthulhu Mythos stories. After his death in 1936, Arkham House re-published most of his work, and his fame has grown immensely.

The Thorntons loved their new house and knew they would be happy there for a long time—if they could just find out why it was haunted.

NINE

A Friendly Exorcise
Talmage Powell

Although located in New Brecon, Vermont, it was not a "New England house." It had no historical flavor, no fanciful gables, no brooding cupolas, no hint of secrets behind darkly staring windows. It was far too sunny and cheerful to remind one of Salem witches and Lizzie Borden axes dripping blood.

But it was a very special house, in that it now belonged to Judy and me, and the mortgage company.

It was our miracle house, our discovery after dogged weeks of searching. Other young couples starting from scratch don't have to be told what I'm talking about, the mind-boggling prices, the magnitude of mortgages. The American Dream time and again hovers agonizingly just out of reach.

"We can go up Shay's Knob, take squatter's rights, and dig a cave," I finally said to Judy.

"Ski back and forth in the winter," she said cheerfully. "Think of the savings in gasoline money. By the time we're fifty we should accumulate enough to satisfy the sellers and lenders."

"If we don't break a leg skiing to the supermarket and blow it all on hospitals."

We munched along on our lunch of 'burgers and fries.

"Wonderful view from the Knob. All the way from the old textile mills to the cliffs of the quarry. Town square. Town hall. Steeple of the Congregational Church. Streets we know so well, sunshine and maple tree shade . . ." Her white, even teeth snapped together. "Damn! It just isn't fair!"

"Hear, hear!"

"All I want is a view from our own front window toward friendly houses along a decent street."

It seemed little enough to ask, and I thought about it while I dropped Judy and returned to my own office. The thinking process brought on a slow burn of frustration, and I barked a hello when the phone shrilled at me.

"Mrs. Reichert here," she said. She was a fiftyish woman, bronzed and iron-gray, who looked like a safari guide or leader of a team of mountain climbers. Her agency moved more real estate than any other in New Brecon. "You want a nice house on a white-collar street, fetch your wife, bring your checkbook, and meet me at four-oh-three Kenilworth Drive. It just hit the market. At the price and terms it will last until about five o'clock, if a speculator doesn't get there first."

Like that.

Homeowners.

And we sent Mrs. Reichert a dozen long-stemmed roses.

Judy and I existed in a sort of breathless, dreamy delirium, trying to realize events as they were occurring, papers being signed, ritual of closing, shopping, planning. In the house at last . . .

I was putting up the traverse rods for the living room draperies when Judy's terrified squeal echoed in an empty room. She sounded like a woman who'd had the world's biggest mouse scurry between her feet.

The sound lifted me off the hassock where I'd been standing to add height to my somewhat bony six-one. I jetted toward the source of the sound, skidding off the hallway into the empty bedroom.

Judy, the delectable, hadn't been frightened by a mouse. Instead, the culprit was a sweatsock. That's right, an ordinary white woolen sweatsock, misshapen and slightly bedraggled from having been laundered many times. It lay in the middle of the bare floor, and it had to be the source of her trouble. Besides Judy there was nothing else in the room. She stood pressed against the wall, elfin face pale, blue eyes round. Pointing at the sock, she tried to talk, getting hung up on the "J" in my name.

"J-J-J-Jim, that darn thing floated out of the closet and g-g-g-gave me a hug across the face!"

She was making no sense whatever to me. I gawked at her, and the expression on my face bugged some of the fright out of her. Her eyes began to flash.

"Don't you care that an old sweatsock floats out of a closet, halfway across an empty room, and nuzzles up to your bride, Jim Thornton?"

"Well, I . . . uh . . . sure I care! But how could it have happened?"

"You tell me. You're the brain. All I know is what happened. When I'd finished putting things away in the bedroom, I came in here. I was thinking how we'd fix this room for a nursery some day. Then that sock . . ." She shuddered. "I wouldn't let my baby take a twenty minute nap in this room."

I detoured the sock, grinning at her. "Baby? Judy, you're pregnant already!"

She shook off my clutching hands. "Don't be silly! We've been married less than a month. I haven't had time to know if I'm pregnant or not. But when we do have a baby, James Arnold Thornton, you'd better have an explanation for anti-gravity sweatsocks, if we stay in this house."

I turned and sank to one knee beside the sock. I poked it with a finger. Nothing supernatural occurred. The sock was as commonplace and ordinary as . . . well, as old sweatsocks.

"When the Bicklefords moved out," I pronounced, "the sock was overlooked. It was probably in a dark corner of the closet shelf."

"Brilliant," said Judy, putting her sunny blonde head next to my drab brown thatch. "Of course it was overlooked by their movers."

"And a breeze happened to blow it across your face."
"Breeze?"
"Capricious breeze."

She tilted her head and gave me a look. "Capricious breeze in an empty room with the windows closed."

Her matter of fact tone was worse than sarcasm. My male ego recoiled. "Naturally," I said with a certain hauteur, "the

131

first home I finagle with a mortgage company for my wife has to be fouled up with a poltergeist!"

She gingerly picked up the sock, stood, held the sock dangling at arm's length. "Now you're a little closer to the beam."

I stood up beside her, dusting my hands. "Come on, you can't be serious. You don't believe in zombies or voices from beyond the grave."

"Nope," she said, "but this sock is real as life. And poltergeists are too well authenticated to deny that *something* every now and then acts up in somebody's house. There have been any number of cases in England. And how about those people in Massachusetts whose house made the newspapers? And the house on Long Island—or was it in the Bronx—that was shown on the television newscast? Crockery flying all over the place in that one—and a team of tough New York cops staked out the joint and saw some of it happen! You going to fly in the face of hard-bitten, super-realistic New York cops?"

"Not me," I said helplessly.

"So there," Judy said. She had riveted her gaze on the sock all this while. Now a strange mood seemed to have overtaken all of her initial fright. "You know, I really don't think he was trying to frighten me. The touch of the sock was ever so gentle, a caress. I think he was trying to say hello and make friends. Still," she glanced about, "I'm not sure we should plan a nursery in here."

That's where the subject rested for the moment. I wandered back to work, more concerned than I cared to show. In our recent college days, Judy and I had both been as far from the LSD crowd as you could polarize. Just a couple of the hard-studying non-jets that made up ninety-five percent of the student body, sans publicity, and floating sweatsocks didn't fit into our pattern of living at all.

I finished hanging the living room draperies, heard Judy safely rattling pots, pans, and crockery from their packing crates in the kitchen, and ambled quietly out the front door.

If it hadn't been for that sweatsock, the day would have been perfect. Up to now, Judy and I had not dared hope to start off in such a house. It was of tasteful antique brick and redwood, half a dozen spacious rooms, built-in cabinets, stone fireplace, thirty-five–forty years old but built in that old New England eye and attitude that puts the foundation on bedrock and thumbs its nose at the on-coming centuries.

Thanks to Mrs. Reichert we had got in for practically nothing down and payments no higher than rent on a decent apartment. Wedding gifts, taken out of storage finally, and carefully budgeted credit would keep us from sleeping on the floor as a starter.

Perfection. Too much so? I couldn't get that sweatsock out of mind, and for the first time I paused to wonder exactly why that Bickleford fellow—the previous owner—had been so anxious to get out.

The house next door, to the west of us, was as quietly white collar as the rest of the neighborhood. The nameplate over the bell button said, "Tate Curzon."

I used the button, and chimes sounded inside. The door opened a few inches and stopped.

"Yes?" he said. He had a voice like a loose violin string being stroked with a scratchy bow.

"Mr. Tate Curzon?"

"So what if I am?"

The door offered no further welcome, remaining just slightly open. From what I could see of him, he was a wiry, narrow shouldered little guy in his late forties or early fifties. He had a long red neck rising out of his starched white collar, a narrow and cruel looking face, and a pinched-up bald pate that was so freckled it looked bloody. It was easy to behold the snappish visage and imagine a vulture's head.

I shuffled a bit uncomfortably. "Just thought I'd say hello. We're your new neighbors, James and Judy Thornton."

He looked me up and down, without approval. "I don't loan tools, carpet sweepers, fuse plugs, or lawn mowers."

"No, sir." I jammed my hands into my slacks pockets. "I didn't want to borrow anything."

"Then you're not disappointed. You got any kids?"

"Not yet, Mr. Curzon."

"Good thing. I hate brats. Always breaking down my rose arbor and throwing trash in my fish pond."

"Yes, well . . . I guess the Bicklefords had kids?"

"One. Stupid oaf. Boy. Eighteen. Always roaring in and out of the driveway in that stupid sports car of his."

"Yes, sir," I said, agreeable as butter. "I guess all boys are that way with their first car."

"His first and last," Mr. Tate Curzon said on a note of malice.

"You mean . . . he smashed it up?"

"And himself with it. Skidded one rainy night and went over the cliffs south of town. They picked up Andrew Bickleford—and his sports car—in little pieces."

"Gee, that's too bad!"

Mr. Curzon's eyes beaded. "You should care. Andy's mother had a nervous breakdown, and that nincompoop father couldn't put the house on the market fast enough."

The inference that I'd profited by a young stranger's death caused the heat to rise. I felt red from cheek to jowl. I let my eyes give Mr. Curzon's gimlet gaze tit for tat, and said stiffly, "Good day."

He slammed the door.

When I carried my burn back into my own premises I heard a couple of female voices in the kitchen. Judy and a blowsy and slightly brassy redhead of middle age were dunking teabags in Judy's new cups.

"Oh, hi, Jim. This is our neighbor, came over to say hello."

"Mrs. Curzon?" I asked, moving out of the doorway toward the kitchen table.

"Heavens, no," the woman laughed. "I'm Mabel Gosness. I live on the other side of you."

She chatted through the ritual of sipping tea and departed with the remark that it was wonderful to have young people in the neighborhood.

Judy carried the cups to the sink and began washing them. "We had real talk before the male presence befell us."

"Did you now?"

"She seemed terribly lonely, eager for someone to talk with. She lives alone—her husband ran away with another woman nearly a year ago."

"Maybe one who talked less."

Judy looked over her shoulder long enough to stick out her tongue. "And guess what else?"

"I give. What?"

"On the other side of us is a mean little man named Tate Curzon. He hates everybody. Had four wives, no less, children by one of them. But even his own kids—they're grown up now—never go near him. Mrs. Gosness says we're to having nothing to do with him."

"Thanks for the advice, but I've met the gentleman."

"Honest?"

"Sure," I said, taking the cups and saucers from her to dry. "Went over and said hello. Wondered if he could tell me why Bickleford was so anxious to sell this house."

Judy practically wriggled. "And did you find out?"

I hesitated, balanced on the point of a fib, then realized she would find out from Mrs. Gosness anyway. So I told her about young Andy Bickleford who'd been picked up in pieces and a mother whose mind hadn't been able to take it and a father-husband to whom the end of the world had come.

"I'll bet that sock was Andy's. The room must have been his." A suspicion of tears touched Judy's eyes.

By bedtime, our first day of settling into our new home had got our minds off the tragic Bicklefords. They were, after all, strangers, and the present was much too vivid. I lounged in the master bedroom in shorts, my sleeping apparel, nonchalantly pretending to read with the pillow stuffed behind my head. Actually I had the dressing room doorway framed in my vision over the edge of the book; and then the door opened and Judy stepped into the soft bedroom lighting wearing a nylon nightgown that was next to nothing. My civilized veneer barely stifled a roar of pleasure.

Hair brushed about her shoulders and a little smile of mystery playing across her mouth, she seemed to glide toward me. A remark on my pulse rate would be needless.

Then as she passed the bureau, a strange thing happened. A ten- by twelve-inch picture of me which Judy had framed suddenly rose, hurled itself across the room and smashed against the wall.

The picture fell to the floor. There was a moment of dead silence, then a whispered tinkle as a bit of glass settled in the wreckage.

I sat up with the dream movements of a man swimming

through molasses. Judy and I knelt beside the picture, neither wanting to touch it.

"Your gown must have brushed against it," I mumbled.

"And knocked it all the way across the room?" Judy said with fearful logic.

I gathered the bits of broken glass, piled them on the picture, and carried the wreckage to the bureau. Judy watched me, wide-eyed and steeped in her own thoughts.

As I turned from the bureau, the murder mystery I'd been pretending to read jumped up and down on the bedside table. The edge of the book cover jarred against the lampshade. The lamp teetered, fell with a crash. Darkness flooded the room.

I wasn't sure whether Judy or I moved first, but in an instant we were standing in shivery embrace.

"Maybe we should check into a motel for the night," I suggested through chattering teeth.

Judy's warmth stirred in my arms. "Nope," she said, "I'm not being chased so easily out of our own house. Anyway, our poltergeist doesn't want to hurt us."

"What makes you so sure?"

"He hasn't thrown anything at us or on us," she said with supreme female logic. "He could have socked you with the picture frame if he were antagonistic."

"He's a sadist," I said, "who'd rather scare people to death a little at a time."

"Or a lonely fellow who's trying to tell us something," Judy mused. "He's certainly picking out a variety of items to toss around, which means he has method and purpose. If we could just get the message, I'm sure he'd go away and rest in peace."

Red-eyed and haggard, I muddled through my junior accountant's job the next day. I was worried about Judy's almost natural acceptance of the existence of a poltergeist. In the warm light of day, I just didn't believe what I had seen for myself. There had to be an explanation, like the juxtaposition of magnetic forces at the spot where our house stood.

I would have welcomed some advice, but could think of no source. My hard-headed, realistic boss was definitely out. If I went to the cops, the newspapers would pick it off the public record. We'd be subjected to the same glare of publicity that had roasted every other family so rash as to reveal acquaintance with a poltergeist. I wondered how many, like myself, had preferred to suffer the inexplicable in silence.

The house looked as normal as peaches and cream when I hurried up the front walk. A bouncy and smiling Judy had a not-very-dry martini waiting, the kind I like. She'd also fractured her grocery budget with a two-inch-thick T-bone steak, but I applauded her.

"No flying crockery today?" I asked as she slipped the steak under the broiler.

"Not even a saucer," she said.

"Maybe the strain proved too much for him," I said hopefully, munching the olive marinated in vermouth and gin.

We dined elegantly by candlelight, the table graced with snowy linen that had been a wedding present from my Aunt Ellen.

I'd had no appetite for lunch, but I worked like a scavenger on the steak. Judy served coffee, and we eyed each other across the table in affectionate silence.

The steak bone made like a Mexican jumping bean all of a sudden, rapping against the plate.

Judy blinked. I jumped. My chair tipped over backward. I grabbed the edge of the table and hung there, watching the bone jump up and down at eye level.

The bone made no threatening motions, but it was a desecration of our privacy. "Enough is enough," I snarled. I rose, cupped my hands, and pounced on the bone. It offered no resistance as I smacked it against the plate. I raised my fingers one at a time, and was a little miffed when the bone just lay there after it was freed.

I sneaked a glance at Judy. "You did see that, too, didn't you?"

Judy nodded an affirmative, her eyes glinting. "I wonder what he meant?"

"Maybe that he's hungry," I growled. "Maybe you should brew him up a spot of newt's eyes over some sulphur and brimstone."

"Don't be facetious, Jim!"

"Facetious? I'm not even rational any longer."

137

While Judy washed the dishes and tidied up after dinner, I did a sneaky search of the house from attic to basement. I didn't find any wires, magnets, or other device remotely resembling the tools of a screwball practical joker.

When I went upstairs from the basement, Judy was curled in our new wing chair before the television set.

"You might have saved your time," she said with wifely forbearance. "I covered every nook and crack myself today. Not that I needed any more proof that we really have a poltergeist."

"I favor selling," I said. "I could put the place on the market by phoning the real estate agent at her home right now."

She sat up. "Don't you dare, Jim Thornton! This poor fellow got stuck here, and when he gets unstuck he will go away and leave us alone."

"Oh, yeah? And I suppose you still think he's trying to deliver a message?"

"More than ever. That rattling bone meant something—if I could just figure out what. Why'd he wait all day until he had the bone to rattle, if he wasn't trying to tell us something?"

I eased to a sitting position on the hassock before her. "Judy," I said gently, "I think I'd better get you out of here before we spend another night in this place."

"Don't be sil! It's a perfectly lovely house."

"But all this talk—"

"He's a perfectly nice poltergeist—and I'm not going to leave." She smiled, leaned forward to pat my cheek. "Be a darling and flip the tuner to channel twelve. There's an hour-long comedy special coming up in about five minutes."

I not only switched the TV, I went and made myself a double-barreled martini, very dry this time. I sipped it and also its big brother while the hour-long was on. Six ounces of nearly straight gin later I settled back in the recliner, a wedding gift of Judy's cousin Ned. I clasped my hands across my midriff comfortably and prepared to think it out.

The TV music faded. The draperies seemed to waver and shake as my heavy lids blotted them out. Lousy draperies, I thought vaguely, with their floral pattern of red roses. Just like Judy's Uncle Horace to give them to us. . . .

I awoke with a muscular jerk that popped a crick out of my neck. I dropped the recliner to sitting position, running my tongue around the inside of my gin-wool mouth. A late newscast was on the television. A crashing mortar attack by guerrillas against an American base overseas seemed to have awakened me.

"Judy?" I said.

She was nowhere in the living-room, bedroom, or kitchen. I made the circuit, beginning to sweat hard by the time I'd come full circle.

The emptiness and silence of the house (except for the insistent TV) began to smother me. I turned off the set with a vicious flip of fingers that were trembling.

"Easy," I ordered myself. "If anything had happened, you'd have heard the ruckus."

Maybe she'd stepped next door to chin a little with Mrs. Gosness and break the boredom of listening to a husband's snore.

I hurried to the east window, pulled the drapery aside; no lights over there. Mrs. Gosness was already off to dreamland, not sipping tea with a next door neighbor.

I took jerky steps back to the middle of the room. My skin was turning icy and exuding a steam of sweat at one and the same time. If the house hadn't been haunted before, it certainly felt so now. The empty wing chair where Judy had been sitting seemed to throb in my vision. Then I saw that something new had been added. On the hassock before the chair, she'd laid a piece of paper, a pencil, and the magazine she'd used for a backing as she'd written.

I snatched up the paper. She hadn't left me a note. Instead, it was a record of her thoughts while I'd slept. Around the margin were curlicues where she'd doodled between words, sentences, phrases.

She'd written:

"The hints—sock—smashed picture—mystery novel—broken lamp—rattling bone—agitated rose-patterned drapes."

So the drapes had really shaken. I steadied the paper and kept reading.

"Sock—friendly—friendly Andy Bickleford—but picture smashed with a great deal of violence—picture of Jim—

Jim's a male—only picture of male in house—male smashed by violence! Friendly Andy trying to say he was smashed violently? Not killed accidentally at all! Slugged, put in sports car, pushed over cliffs!—Why? Because of something he'd done?—done bone—bone did—bone does—darn you, bone!—Well, let's see . . . If Andy didn't do anything, maybe he was undone because of something he'd witnessed—see bone—bone from T-bone steak, useless—except to a doggie—doggie would go out and bury bone—BURIED BONE—hidden weapon?—Buried weapon that killed Andy before he was stuffed in sports car and driven to those dreadful cliffs?—Buried where—Next hint, final clue, quaking draperies—draped for burial—nope—bedroom draperies weren't chosen—specific draperies—those in the living room with roses—buried with roses—buried under roses—weapon buried under only rose arbor in neighborhood!"

I dropped the paper. The gimlet eyes and the scratchy violin-string voice flashed through my mind, "—hate brats. Always throwing trash in my fish pond and breaking my rose arbor."

The night coolness washed across my face before I even realized I'd run outside. A pale moon bathed our backyards, ours and Mr. Tate Curzon's. I slipped through the shadows cast by our house, my eyes seeking and searching.

Then I heard a muffled cry and jerked my attention from the rose arbor next door. I saw the struggling shadows near Mr. Curzon's basement door. He heard my pounding footsteps, and as my presence loomed over him, Curzon shoved Judy sprawling and laid a hard little fist in my kisser.

My knees buckled and my nose dug a furrow. He kicked me hard in the ribs. Breath whoofed out, but as he spun and started to run away, my grabbing hand found an ankle. I yanked, and this time Mr. Curzon fell. He writhed around and started lashing me with his fists. I disliked picking on such a little fellow, but he ignored my orders to lie still, so I grabbed him by his thin neck and popped his head against the hard ground. It proved to be an anesthetizing measure. He would remain unconscious for several minutes at least.

Judy grabbed my arms, helped me to my feet. Then she put her arms around me and collapsed against my chest.

"Oh, Jim! I was peeping about his rose arbor and suddenly he was there. He grabbed me, and I screamed just once before he—"

I tipped her face up and kissed her. She began to sob with relief. I picked her up and my shoulder was a very nice cradle for her head.

"I think we'd better call the police," I said.

We thought it discreet to omit mention of the poltergeist, inferring to the police that Mr. Curzon had been acting strangely around his roses and launched his murderous attack when Judy's curiosity got the better of her.

It turned out that the police had previously questioned Mr. Curzon in the disappearance of one of his wives. Their probe of the rose arbor turned up the remains of the fourth Mrs. Curzon. Perhaps it was suspicion or evidence of this that led to Andy Bickleford's untimely demise.

We can't know for sure. The poltergeist hasn't been around since that fateful night, and if the subject came up, Judy and I would be first to agree that nobody in his right mind could believe in poltergeists. Like all the silent others who've shared similar experiences, we don't want our friends thinking we are soft in the head.

I do, however, feel the poltergeist should have assisted a bit longer. An army of cops and insurance investigators are going nuts trying to find out what happened to Mrs. Curzons, numbers one, two, three.

Talmage Powell has written nineteen novels under several names. Born in North Carolina in 1920, he was educated in several schools before finishing at the University of North Carolina. He worked as a police reporter before selling his first story, and he has now written more than five hundred stories, including such tales as "Last Run of the Night," "Sunstroke at Midnight," and the western "Star for a Warrior." Several of his better stories have been collected in Written for Hitchcock. *His novel,* The Smasher, *shows his virtues of tight construction and careful plotting.*

Every guy in the bar had tried to pick up Donna, but Howard only wanted to talk. He had a message that some living person must understand.

TEN

Safety Zone
Barry Malzberg

The view that human relations exist only as engulfment is a serious limitation on a narrative artist. Toward the end of his life, Lovecraft seems to have been unhappily aware of this.

—Joanna Russ

On the singles circuit in Providence, every night a new night. The most densely populated state, of course. Every night a new disaster, I should have said. Some are tall and some are short, some are thin and some are rich (but never those who come on to you) but there is, as they say, a common denominator. That common denominator is not sex, however, it is craziness. Why do I partake? This is a question for the tombstone. In the meantime, I move around. It keeps me interested.

On the left, that night, two guys were arguing about craft. Love craft, they said, he would have been a hundred years old this year. Can you imagine that guy being a hundred? They giggled. Love craft, I want to respond, love craft is not a hundred years old, love craft has not been *born* in this place. But I deduced from the conversation that the subject was some writer, not sex. Supernatural writer. Love craft is the most supernatural thing around, I wanted to say, but starting a conversation is always risky. They went on to talk about dogs and then colors in space. It takes all kinds.

Engulfment, this guy on my right said, a strange-looking dude with big eyeballs and hands, the hands floundering into one another. He leaned forward. That's what I wanted, don't you see? But of course that was the mistake.

What mistake? I said, not to be encouraging, just to give him a place to hang his hat.

Just one of them, he said. To embrace one another, it is necessary that we give, not merely entrap. What's your name?

Not a terrific night at Dancer's Lounge. The two on my left were already getting ready to split, maybe to try out some love craft on each other, a few of the bowling machine boys behind me pounding on each other, giving high signs, another cluster at the machine itself. Nowhere really to hide then and all of them had hit on me and knew enough to stay away.

Well, I should quit weekday nights, sure. I really should, go to community college, improve my mind, but what is the point? What is the point, really? Community college is full of guys like this too and nothing to drink and the other way is to stay in the apartment and look at George and look at George and look at George until I want to throw an ashtray or worse. It is best to get out. Before his agoraphobia stopped him cold as George put it, he felt the same way. Now he feels the other way. He is into chapters of his auto-biography.

What's it to you? I said to the guy with the eyeballs. What's your name?

Howard Phillips, he said. I'm forty-seven years old. He put a hand on my arm, ran his fingers up and down. It's not engulfment, he said. I was looking for a little tenderness, that was all. You still haven't told me—

I'm Donna, I said. Just Donna. Do you have to touch my arm?

Well, no, he said. He raised his hand, shrugged his shoulders, moved back on the stool. I don't have to do anything. You're pretty, he said. Do you want to go for a walk?

A walk? I said, you have to be kidding. In the faint light he seemed to have a certain charm, maybe an intensity, but he was an old guy and no way around it. On the other hand, this was the first time at Dancer's in months that I had been offered anything but a drink or the chance to have a heavenly experience. No, I said, I don't want to walk. I just got here. I want to sit a while, make the scene. I haven't seen you here before.

I live in the neighborhood, he said. I just haven't been around for a while. I kind of keep to myself.

Right, I say, there's a lot of that around. People are keeping to themselves a lot these days. It has to do with the times.

But you're pretty, Donna, he said. I look at you and I wish I had come here a long time ago. Engulfment, that was all wrong. I should have been trying to get out of myself, to really give. You know what I mean?

Is your first name Howard and your last name Phillips? I said. Or are you Howard Phillips something else?

Oh, he said. I'm just Howard Phillips. He shook his head, thought of leaning forward, then seemed to consider it too dangerous and half turned. Tell me about yourself, he said. I want to get to know you, Donna.

There's nothing to know. I come and sit on stools and listen to the music. What is this about engulfment?

Oh, never mind, he said. That's something else. I shouldn't have brought it up. He reached out, touched my hand. You have nice hands, he said.

Let it go, I said. I might have said it a little loudly. He dropped my hand fast, picked up his glass, seemed to shudder. You don't start touching someone you don't know, I said.

One of the guys behind me said, This guy bothering you, Donna? You want us to talk to him? Richie will straighten him right out.

Leave him out of it, I said. I need help, I'll tell you.

Because we're always ready to serve, Donna. We're here to help you. You're our mascot.

I listened to them laugh. I heard that laugh a lot without ever wanting to go anywhere with it. Hey, guy, what's your name? Richie said, looking at Howard Phillips, you got an agenda? You got business? They all laughed again.

I waved at Richie. Go away. I said. I can handle this. Howard Phillips just wants to talk, isn't that right?

Howard Phillips nodded, both hands flat on the bar. Talk, he said, that's right. Nothing else. He hunched over as if under attack. I don't want to hurt anyone, he said. I just wanted to talk to you, that's all, see what I was missing. See what was going on here.

That's all right, Richie, I said. You hear him now? He just wants conversation.

Well, you're the girl, Richie said. Donna's the conversation girl.

Providence has sure changed, Howard Phillips said. It's changed a lot.

Since when? I said. Since last night?

Oh, something like that, he said. He stood suddenly, loomed over me. I wonder what Sonia would have made of this, he said. I wonder what would have happened to her here.

Sonia? A girlfriend of yours?

My wife, Howard Phillips said. I mean, she used to be my wife. I've been divorced for years and years. You don't think that I'd dishonor her by coming out to drink alone and talking to a young lady if I were still married, do you? Come on, he said, with a sudden change of expression, that kind of shift I had already come to understand. A very peculiar guy. Let me take you outside. I just want to walk with you. I can't take too much of being inside places. I have to move around. And I write too many letters. I won't hurt you, he said. I'll pay for your drink, here. He reached into his pocket, put a twenty on the bar. I have plenty of money, he said. Money was never a problem for me, Donna. Can we walk?

It was all too much for me. One minute you are sitting in a dark place, trying to make a little open channel for yourself and the next some strange tall guy is all over you, making demands. You ought to meet George, I said. You and he should really get together.

George?

The guy I live with, I said. He can't stand to go outdoors. You say you can't stand being in small spaces. Maybe the two of you could trade off, strike a happy medium. I don't mind, I said, I'll go for a walk with you. It's all the same to me. It's Tuesday night and I don't want to go anywhere.

You live with someone? Howard Phillips said.

Last time I looked, I said. I stood, moved toward the door. You want to walk or something then? It's up to you. I waved to the guys clumped around the machine, two of them waved back. Up to her old tricks, they were thinking. They

145

should only know, I thought. They should know what I got here.

Howard Phillips waited at the door, opened it for me, gently eased me into the parking lot. A nice night, he said, looking up and then at the ground, cobblestones and stars, splitting the difference, looking at me. But it's changed all right, Providence. It's not what it was.

You said that before, I said. You didn't tell me how it's changed. Since when?

Actually I've been away for a long time, he said. I've been out of the city for years. I don't live here any more. I came to have a look at it, that was all. He took my wrist, led me through the parking lot, past my car, onto the path, then we went through the fence. It wasn't like this when I was here before, he said. All that light. The cars.

Looking for Sonia? I said.

What's that?

Is that another reason you came back? To look for Sonia?

Oh, he said. That seemed to stop him flat for a minute. Cobblestones and stars. We walked down the sidewalk, his hand on my wrist curiously delicate but old, *old*. There is something about a guy past forty, his touch, that I really cannot stand. I'm not looking for Sonia, he said. That's all behind me. I lost interest in that a long, long time ago, even when she was still around.

You and George, I said. It was a mistake to go walking with Howard Phillips, I decided and stopped on the sidewalk, then turned him around. I've had enough air, I said. Let's go back inside.

We're barely *out*, Howard Phillips said, and you want to go back. Are you afraid of me? You shouldn't be, you know.

I'm not afraid of anyone, I said.

His hands were on my shoulders. There's nothing to be afraid of, he said. Not engulfment, not the hounds, not the creatures. Nothing at all. It's all gone, don't you understand? I've checked it out here and back and there's just nothing. That's all I wanted to say.

Well, you said it.

I had big ideas, he said. I thought that there was something else. But there really isn't, you know. Which is what I wanted to tell you.

You told me, I said. I began to pull him back toward the bar. We've had our walk and our night on the stars and you've told me about that and about engulfment and about Sonia, too. Now why don't you go home and sleep it off? It was a hard thing to say but that was the only way to put it. I was thinking of the night, another night with George come back to the apartment to watch him staring at the mini-series and making little cutouts of his life on the table. Come and go, try to stay out of it, but you always had to come back, just like Howard Phillips. Engulfment, maybe that was a good word for it.

I've been sleeping, he said. I've slept and I've slept. I can't sleep any more. His grasp was huge and sudden upon me. I could feel his big hands pressing me into him and then the smell of him rising in the crushed space between us, a smell which might have been sex, might have been dank, like nothing I had ever known. Can't you hear the hounds? he said. Can't you hear them beyond the horizon?

I can't hear anything, I said. Let me go. You're starting to hurt me now and you're scaring me. Sometimes it is best to take the direct approach. Let me go, I said, or I'll scream.

He dropped his hands right away, backed away from me. You too, he said, you're another. You're like the rest of them.

I've had enough, I said. One yell and all of the boys would have been at the door, then in the parking lot, fighting for me regardless of the hard times I had given some of them, but I could tell that this was not necessary. You can sense when they are broken and aren't going to give you trouble any more. That's all right, I said. Just go home. It will feel better later on.

It will never feel better, he said. It is better to give than to receive.

Well, sure, I said. Sure, absolutely. Now that he was standing there sniveling I could even feel a little pity for him. It comes and it goes. Take care, I said. I'll see you around sometime.

I could come back in with you.

That wouldn't be a good idea, I said. That definitely would not be a good idea. There are some people there who don't want to see you, who wouldn't be so glad to see you, I think, if I told them.

All right, he said. You don't hear the hounds, he said. You don't hear the dogs, the sound beyond the horizon? You're too young yet, he said. You'll hear them.

Pal, I said, I don't hear a fucking thing and turned and went away from him, walked the walk into the place and went up to the bar and waited for Sam to drop the napkin around. The guys looked at me, shrugged, went back to the machine. That was fast, Richie said. Faster than your regular.

Yeah, I said, well go shove it, you and your foul mouth and went on to say some other stuff, the kind of stuff I can say to Richie, thinking about this and that and nothing at all and the strange guy in the parking lot who found that Providence had changed. Oh, it's changed, Howard Phillips, I said, it's changed all right. But not enough for you, I think, not the way you wanted it to. It's *never* going to change the way you want it. What you want, I think, is a fucking AS-PCA.

Later, some drinks later, I went out to my car, no sign of Howard Phillips of course and drove back to the place, found George passed out, his mouth an open *O*, stretched next to his half-done puzzle, the Carson show bouncing and flickering along on the network. I would like to say I got engulfed but that was not my fate. It is no fate for a serious person, say I, but lying down in the other room, listening to George breathe, thinking of my life and all of the sounds and spaces of it, I thought I heard, for the first time, the sound of the dogs in the distance.

Strange. A strange guy. I wonder what happened to Sonia.

One of science fiction's most critically admired and prolific authors, Barry Malzberg was born in New York City in 1939 and educated at Syracuse University. He has written nearly two hundred short stories and sixty novels; Beyond Apollo *won the John W. Campbell Award in 1972. His critical history of science fiction from the 1950s to the 1980s,* The Engines of Night, *is acclaimed for its authoritativeness. Most of his work is in science fiction, but his suspense stories are also notable.*

John fell in love with the farmer's daughter, even though everyone told him that the farmhouse and the family who lived there had been destroyed years ago.

ELEVEN

The Phantom Farmhouse

Seabury Quinn

I had been at the New Briarcliff Sanitarium nearly three weeks before I actually saw the house.

Every morning, as I lay abed after the nurse had taken my temperature, I wondered what was beyond the copse of fir and spruce at the turn of the road. The picture seemed incomplete without chimneys rising among the evergreens. I thought about it so much I finally convinced myself there really was a house in the wood. A house where people lived and worked and were happy.

All during the long, trying days when I was learning to navigate a wheelchair, I used to picture the house and the people who lived in it. There would be a father, I was sure; a stout, good-natured father, somewhat bald, who sat on the porch and smoked a cob pipe in the evening. And there was a mother, too; a waistless, plaid-skirted mother with hair smoothly parted over her forehead, who sat beside the father as he rocked and smoked, and who had a brown workbasket in her lap. She spread the stocking feet over her outstretched fingers and her vigilant needle spied out and closed every hole with a cunning no mechanical loom could rival.

Then there was a daughter. I was a little hazy in my conception of her; but I knew she was tall and slender as a hazel wand, and that her eyes were blue and wide and sympathetic.

Picturing the house and its people became a favorite pastime with me during the time I was acquiring the art of walking all over again. By the time I was able to trust my legs on the road I felt I knew my way to my vision-friends' home as well as I knew the byways of my own parish; though I had as yet not set foot outside the sanitarium.

Oddly enough, I chose the evening for my first long stroll. It was unusually warm for September in Maine, and some of the sturdier of the convalescents had been playing tennis during the afternoon. After dinner they sat on the veranda, comparing notes on their respective cases of influenza, or matching experiences in appendicitis operations.

After building the house bit by bit from my imagination, as a child pieces together a picture puzzle, I should have been bitterly disappointed if the woods had proved empty; yet when I reached the turn of the road and found my dream house a reality, I was almost afraid. Bit for bit and part for part, it was as I had visualized it.

A long, rambling, comfortable-looking farmhouse it was, with a wide porch screened by vines, and a whitewashed picket fence about the little clearing before it. There was a tumbledown gate in the fence, one of the kind that is held shut with a weighted chain. Looking closely, I saw the weight was a disused ploughshare. Leading from gate to porch was a path of flat stones, laid unevenly in the short grass, and bordered with a double row of clam shells. A lamp burned in the front room, sending out cheerful golden rays to meet the silver moonlight.

A strange, eerie sensation came over me as I stood there. Somehow, I felt I had seen that house before; many, many times before; yet I had never been in that part of Maine till I came to Briarcliff, nor had anyone ever described the place to me. Indeed, except for my idle dreams, I had had no intimation that there was a house in those pines at all.

"Who lives in the house at the turn of the road?" I asked the fat man who roomed next to me.

He looked at me as blankly as if I had addressed him in Choctaw, then countered, "What road?"

"Why, the south road," I explained. "I mean the house in the pines—just beyond the curve, you know."

If such a thing had not been obviously absurd, I should have thought he looked frightened at my answer. Certainly his already prominent eyes started a bit further from his face.

"Nobody lives there," he assured me. "Nobody's lived there for years. There isn't any house there."

I became angry. What right had this fellow to make my civil question the occasion for an ill-timed jest? "As you please," I replied. "Perhaps there isn't any house there for you; but I saw one there last night."

"My God!" he ejaculated, and hurried away as if I'd just told him I was infected with smallpox.

Later in the day I overheard a snatch of conversation between him and one of his acquaintances in the lounge.

"I tell you it's so," he was saying with great earnestness. "I thought it was a lot of poppycock, myself; but that clergyman saw it last night. I'm going to pack my traps and get back to the city, and not waste any time about it, either."

"Rats!" his companion scoffed. "He must have been stringing you."

Turning to light a cigar, he caught sight of me. "Say, Mr. Weatherby," he called, "you didn't mean to tell my friend here that you really saw a house down by those pines last night, did you?"

"I certainly did," I answered, "and I tell you, too. There's nothing unusual about it, is there?"

"Is there!" he repeated. "*Is* there? Say, what'd it look like?"

I described it to him as well as I could, and his eyes grew as wide as those of a child hearing the story of Bluebeard.

"Well, I'll be a Chinaman's uncle!" he declared as I finished. "I sure will!"

"See here," I demanded. "What's all the mystery about that farmhouse? Why shouldn't I see it? It's there to be seen, isn't it?"

He gulped once or twice, as if there were something hot in his mouth, before he answered:

"Look here, Mr. Weatherby, I'm telling you this for your own good. You'd better stay in nights; and you'd better stay away from those pines in particular."

Nonplussed at this unsolicited advice, I was about to ask an explanation, when I detected the after-tang of whisky on his breath. I understood, then. I was being made the butt of a drunken joke by a pair of race course followers.

"I'm very much obliged, I'm sure," I replied with dignity, "but if you don't mind, I'll choose my own comings and goings."

"Oh, go as far as you like"—he waved his arms wide in token of my complete free-agency—"go as far as you like. I'm going to New York."

And he did. The pair of them left the sanitarium that afternoon.

A slight recurrence of my illness held me housebound for several days after my conversation with the two sportively inclined gentlemen, and the next time I ventured out at night the moon had waxed to the full, pouring a flood of light upon the earth that rivaled midday. The minutest objects were as readily distinguished as they would have been before sunset; in fact, I remember comparing the evening to a silver-plated noon.

As I trudged along the road to the pine copse I was busy formulating plans for intruding into the family circle at the farmhouse; devising all manner of pious frauds by which to scrape acquaintance.

"Shall I feign having lost my way, and inquire direction to the sanitarium; or shall I ask if some mythical acquaintance, a John Squires, for instance, lives there?" I asked myself as I neared the turn of the road.

Fortunately for my conscience, all these subterfuges were unnecessary, for as I neared the whitewashed fence, a girl left the porch and walked quickly to the gate, where she stood gazing pensively along the moonlit road. It was almost as if she were coming to meet me, I thought, as I slacked my pace and assumed an air of deliberate casualness.

Almost abreast of her, I lessened my pace still more, and looked directly at her. Then I knew why my conception of the girl who lived in that house had been misty and indistinct. For the same reason the venerable John had faltered in his description of the New Jerusalem until his vision in the Isle of Patmos.

From the smoothly parted hair above her wide, forget-me-not eyes, to the hem of her white cotton frock, she was

152

as slender and lovely as a Rossetti saint; as wonderful to the eye as a medieval poet's vision of his lost love in paradise. Her forehead, evenly framed in the beaten bronze of her hair, was wide and high, and startlingly white, and her brows were delicately penciled as if laid on by an artist with a camel's hair brush. The eyes themselves were sweet and clear as forest pools mirroring the September sky, and lifted a little at the corners, like an Oriental's, giving her face a quaint, exotic look in the midst of these Maine woods.

So slender was her figure that the swell of her bosom was barely perceptible under the light stuff of her dress, and, as she stood immobile in the nimbus of moon rays, the undulation of the line from her shoulders to ankles was what painters call a "curve of motion."

One hand rested lightly on the gate, a hand as finely cut as a bit of Italian sculpture, and scarcely less white than the limed wood supporting it. I noticed idly that the forefinger was somewhat longer than its fellows, and that the nails were almond shaped and very pink—almost red—as if they had been rouged and brightly polished.

No man can take stock of a woman thus, even in a cursory, fleeting glimpse, without her being aware of the inspection, and in the minute my eyes drank up her beauty, our glances crossed and held.

The look she gave back was as calm and unperturbed as though I had been nonexistent; one might have thought I was an invisible wraith of the night; yet the faint suspicion of a flush quickening in her throat and cheeks told me she was neither unaware nor unappreciative of my scrutiny.

Mechanically, I raised my cap, and, wholly without conscious volition, I heard my own voice asking:

"May I trouble you for a drink from your well? I'm from the sanitarium—only a few days out of bed, in fact—and I fear I've overdone myself in my walk."

A smile flitted across her rather wide lips, quick and sympathetic as a mother's response to her child's request, as she swung the gate open for me.

"Surely—" she answered, and her voice had all the sweetness of the south wind soughing through her native pines—"surely you may drink at our well, and rest yourself, too—if you wish."

She preceded me up the path, quickening her pace as she neared the house, and running nimbly up the steps to the porch. From where I stood beside the old-fashioned well, fitted with windlass and bucket, I could hear the sound of whispering voices in earnest conversation. Hers I recognized, lowered though it was, by the flutelike purling of its tones; the other two were deeper, and, it seemed to me, hoarse and throaty. Somehow, odd as it seemed, there was a queer, canine note in them, dimly reminding me of the muttering of not too friendly dogs—such fractious growls I had heard while doing missionary duty in Alaska, when the savage, half-wolf malemutes were not fed promptly at the relay stations.

Her voice rose a trifle higher, as if in argument, and I fancied I heard her whisper, "This one is mine, I tell you; mine. I'll brook no interference. Go to your own hunting."

An instant later there was a reluctant assenting growl from the shadow of the vines curtaining the porch, and a light laugh from the girl as she descended the steps, swinging a bright tin cup in her hand. For a second she looked at me, as she sent the bucket plunging into the stone-curbed well; then she announced, in explanation:

"We're great hunters here, you know. The season is just in, and Dad and I have the worst quarrels about whose game is whose."

She laughed in recollection of their argument, and I laughed with her. I had been quite a Nimrod as a boy, myself, and well I remembered the heated controversies as to whose charge of shot was responsible for some luckless bunny's demise.

The well was very deep, and my breath was coming fast by the time I had helped her wind the bucket-rope upon the windlass; but the water was cold as only spring-fed well water can be. As she poured it from the bucket it shone almost like foam in the moonlight, and seemed to whisper with a half-human voice, instead of gurgling as other water does when poured.

I had drunk water in nearly every quarter of the globe; but never such water as that. Cold as the breath from a glacier, limpid as visualized air, it was yet so light and tasteless in substance that only the chill in my throat and the sight of the liquid in the cup told me that I was doing more than going through the motions of drinking.

"And now, will you rest?" she invited, as I finished my third draught. "We've an extra chair on the porch for you."

Behind the screen of vines I found her father and mother seated in the rays of the big kitchen lamp. They were just as I had expected to find them: plain, homely, sincere country folk, courteous in their reception and anxious to make a sick stranger welcome. Both were stout, with the comfortable stoutness of middle age and good health; but both had surprisingly slender hands. I noticed, too, that the same characteristic of an over-long forefinger was apparent in their hands as in their daughter's, and that both their nails were trimmed to points and stained almost a brilliant red.

"My father, Mr. Squires," the girl introduced, "and my mother, Mrs. Squires."

I could not repress a start. These people bore the very name I had casually thought to use when inquiring for some imaginary person. My lucky stars had surely guided me away from that attempt to scrape an acquaintance. What a figure I should have cut if I had actually asked for Mr. Squires!

Though I was not aware of it, my curious glance must have stayed longer on their reddened nails than I had intended, for Mrs. Squires looked deprecatingly at her hands. "We've all been turning, putting up fox grapes"—she included her husband and daughter with a comprehensive gesture. "And the stain just won't wash out; has to wear off, you know."

I spent, perhaps, two hours with my new-found friends, talking of everything from the best methods of potato culture to the surest way of landing a nine-pound bass. All three joined in the conversation and took a lively interest in the topics under discussion. After the vapid talk of the guests at the sanitarium, I found the simple, interested discourse of these country people as stimulating as wine, and when I left them it was with a hearty promise to renew my call at an early date.

"Better wait until after dark," Mr. Squires warned. "We'd be glad to see you any time; but we're so busy these fall days, we haven't much time for company."

I took the broad hint in the same friendly spirit it was given.

It must have grown chillier than I realized while I sat there, for my new friends' hands were clay-cold when I took them in mine at parting.

Homeward bound, a whimsical thought struck me so suddenly I laughed aloud. There was something suggestive of the dog tribe about the Squires family, though I could not for the life of me say what it was. Even Mildred, the daughter, beautiful as she was, with her light eyes, her rather prominent nose and her somewhat wide mouth, reminded me in some vague way of a lovely silver collie I had owned as a boy.

I struck a tassel of dried leaves from a cluster of weeds with my walking stick as I smiled at the fanciful conceit. The legend of the werewolf—those horrible monsters, formed as men, but capable of assuming bestial shape at will, and killing and eating their fellows—was as old as mankind's fear of the dark, but no mythology I had ever read contained a reference to dog-people.

Strange fancies strike up in the moonlight, sometimes.

September ripened to October, and the moon, which had been as round and bright as an exchange-worn coin when I first visited the Squires house, waned as thin as a shaving from a silversmith's lathe.

I became a regular caller at the house in the pines. Indeed, I grew to look forward to my nightly visits with those homely folk as a welcome relief from the tediously gay companionship of the over-sophisticated people at the sanitarium.

My habit of slipping away shortly after dinner was the cause of considerable comment and no little speculation on the part of my fellow convalescents, some of whom set it down to the eccentricity which, to their minds, was the inevitable concomitant of a minister's vocation, while others were frankly curious. Snatches of conversation I overheard now and then led me to believe that the objective of my strolls was the subject of wagering, and the guarded questions put to me in an effort to solve the mystery became more and more annoying.

I had no intention of taking any of them to the farmhouse with me. The Squires were my friends. Their cheerful talk and unassuming manners were as delightful a contrast to the atmosphere of the sanitarium as a breath of mountain balsam after the fetid air of a hothouse; but to the city-centered crowd at Briarcliff they would have been only the objects of less than half scornful patronage, the source of pitying amusement.

It was Miss Leahy who pushed the impudent curiosity further than any of the rest, however. One evening, as I was setting out, she met me at the gate and announced her intention of going with me.

"You must have found something *dreadfully* attractive to take you off *every* evening this way, Mr. Weatherby," she hazarded as she pursed her rather pretty, rouged lips at me and caught step with my walk. "We girls really *can't* let some little country lass take you away from us, you know. We simply can't."

I made no reply. It was scarcely possible to tell a pretty girl, even such a vain little flirt as Sara Leahy, to go home and mind her business. Yet that was just what I wanted to do. But I would not take her with me; to that I made up my mind. I would stop at the turn of the road, just out of sight of the farmhouse, and cut across the fields. If she wanted to accompany me on a cross-country hike in high-heeled slippers, she was welcome to do so.

Besides, she would tell the others that my wanderings were nothing more mysterious than nocturnal explorations of the nearby woods; which bit of misinformation would satisfy the busybodies at Briarcliff and relieve me of the espionage to which I was subjected, as well.

I smiled grimly to myself as I pictured her climbing over fences and ditches in her flimsy party frock and beaded pumps, and lengthened my stride toward the woods at the road's turn.

We marched to the limits of the field bordering the Squires' grove in silence, I thinking of the mild revenge I should soon wreak upon the pretty little busybody at my side, Miss Leahy too intent on holding the pace I set to waste breath in conversation.

As we neared the woods she halted, an expression of worry, almost fear, coming over her face.

"I don't believe I'll go any farther," she announced.

"No?" I replied, a trifle sarcastically. "And is your curiosity so easily satisfied?"

"It's not that." She turned half round, as if to retrace her steps. "I'm afraid of those woods."

"Indeed?" I queried. "And what is there to be afraid of? Bears, Indians, or wildcats? I've been through them several times without seeing anything terrifying." Now she had come this far, I was anxious to take her through the fields and underbrush.

"No-o," Miss Leahy answered, a nervous quaver in her voice, "I'm not afraid of anything like that; but—oh, I don't know what you call it. Pierre told me all about it the other day. Some kind of dreadful thing—loop—loop—something or other. It's a French word, and I can't remember it."

I was puzzled. Pierre Geronte was the ancient French-Canadian gardener at the sanitarium, and, like all doddering old men, would talk for hours to anyone who would listen. Also, like all *habitants*, he was full of wild folklore his ancestors brought overseas with them generations ago.

"What did Pierre tell you?" I asked.

"Why, he said that years ago some terrible people lived in these woods. They had the only house for miles 'round; and travelers stopped there for the night, sometimes. But no stranger was ever seen to leave that place, once he went in. One night the farmers gathered about the house and burned it, with the family that lived there. When the embers had cooled down they made a search, and found nearly a dozen bodies buried in the cellar. That was why no one ever came away from that dreadful place.

"They took the murdered men to the cemetery and buried them; but they dumped the charred bodies of the murderers into graves in the barnyard, without even saying a prayer over them. And Pierre says—Oh, Look! *Look!*"

She broke off her recital of the old fellow's story, and pointed a trembling hand across the field to the edge of the woods. A second more and she shrank against me, clutching at my coat with fear-stiffened fingers and crying with excitement and terror.

I looked in the direction she indicated, myself a little startled by the abject fear that had taken such sudden hold on her.

Something white and ungainly was running diagonally across the field from us, skirting the margin of the woods and making for the meadow that adjoined the sanitarium pasture. A second glance told me it was a sheep; probably one of the flock kept to supply our table with fresh meat.

I was laughing at the strength of the superstition that could make a girl see a figure of horror in an innocent mutton that had strayed away from its fellows and was scared out of its silly wits, when something else attracted my attention.

Loping along in the trail of the fleeing sheep, somewhat to the rear and a little to each side, were two other animals. At first glance they appeared to be a pair of large collies; but as I looked more intently, I saw that these animals were like nothing I had ever seen before. They were much larger than any collie—nearly as high as St. Bernards—yet shaped in a general way like Alaskan sledge dogs—huskies.

The farther one was considerably the larger of the two, and ran with a slight limp, as if one of its hind paws had been injured. As nearly as I could tell in the indifferent light, they were a rusty brown color, very thick-haired and unkempt in appearance. But the strangest thing about them was the fact that both were tailless, which gave them a terrifyingly grotesque look.

As they ran, a third form, similar to the other two in shape, but smaller, slender as a greyhound, with much lighter-hued fur, broke from the thicket of short brush edging the wood and took up the chase, emitting a series of short, sharp yelps.

"Sheep-killers," I murmured, half to myself. "Odd. I've never seen dogs like that before."

"They're not dogs," wailed Miss Leahy against my coat. "They're not dogs. Oh, Mr. Weatherby, let's go away. Please, please take me home."

She was rapidly becoming hysterical, and I had a difficult time with her on the trip back. She clung whimpering to me, and I had almost to carry her most of the way. By the time we reached the sanitarium, she was crying bitterly, shivering, as if with a chill, and went in without stopping to thank me for my assistance.

I turned and made for the Squires farm with all possible speed, hoping to get there before the family had gone to bed. But when I arrived the house was in darkness, and my knock at the door received no answer.

As I retraced my steps to the sanitarium I heard faintly, from the fields beyond the woods, the shrill, eerie cry of the sheep-killing dogs.

A torrent of rain held us marooned the next day. Miss Leahy was confined to her room, with a nurse in constant attendance and the house doctor making hourly calls. She was on the verge of a nervous collapse, he told me, crying with a persistence that bordered on hysteria, and responding to treatment very slowly.

An impromptu dance was organized in the great hall and half a dozen bridge tables set up in the library; but as I was skilled in neither of these rainy day diversions, I put on a waterproof and patrolled the veranda for exercise.

On my third or fourth trip around the house I ran into old Geronte shuffling across the porch, wagging his head and muttering portentously to himself.

"See here, Pierre," I accosted him, "what sort of nonsense have you been telling Miss Leahy about those pine woods down the south road?"

The old fellow regarded me unwinkingly with his beady eyes, wrinkling his age-yellowed forehead for all the world like an elderly baboon inspecting a new sort of edible. "*M'sieur* goes out alone much at nights, *n'est ce pas?*" he asked, at length.

"Yes, Monsieur goes out alone much at night," I echoed, "but what Monsieur particularly desires to know is what sort of tales have you been telling Mademoiselle Leahy. *Comprenez vous?*"

The network of wrinkles about his lips multiplied as he smiled enigmatically, regarding me askance from the corners of his eyes.

"*M'sieur is anglais,*" he replied. "He would not understand—or believe."

"Never mind what I'd believe," I retorted. "What is this

story about murder and robbery being committed in those woods? Who were the murderers, and where did they live? *Hein?*"

For a few seconds he looked fixedly at me, chewing the cud of senility between his toothless gums, then, glancing carefully about, as if he feared being overheard, he tiptoed up to me and whispered:

"*M'sieur* mus' stay indoors these nights. There are evil things abroad at the dark of the moon, *M'sieur*. Even las' night they keel t'ree of my bes' sheep. Remembair, *M'sieur*, the *loup-garou*, he is out when the moon hide her light."

And with that he turned and left me; nor could I get another word from him save his cryptic warning, "Remembair, *M'sieur;* the *loup-garou*. Remembair."

In spite of my annoyance, I could not get rid of the unpleasant sensation the old man's words left with me. The *loup-garou*—werewolf—he had said, and to prove his goblin-wolf's presence, he had cited the death of his three sheep.

As I paced the rain-washed porch I thought of the scene I had witnessed the night before, when the sheep-killers were at their work.

"Well," I reflected, "I've seen the *loup-garou* on his native heath at last. From causes as slight as this, no doubt, the horrible legend of the werewolf had sprung. Time was when all France quaked at the sound of the *loup-garou*'s hunting call and the bravest knights in Christendom trembled in their castles and crossed themselves fearfully because some renegade shepherd dog quested his prey in the night. On such a foundation are the legends of a people built."

Whistling a snatch from *Pinafore* and looking skyward in search of a patch of blue in the clouds, I felt a tug at my raincoat sleeve, such as a neglected terrier might give. It was Geronte again.

"*M'sieur*," he began in the same mysterious whisper, "the *loup-garou* is a verity, certainly. I, myself, have nevair seen him"—he paused to bless himself—"but my cousin, Baptiste, was once pursued by him. Yes.

"It was near the shrine of the good Sainte Anne that Baptiste lived. One night he was sent to fetch the curé for a dying woman. They rode fast through the trees, the curé and my cousin Baptiste, for it was at the dark of the moon, and the evil forest folk were abroad. And as they galloped, there came a *loup-garou* from the woods, with eyes as bright as hell fire. It followed hard, this tailless hound from the devil's kennel; but they reached the house before it, and the curé put his book, with the Holy Cross on its cover, at the doorstep. The *loup-garou* wailed under the windows like a child in pain until the sun rose; then it slunk back to the forest.

"When my cousin Baptiste and the curé came out, they found its hand marks in the soft earth around the door. Very like your hand, or mine, they were, *M'sieur*, save that the first finger was longer than the others."

"And did they find the *loup-garou*?" I asked, something of the old man's earnestness communicated to me.

"Yes, *M'sieur*; but of course," he replied gravely. "T'ree weeks before a stranger, drowned in the river, had been buried without the office of the Church. W'en they opened his grave they found his fingernails as red as blood, and sharp. Then they knew. The good curé read the burial office over him, and the poor soul that had been snatched away in sin slept peacefully at last."

He looked quizzically at me, as if speculating whether to tell me more; then, apparently fearing I would laugh at his outburst of confidence, started away toward the kitchen.

"Well, what else, Pierre?" I asked, feeling he had more to say.

"*Non, non, non,*" he replied. "There is nothing more, *M'sieur.* I did but want M'sieur should know my own cousin, Baptiste Geronte, had seen the *loup-garou* with his very eyes."

"Hearsay evidence," I commented, as I went in to dinner.

During the rainy week that followed I chafed at my confinement like a privileged convict suddenly deprived of his liberties, and looked as wistfully down the south road as any prisoned gypsy ever gazed upon the open trail.

The quiet home circle at the farmhouse, the unforced conversation of the old folks, Mildred's sweet companionship, all beckoned me with an almost irresistible force.

162

For in this period of enforced separation I discovered what I had dimly suspected for some time. I loved Mildred Squires. And, loving her, I longed to tell her of it.

No lad intent on visiting his first sweetheart ever urged his feet more eagerly than I when, the curtains of rain at last drawn up, I hastened toward the house at the turn of the road.

As I hoped, yet hardly dared expect, Mildred was standing at the gate to meet me as I rounded the curve, and I yearned toward her like a hummingbird seeking its nest.

She must have read my heart in my eyes, for her greeting smile was as tender as a mother's as she bends above her babe.

"At last you have come, my friend," she said, putting out both hands in welcome. "I am very glad."

We walked silently up the path, her fingers still resting in mine, her face averted. At the steps she paused, a little embarrassment in her voice as she explained, "Father and Mother are out; they have gone to a—meeting. But you will stay?"

"Surely," I acquiesced. And to myself I admitted my gratitude for this chance of Mildred's unalloyed company.

We talked but little that night. Mildred was strangely distrait, and, much as I longed to, I could not force a confession of my love from my lips. Once, in the midst of a long pause between our words, the cry of the sheep-killers came faintly to us, echoed across the fields and woods, and as the weird, shrill sound fell on our ears, she threw back her head, with something of the gesture of a hunting dog scenting its quarry.

Toward midnight she turned to me, a panic of fear having apparently laid hold of her.

"You must go!" she exclaimed, rising and laying her hand on my shoulder.

"But your father and mother have not returned," I objected. "Won't you let me stay until they get back?"

"Oh, no, no," she answered, her agitation increasing. "You must go at once—please." She increased her pressure on my shoulder, almost as if to shove me from the porch.

Taken aback by her sudden desire to be rid of me, I was picking up my hat, when she uttered a stifled little scream and ran quickly to the edge of the porch, interposing herself between me and the yard. At the same moment, I heard a muffled sound from the direction of the front gate, a sound like a growling and snarling of savage dogs.

I leaped forward, my first thought being that the sheep-killers I had seen the other night had strayed to the Squires place. Crazed with blood, I knew, they would be almost as dangerous to men as to sheep, and every nerve in my sickness-weakened body cried out to protect Mildred.

To my blank amazement, as I looked from the porch I beheld Mr. and Mrs. Squires walking sedately up the path, talking composedly together. There was no sign of the dogs or any other animals about.

As the elderly couple neared the porch I noticed that Mr. Squires walked with a pronounced limp, and that both their eyes shone very brightly in the moonlight, as though they were suffused with tears.

They greeted me pleasantly enough; but Mildred's anxiety seemed increased, rather than diminished, by their presence, and I took my leave after a brief exchange of civilities.

On my way back I looked intently in the woods bordering the road for some sign of the house of which Pierre had told Miss Leahy; but everywhere the pines grew as thickly as though neither axe nor fire had ever disturbed them.

"Geronte is in his second childhood," I reflected, "and like an elder child, he loves to terrify his juniors with fearsome witch-tales."

Yet an uncomfortable feeling was with me till I saw the gleam of the sanitarium's lights across the fields; and as I walked toward them it seemed to me that more than once I heard the baying of the sheep-killers in the woods behind me.

A buzz of conversation, like the sibilant arguments of a cloud of swarming bees, greeted me as I descended the stairs to breakfast next morning.

It appeared that Ned, one of the pair of great mastiffs attached to the sanitarium, had been found dead before his kennel, his throat and brisket torn open and several gaping wounds in his flanks. Boris, his fellow, had been discovered whimpering and trembling in the extreme corner of the doghouse, the embodiment of canine terror.

Speculation as to the animal responsible for the outrage was rife, and, as usual, it ran the gamut of possible and impossible surmises. Every sort of beast from a grizzly bear to a lion escaped from the circus was in turn indicted for the crime, only to have a complete alibi straightway established.

The only one having no suggestion to offer was old Geronte, who stood Sphinx-like in the outskirts of the crowd, smiling sardonically to himself and wagging his head sagely. As he caught sight of me he nodded, sapiently, as if to include me in the joint tenancy to some weighty secret.

Presently he worked his way through the chattering group and whispered, *"M'sieur,* he was here last night—and with him was the other tailless one. Come and see."

Plucking me by the sleeve, he led me to the rear of the kennels, and, stooping, pointed to something in the moist earth. "You see?" he asked, as if a printed volume lay for my reading in the mud.

"I see that someone has been on his hands and knees here," I answered, inspecting the hand prints he indicated.

"Something," he corrected, as if reasoning with an obstinate child. "Does not *M'sieur* behol' that the first finger is the longest?"

"Which proves nothing," I defended. "There are many hands like that."

"Oh—yes?" he replied with that queer upward accent of his. "And where has *M'sieur* seen hands like that before?"

"Oh, many times," I assured him somewhat vaguely, for there was a catch at the back of my throat as I spoke. Try as I would, I could recall only three pairs of hands with that peculiarity.

His little black eyes rested steadily on me in an unwinking stare, and the corners of his mouth curved upward in a malicious grin. It seemed, almost, as if he found a grim pleasure in thus driving me into a corner.

"See here, Pierre," I began testily, equally annoyed at myself and him, "you know as well as I that the *loup-garou* is an old woman's tale. Someone was looking here for tracks, and left his own while doing it. If we look among the patients here we shall undoubtedly find a pair of hands to match these prints."

"God forbid!" he exclaimed, crossing himself. "That would be an evil day for us, *M'sieur.* Here, Bor-ees," he snapped his fingers to the surviving mastiff, "come and eat."

The huge beast came wallowing over to him with the ungainly gait of all heavily-muscled animals, stopping on his way to make a nasal investigation of my knees. Scarcely had his nose come into contact with my trousers when he leaped back, every hair in his mane and along his spine stiffly erect, every tooth in his great mouth bared in a savage snarl. But instead of the mastiff's fighting growl, he emitted only a low, frightened whine, as though he were facing some animal of greater power than himself, and knew his own weakness.

"Good heavens!" I cried, thoroughly terrified at the friendly brute's sudden hostility.

"Yes, *M'sieur,*" Geronte cut in quickly, putting his hand on the dog's collar and leading him a few paces away. "It is well you should call upon the heavenly ones; for surely you have the odor of hell upon your clothes."

"What do you mean?" I demanded angrily. "How dare you—?"

He raised a thin hand deprecatingly. "*M'sieur* knows that he knows," he replied evenly; "and what I also know."

And leading Boris by the collar, he shuffled to the house.

Mildred was waiting for me at the gate that evening, and again her father and mother were absent at one of their meetings.

We walked silently up the path and seated ourselves on the porch steps where the waning moon cast oblique rays through the pine branches.

I think Mildred felt the tension I was drawn to, for she talked trivialities with an almost feverish earnestness, stringing her sentences together, and changing her subjects as a Navajo rug weaver twists and breaks her threads.

At last I found an opening in the abatis of her small talk.

"Mildred," I said, very simply, for great emotions tear the ornaments from our speech, "I love you, and I want you for my wife. Will you marry me, Mildred?" I laid my hand on hers. It was cold as lifeless flesh, and seemed to shrink beneath my touch.

"Surely, dear, you must have read the love in my eyes," I urged, as she averted her face in silence. "Almost from the night I first saw you. I've loved you! I—"

"O-o-h, don't!" Her interruption was a strangled moan, as if wrung from her by my words.

I leaned nearer her. "Don't you love me, Mildred?" I asked. As yet she had not denied it.

For a moment she trembled, as if a sudden chill had come on her, then, leaning to me, she clasped my shoulders in her arms, hiding her face against my jacket.

"John, John, you don't know what you say," she whispered disjointedly, as though a sob had torn the words before they left her lips. Her breath was on my cheek, moist and cold as air from a vault.

I could feel the litheness of her through the thin stuff of her gown, and her body was as devoid of warmth as a dead thing.

"You're cold," I told her, putting my arms shieldingly about her. "The night has chilled you."

A convulsive sob was her only answer.

"Mildred," I began again, putting my hand beneath her chin and lifting her face to mine, "tell me, dear, what is the matter?" I lowered my lips to hers.

With a cry that was half scream, half weeping, she thrust me suddenly from her, pressing her hands against my breast and lowering her head until her face was hidden between her outstretched arms. I, too, started back, for in the instant our lips were about to meet, hers had writhed back from her teeth, like a dog's when he is about to spring, and a low, harsh noise, almost a growl, had risen in her throat.

"For God's sake," she whispered hoarsely, agony in every note of her shaking voice, "never do that again! Oh, my dear, dear love, you don't know how near to a horror worse than death you were."

"A—horror—worse—than—death?" I echoed dully, pressing her cold little hands in mine. "What do you mean, Mildred?"

"Loose my hands," she commanded with a quaint rever-

167

sion to the speech of our ancestors, "and hear me. I do love you. I love you better than life. Better than death. I love you so I have overcome something stronger than the walls of the grave for your sake, but John, my very love, this is our last night together. We can never meet again. You must go, now, and not come back until tomorrow morning."

"Tomorrow morning?" I repeated blankly. What wild talk was this?

Heedless of my interruption, she hurried on. "Tomorrow morning, just before the sun rises over those trees, you must be here, and have your prayer book with you."

I listened speechless, wondering which of us was mad.

"By that corncrib there"—she waved a directing hand—"you will find three mounds. Stand beside them and read the office for the burial of the dead. Come quickly, and pause for nothing on the way. Look back for nothing; heed no sound from behind you. And for your own safety, come no sooner than to allow yourself the barest time to read your office."

Bewildered, I attempted to reason with the mad woman; begged her to explain this folly; but she refused all answer to my fervid queries, nor would she suffer me to touch her.

Finally, I rose to go. "You will do what I ask?" she implored.

"Certainly not," I answered firmly.

"John, John, have pity!" she cried, flinging herself to the earth before me and clasping my knees. "You say you love me. I only ask this one favor of you; only this. Please, for my sake, for the peace of the dead and the safety of the living, promise you will do this thing for me."

Shaken by her abject supplication, I promised, though I felt myself a figure in some grotesque nightmare as I did it.

"Oh, my love, my precious love," she wept, rising and taking both my hands. "At last I shall have peace, and you shall bring it to me. No," she forbade me as I made to take her in my arms at parting. "The most I can give you, dear, is this." She held her icy hands against my lips. "It seems so little, dear, but oh! it is so much."

Like a drunkard in his cups I staggered along the south road, my thoughts gone wild with the strangeness of the play I had just acted.

Across the clearing came the howls of the sheep-killers, a sound I had grown used to of late. But tonight there was a deeper, fiercer *timbre* in their bay; a note that boded ill for man as well as beast. Louder and louder it swelled; it was rising from the field itself, now, drawing nearer and nearer the road.

I turned and looked. The great beasts I had seen pursuing the luckless sheep the other night were galloping toward me. A cold finger seemed traced down my spine; the scalp crept and tingled beneath my cap. There was no other object of their quest in sight. I was their elected prey.

My first thought was to turn and run; but a second's reasoning told me this was worse than useless. Weakened with long illness, with an uphill road to the nearest shelter, I should soon be run down.

No friendly tree offered asylum; my only hope was to stand and fight. Grasping my stick, I spread my feet, bracing myself against their charge.

And as I waited their onslaught, there came from the shadow of the pines the shriller, sharper cry of the third beast. Like the crest of a flying, wind-lashed wave, the slighter, silver-furred brute came speeding across the meadow, its ears laid back, its slender paws spurning the sod daintily. Almost, it seemed as if the pale shadow of a cloud were racing toward me.

The thing dashed slantwise across the field, its flight converging on the line of the other two's attack. Midway between me and them it paused; hairs bristling, limbs bent for a spring.

All the savageness of the larger beasts' hunting cry was echoed in the smaller creature's bay, and with it a defiance that needed no interpretation.

The attackers paused in their rush; halted, and looked speculatively at my ally. They took a few tentative steps in my direction; and a fierce whine, almost an articulate curse, went up from the silver-haired beast. Slowly the tawny pair circled and trotted back to the woods.

I hurried toward the sanitarium, grasping my stick firmly in readiness for another attack.

But no further cries came from the woods, and once, as I

glanced back, I saw the light-haired beast trotting slowly in my wake, looking from right to left, as if to ward off danger.

Half an hour later I looked from my window toward the house in the pines. Far down the south road, its muzzle pointed to the moon, the bright-furred animal crouched and poured out a lament to the night. And its cry was like the wail of a child in pain.

Far into the night I paced my room, like a condemned convict when the vigil of the death watch is on him. Reason and memory struggled for the mastery; one urging me to give over my wild act, the other bidding me obey my promise to Mildred.

Toward morning I dropped into a chair, exhausted with my objectless marching. I must have fallen asleep, for when I started up the stars were dimming in the zenith, and bands of slate, shading to amethyst, slanted across the horizon.

A moment I paused, laughing cynically at my fool's errand, then, seizing cap and book, I bolted down the stairs, and ran through the paling dawn to the house in the pines.

There was something ominous and terrifying in the two-toned pastel of the house that morning. Its windows stared at me with blank malevolence, like the half-closed eyes of one stricken dead in mortal sin. The little patches of hoarfrost on the lawn were like leprous spots on some unclean thing. From the trees behind the clearing an owl hooted mournfully, as if to say, "Beware, beware!" and the wind soughing through the black pine boughs echoed the refrain ceaselessly.

Three mounds, sunken and weed-grown, lay in the unkempt thicket behind the corncrib. I paused beside them, throwing off my cap and adjusting my stole hastily. Thumbing the pages to the committal service, I held the book close, that I might see the print through the morning shadows, and commenced: "I know that my redeemer liveth—"

Almost beside me, under the branches of the pines, there rose such a chorus of howls and yelps I nearly dropped my book. Like all the hounds in the kennels of hell, the sheep-killers clamored at me, rage and fear and mortal hatred in their cries. Through the bestial cadences, too, there seemed to run a human note; the sound of voices heard before beneath these very trees. Deep and throaty, and raging mad, two of the voices came to me, and, like the tremolo of a violin lightly played in an orchestra of brass, the shriller cry of a third beast sounded.

As the infernal hubbub rose at my back, I half turned to fly. Next instant I grasped my book more firmly and resumed my office, for like a beacon in the dark, Mildred's words flashed on my memory: *"Look back for nothing; heed no sound behind you."*

Strangely, too, the din approached no nearer; but as though held by an invisible bar, stayed at the boundary of the clearing.

"Man that is born of a woman hath but a short time to live and is full of misery—deliver us from all our offenses—O, Lord, deliver us not into the bitter pains of eternal death—" and to such an accompaniment, surely, as no priest ever before chanted the office, I pressed through the brief service to the final *Amen*.

Tiny grouts of moisture stood out on my forehead, my breath struggled in my throat as I gasped out the last word. My nerves were frayed to shreds and my strength nearly gone as I let fall my book, and turned upon the beasts among the trees.

They were gone. Abruptly as it had begun, their clamor stopped, and only the rotting pine needles, lightly gilded by the morning sun, met my gaze. A light touch fell in the palm of my open hand, as if a pair of cool, sweet lips had laid a kiss there.

A vaporlike swamp-fog enveloped me. The outbuildings, the old, stone-curbed well where I had drunk the night I first saw Mildred, the house itself—all seemed fading into mist and swirling away in the morning breeze.

"Eh, eh, eh; but *M'sieur* will do himself an injury, sleeping on the wet earth!" Old Geronte bent over me, his arm beneath my shoulders. Behind him, great Boris, the mastiff, stood wagging his tail, regarding me with doggish good humor.

"Pierre," I muttered thickly, "how came you here?"

"This morning, going to my tasks, I saw *M'sieur* run down the road like a thing pursued. I followed quickly, for the woods hold terrors in the dark, *M'sieur*."

I looked toward the farmhouse. Only a pair of chimneys,

rising stark and bare from a crumbling foundation were there. Fence, well, barn—all were gone, and in their place a thicket of sumac and briars, tangled and overgrown as though undisturbed for thirty years.

"The house, Pierre! Where is the house?" I croaked, sinking my fingers into his withered arm.

"'Ouse?" he echoed. "Oh, but of course. There is no 'ouse here, *M'sieur;* nor has there been for years. This is an evil place, *M'sieur;* it is best we quit it, and that quickly. There be evil things that run by night—"

"No more," I answered, staggering toward the road, leaning heavily on him. "I brought them peace, Pierre."

He looked dubiously at the English prayer book I held. A Protestant clergyman is a thing of doubtful usefulness to the orthodox French-Canadian. Something of the heartsick misery in my face must have touched his kind old heart, for at last he relented, shaking his head pityingly and patting my shoulder gently, as one would soothe a sorrowing chid.

"Per'aps, *M'sieur,*" he conceded. "Per'aps; who shall say no? Love and sorrow are the purchase price of peace. Yes. Did not *le bon Dieu* so buy the peace of the world?"

The creator of one of the most famous of all occult detectives, Dr. Jules de Grandin, Seabury Quinn was born in Washington, D.C., in 1889. A man of several careers, Quinn was a lawyer, editor of trade journals for funeral directors, and was an expert on mortuary science. Most of his more than 160 stories appeared in Weird Tales, *and many of his de Grandin tales have been collected in six volumes, beginning with* The Adventures of Jules de Grandin. *The best of his non-de Grandin works are collected in* Is the Devil a Gentleman?

Perry Moore was a scientist, an objective researcher into fraudulent psychic mediums—until a voice from his own past spoke out of the darkness.

TWELVE

Night-Side

Joyce Carol Oates

ⓢ *February 1887. Quincy, Massachusetts. Montague House.*

Disturbing experience at Mrs. A——'s home yesterday evening. Few theatrics—comfortable though rather pathetically shabby surroundings—an only mildly sinister atmosphere (especially in contrast to the Walpurgis Night presented by that shameless charlatan in Portsmouth: the Dwarf Eustace who presumed to introduce me to Swedenborg himself, under the erroneous impression that I am a member of the Church of the New Jerusalem—*I!*). Nevertheless I came away disturbed, and my conversation with Dr. Moore afterward, at dinner, though dispassionate and even, at times, a bit flippant, did not settle my mind. Perry Moore is of course a hearty materialist, an Aristotelian-Spencerian with a love of good food and drink, and an appreciation of the more nonsensical vagaries of life; when in his company I tend to support that general view, as I do at the University as well—for there is a terrific pull in my nature toward the gregarious that I cannot resist. (That I do not wish to resist.) Once I am alone with my thoughts, however, I am accursed with doubts about my own position and nothing seems more precarious than my intellectual "convictions."

The more hardened members of our Society, like Perry Moore, are apt to put the issue bluntly: Is Mrs. A—— of Quincy a conscious or unconscious fraud? The conscious frauds are relatively easy to deal with; once discovered, they prefer to erase themselves from further consideration. The unconscious frauds are not, in a sense, "frauds" at all. It would certainly be difficult to prove criminal intention. Mrs. A—— for instance, does not accept money or gifts so far as we have been able to determine, and both Perry Moore and I noted her courteous but firm refusal of the Judge's offer to send her and her husband (presumably ailing?) on holiday to England in the spring. She is a mild, self-effacing, rather stocky woman in her mid-fifties who wears her hair parted in the center, like several of my maiden aunts, and whose sole item of adornment was an old-fashioned cameo brooch; her black dress had the appearance of having been homemade, though it was attractive enough, and freshly ironed. According to the Society's records she has been a practicing medium now for six years. Yet she lives, still, in an undistinguished section of Quincy, in a neighborhood of modest frame dwellings. The A——s' house is in fairly good condition, especially considering the damage routinely done by our winters, and the only room we saw, the parlor, is quite ordinary, with overstuffed chairs and the usual cushions and a monstrous horsehair sofa and, of course, the oaken table; the atmosphere would have been so conventional as to have seemed disappointing had not Mrs. A—— made an attempt to brighten it, or perhaps to give it a glamourously occult air, by hanging certain watercolors about the room. (She claims that the watercolors were "done" by one of her contact spirits, a young Iroquois girl who died in the seventeen seventies of smallpox. They are touchingly garish—mandalas and triangles and stylized eyeballs and even a transparent Cosmic Man with Indian-black hair.)

At last night's sitting there were only three persons in addition to Mrs. A——. Judge T—— of the New York State Supreme Court (now retired); Dr. Moore; and I, Jarvis Williams. Dr. Moore and I came out from Cambridge under the aegis of the Society for Psychical Research in order to make a preliminary study of the kind of mediumship Mrs. A—— affects. We did not bring a stenographer along this time though Mrs. A—— indicated her willingness to have the sitting transcribed; she struck me as being rather warmly cooperative, and even interested in our formal procedures, though Perry Moore remarked afterward at dinner that she had struck him as "noticeably reluctant." She was, however, flustered at the start of the séance and for a while it seemed as if we and the Judge might have made the trip for nothing. (She kept waving her plump hands about like an embarrassed hostess, apologizing for the fact that the spirits were evidently in a "perverse uncommunicative mood tonight.")

She did go into a trance eventually, however. The four of us were seated about the heavy round table from approximately 6:50 P.M. to 9:00 P.M. For nearly forty-five minutes Mrs. A—— made abortive attempts to contact her Chief Communicator and then slipped abruptly into trance (dramatically, in fact: her eyes rolled back in her head in a manner that alarmed me at first), and a personality named Webley appeared. "Webley's" voice appeared to be coming from several directions during the course of the sitting. At all times it was at least three yards from Mrs. A——; despite the semi-dark of the parlor I believe I could see the woman's mouth and throat clearly enough, and I could not detect any obvious signs of ventriloquism. (Perry Moore, who is more experienced than I in psychical research, and rather more casual about the whole phenomenon, claims he has witnessed feats of ventriloquism that would make poor Mrs. A—— look quite shabby in comparison.) "Webley's" voice was raw, singsong, peculiarly disturbing. At times it was shrill and at other times so faint as to be nearly inaudible. Something brattish about it. Exasperating. "Webley" took care to pronounce his final g's in a self-conscious manner, quite unlike Mrs. A——. (Which could be, of course, a deliberate ploy.)

This Webley is one of Mrs. A——'s most frequent manifesting spirits, though he is not the most reliable. Her Chief Communicator is a Scots patriarch who lived "in the time of Merlin" and who is evidently very wise; unfortunately he did not choose to appear yesterday evening. Instead, Webley presided. He is supposed to have died some seventy-five years ago at the age of nineteen in a house just up the street from the A——s'. He was either a butcher's helper or an apprentice tailor. He died in a fire—or by a "slow dreadful crippling disease"—or beneath a horse's hooves, in a freakish accident; during the course of the sitting he alluded self-pityingly to his death but seemed to have forgotten the exact details. At the very end of the evening he addressed me directly as Dr. Williams of Harvard University, saying that since I had influential friends in Boston I could help him with his career—it turned out he had written hundreds of songs and poems and parables but none had been published; would I please find a publisher for his work? Life had treated him so unfairly. His talent—his genius—had been lost to humanity. I had it within my power to help him, he claimed, was I not *obliged* to help him . . .? He then sang one of his songs, which sounded to me like an old ballad; many of the words were so shrill as to be unintelligible, but he sang it just the same, repeating the verses in a haphazard order:

> *This ae nighte, this ae nighte,*
> * —Every nighte and alle,*
> *Fire and fleet and candle-lighte,*
> * And Christe receive thy saule.*
>
> *When thou from hence away art past,*
> * —Every nighte and alle,*
> *To Whinny-muir thou com'st at last:*
> * And Christe receive thy saule.*
>
> *From Brig o' Dread when thou may'st pass,*
> * —Every nighte and alle,*
> *The whinnes sall prick thee to the bare bane:*
> * And Christe receive thy saule.*

The elderly Judge T—— had come up from New York City in order, as he earnestly put it, to "speak directly to his deceased wife as he was never able to do while she was living"; but Webley treated the old gentleman in a high-handed, cavalier manner, as if the occasion were not at all serious. He kept saying, "Who is there tonight? *Who* is there? Let them introduce themselves again—I don't *like* strangers! I tell you I don't *like* strangers!" Though Mrs. A—— had informed us beforehand that we would witness no physical phenomena, there were, from time to time, glimmerings of light in the darkened room, hardly more than the tiny pulsations of light made by fireflies; and both Perry Moore and I felt the table vibrating beneath our fingers. At about the time when Webley gave way to the spirit of Judge T——'s wife, the temperature in the room seemed to drop suddenly and I remember being gripped by a sensation of panic—but it lasted only an instant and I was soon myself again. (Dr. Moore claimed not to have noticed any drop in temperature and Judge T—— was so rattled after the sitting that it would have been pointless to question him.)

The séance proper was similar to others I have attended. A spirit—or voice—laid claim to being the late Mrs. T——; this spirit addressed the survivor in a peculiarly intense, urgent manner, so that it was rather embarrassing to be present. Judge T—— was soon weeping. His deeply creased face glistened with tears like a child's.

"Why Darrie! *Darrie!* Don't cry! Oh, don't cry!" the spirit said. "No one is dead, Darrie. There is no death. No death! . . . Can you hear me, Darrie? Why are you so frightened? So upset? No need, Darrie, no need! Grandfather and Lucy and I are together here—happy together. Darrie, look up! Be brave, my dear! My poor frightened dear! We never knew each other, did we? My poor dear! My love! . . . I saw you in a great transparent house, a great burning house; poor Darrie, they told me you were ill, you were weak with fever; all the rooms of the house were aflame and the staircase was burnt to cinders, but there were figures walking up and down, Darrie, great numbers of them, and you were among them, dear, stumbling in your fright—so clumsy! Look up, dear, and shade your eyes, and you will see me. Grandfather helped me—did you know? Did I call out his name at the end? My dear, my darling, it all happened so quickly—we never knew each other, did we? Don't be hard on Annie! Don't be cruel! Darrie? Why are you crying?" And gradually the spirit voice grew fainter; or perhaps something went wrong and the channels of communication were no longer clear. There were repetitions, garbled phrases, meaningless queries of "Dear? Dear?" that the Judge's replies did not seem to placate. The spirit spoke of her gravesite, and of a trip to Italy taken many years before, and of a dead or unborn baby, and again of Annie—evidently Judge T——'s daughter; but the jumble of words did not always make sense and it was a great relief when Mrs. A—— suddenly woke from her trance.

177

Judge T—— rose from the table, greatly agitated. He wanted to call the spirit back; he had not asked her certain crucial questions; he had been overcome by emotion and had found it difficult to speak, to interrupt the spirit's monologue. But Mrs. A—— (who looked shockingly tired) told him the spirit would not return again that night and they must not make any attempt to call it back.

"The other world obeys its own laws," Mrs. A—— said in her small, rather reedy voice.

We left Mrs. A——'s home shortly after 9:00 P.M. I too was exhausted; I had not realized how absorbed I had been in the proceedings.

Judge T—— is also staying at Montague House, but he was too upset after the sitting to join us for dinner. He assured us, though, that the spirit was authentic—the voice had been his wife's, he was certain of it, he would stake his life on it. She had never called him "Darrie" during her lifetime, wasn't it odd that she called him "Darrie" now?—and was so concerned for him, so loving?—and concerned for their daughter as well? He was very moved. He had a great deal to think about. (Yes, he'd had a fever some weeks ago—a severe attack of bronchitis and a fever; in fact, he had not completely recovered.) What was extraordinary about the entire experience was the wisdom revealed: There is no death.

There is no death.

Dr. Moore and I dined heartily on roast crown of lamb, spring potatoes with peas, and buttered cabbage. We were served two kinds of bread—German rye and sour cream rolls; the hotel's butter was superb; the wine excellent; the dessert—crepes with cream and toasted almonds—looked marvelous, though I had not any appetite for it. Dr. Moore was ravenously hungry. He talked as he ate, often punctuating his remarks with rich bursts of laughter. It was his opinion, of course, that the medium was a fraud—and not a very skillful fraud, either. In his fifteen years of amateur, intermittent investigations he had encountered far more skillful mediums. Even the notorious Eustace with his levitating table and hobgoblin chimes and shrieks was cleverer than Mrs. A——; one knew of course that Eustace was a cheat, but one was hard pressed to explain his method. Whereas Mrs. A—— was quite transparent.

Dr. Moore spoke for some time in his amiable, dogmatic way. He ordered brandy for both of us, though it was nearly midnight when we finished our dinner and I was anxious to get to bed. (I hoped to rise early and work on a lecture dealing with Kant's approach to the problem of Free Will, which I would be delivering in a few days.) But Dr. Moore enjoyed talking and seemed to have been invigorated by our experience at Mrs. A——'s.

At the age of forty-three Perry Moore is only four years my senior, but he has the air, in my presence at least, of being considerably older. He is a second cousin of my mother, a very successful physician with a bachelor's flat and office in Louisburg Square; his failure to marry, or his refusal, is one of Boston's perennial mysteries. Everyone agrees that he is learned, witty, charming, and extraordinarily intelligent. Striking rather than conventionally handsome, with a dark, lustrous beard and darkly bright eyes, he is an excellent amateur violinist, an enthusiastic sailor, and a lover of literature—his favorite writers are Fielding, Shakespeare, Horace, and Dante. He is, of course, the perfect investigator in spiritualist matters since he is detached from the phenomena he observes and yet he is indefatigably curious; he has a positive love, a mania, for facts. Like the true scientist he seeks facts that, assembled, may possibly give rise to hypotheses: he does not set out with a hypothesis in mind, like a sort of basket into which certain facts may be tossed, helter-skelter, while others are conveniently ignored. In all things he is an empiricist who accepts nothing on faith.

"If the woman is a fraud, then," I say hesitantly, "you believe she is a self-deluded fraud? And her spirits' information is gained by means of telepathy?"

"Telepathy indeed. There can be no other explanation," Dr. Moore says emphatically. "By some means not yet known to science—by some uncanny means she suppresses her conscious personality—and thereby releases other, secondary personalities that have the power of seizing upon others' thoughts and memories. It's done in a way not understood by science at the present time. But it will be

179

understood eventually. Our investigations into the unconscious powers of the human mind are just beginning; we're on the threshold, really, of a new era."

"So she simply picks out of her clients' minds whatever they want to hear," I say slowly. "And from time to time she can even tease them a little—insult them, even: she can unloose a creature like that obnoxious Webley upon a person like Judge T—— without fear of being discovered. Telepathy . . . Yes, that would explain a great deal. Very nearly everything we witnessed tonight."

"*Everything*, I should say," Dr. Moore says.

In the coach returning to Cambridge I set aside Kant and my lecture notes and read Sir Thomas Browne: *Light that makes all things seen, makes some things invisible. The greatest mystery of Religion is expressed by adumbration.*

19 March 1887. Cambridge. 11 P.M.

Walked ten miles this evening; must clear cobwebs from mind.

Unhealthy atmosphere. Claustrophobic. Last night's sitting in Quincy—a most unpleasant experience.

(Did not tell my wife what happened. Why is she so curious about the Spirit World?—about Perry Moore?)

My body craves more violent physical activity. In the summer, thank God, I will be able to swim in the ocean: the most strenuous and challenging of exercises.

Jotting down notes re the Quincy experience:

I. Fraud

Mrs. A——, possibly with accomplices, conspires to deceive: she does research into her clients' lives beforehand, possibly bribes servants. She is either a very skillful ventriloquist or works with someone who is. (Husband? Son? The husband is a retired cabinetmaker said to be in poor health; possibly consumptive. The son, married, lives in Waterbury.)

Her stated wish to avoid publicity and her declining of payment may simply be ploys; she may intend to make a great deal of money at some future time.

(Possibility of blackmail?—might be likely in cases similar to Perry Moore's.)

II. Non-fraud

Naturalistic
1. Telepathy. She reads minds of clients.
2. "Multiple personality" of medium. Aspects of her own buried psyche are released as her conscious personality is suppressed. These secondary beings are in mysterious rapport with the "secondary" personalities of the clients.

Spiritualistic
1. The controls are genuine communicators, intermediaries between our world and the world of the dead. These spirits give way to other spirits, who then speak through the medium; or
2. These spirits *influence* the medium, who relays their messages using her own vocabulary. Their personalities are then filtered through and limited by hers.
3. The spirits are not those of the deceased; they are perverse, willful spirits. (Perhaps demons? But there are no demons.)

III. Alternative hypothesis
Madness: the medium is mad, the clients are mad, even the detached, rationalist investigators are mad.

Yesterday evening at Mrs. A——'s home, the second sitting Perry Moore and I observed together, along with Miss Bradley, a stenographer from the Society, and two legitimate clients—a Brookline widow, Mrs. P——, and her daughter Clara, a handsome young woman in her early twenties. Mrs. A—— exactly as she appeared to us in February; possibly a little stouter. Wore black dress and cameo brooch. Served Lapsang tea, tiny sandwiches, and biscuits when we arrived shortly after 6:00 P.M. Seemed quite friendly to Perry, Miss Bradley, and me; fussed over us, like any hostess, chattered a bit about the cold spell. Mrs. P—— and her daughter arrived at six-thirty and the sitting began shortly thereafter.

Jarring from the very first. A babble of spirit voices. Mrs.

181

A—— in trance, head flung back, mouth gaping, eyes rolled upward. Queer. Unnerving. I glanced at Dr. Moore but he seemed unperturbed, as always. The widow and her daughter, however, looked as frightened as I felt.

Why are we here, sitting around this table?

What do we believe we will discover?

What are the risks we face . . .?

"Webley" appeared and disappeared in a matter of minutes. His shrill, raw, aggrieved voice was supplanted by that of a creature of indeterminate sex who babbled in Gaelic. This creature in turn was supplanted by a hoarse German, a man who identified himself as Felix; he spoke a curiously ungrammatical German. For some minutes he and two or three other spirits quarreled. (Each declared himself Mrs. A——'s Chief Communicator for the evening.) Small lights flickered in the semi-dark of the parlor and the table quivered beneath my fingers and I felt, or believed I felt, something brushing against me, touching the back of my head. I shuddered violently but regained my composure at once. An unidentified voice proclaimed in English that the Spirit of our Age was Mars: there would be a catastrophic war shortly and most of the world's population would be destroyed. All atheists would be destroyed. Mrs. A—— shook her head from side to side as if trying to wake. Webley appeared, crying "Hello? Hello? I can't see anyone! Who is there? Who has called me?" but was again supplanted by another spirit who shouted long strings of words in a foreign language. [Note: I discovered a few days later that this language was Walachian, a Romanian dialect. Of course Mrs. A——, whose ancestors are English, could not possibly have known Walachian, and I rather doubt that the woman has ever heard of the Walachian people.]

The sitting continued in this chaotic way for some minutes. Mrs. P—— must have been quite disappointed, since she had wanted to be put in contact with her deceased husband. (She needed advice on whether or not to sell certain pieces of property.) Spirits babbled freely in English, German, Gaelic, French, even in Latin, and at one point Dr. Moore queried a spirit in Greek, but the spirit retreated at once as if not equal to Dr. Moore's wit. The atmosphere was alarming but at the same time rather manic; almost jocular. I found myself suppressing laughter. Something touched the back of my head and I shivered violently and broke into perspiration, but the experience was not altogether unpleasant; it would be very difficult for me to characterize it.

And then . . .

And then, suddenly, everything changed. There was complete calm. A spirit voice spoke gently out of a corner of the room, addressing Perry Moore by his first name in a slow, tentative, groping way. "Perry? Perry . . .?" Dr. Moore jerked about in his seat. He was astonished; I could see by his expression that the voice belonged to someone he knew.

"Perry . . .? This is Brandon. I've waited so long for you, Perry, how could you be so selfish? I forgave you. Long ago. You couldn't help your cruelty and I couldn't help my innocence. Perry? My glasses have been broken . . . I can't see. I've been afraid for so long, Perry, please have mercy on me! I can't bear it any longer. I didn't *know* what it would be like. There are crowds of people here, but we can't see one another, we don't know one another, we're strangers, there is a universe of strangers. . . . I can't see anyone clearly . . . I've been lost for twenty years, Perry. I've been waiting for you for twenty years! You don't dare turn away again, Perry! Not again! Not after so long!"

Dr. Moore stumbled to his feet, knocking his chair aside.

"No . . . Is it . . . I don't believe . . ."

"Perry? Perry? Don't abandon me again, Perry! Not again!"

"What is this?" Dr. Moore cried.

He was on his feet now; Mrs. A—— woke from her trance with a groan. The women from Brookline were very upset and I must admit that I was in a mild state of terror, my shirt and my underclothes drenched with perspiration.

The sitting was over. It was only seven-thirty.

"Brandon?" Dr. Moore cried. "Wait. Where are . . .? Brandon? Can you hear me? Where are you? Why did you do it, Brandon? Wait! Don't leave! Can't anyone call him back—Can't anyone help me . . .?"

Mrs. A—— rose unsteadily. She tried to take Dr. Moore's hands in hers but he was too agitated.

"I heard only the very last words," she said. "They're always that way . . . so confused, so broken . . . the poor

183

things. . . . Oh, what a pity! It wasn't murder, was it? Not murder! Suicide . . .? I believe suicide is even worse for them! The poor broken things, they wake in the other world and are utterly, utterly lost—they have no guides, you see—no help in crossing over. . . . They are completely alone for eternity . . ."

"Can't you call him back?" Dr. Moore asked wildly. He was peering into a corner of the parlor, slightly stooped, his face distorted as if he were staring into the sun. "Can't someone help me? . . . Brandon? Are you here? Are you here somewhere? For God's sake can't someone help!"

"Dr. Moore, please, the spirits are gone—the sitting is over for tonight—"

"You foolish old woman, leave me alone! Can't you see I . . . I . . . I must not lose him . . . Call him back, will you? I insist! I insist!"

"Dr. Moore, please . . . You mustn't shout . . ."

"I said call him back! At once! *Call him back!*"

Then he burst into tears. He stumbled against the table and hid his face in his hands and wept like a child; he wept as if his heart had been broken.

And so today I have been reliving the séance. Taking notes, trying to determine what happened. A brisk windy walk of ten miles. Head buzzing with ideas. Fraud? Deceit? Telepathy? Madness?

What a spectacle! Dr. Perry Moore calling after a spirit, begging it to return . . . and then crying, afterward, in front of four astonished witnesses.

Dr. Perry Moore of all people.

My dilemma: whether I should report last night's incident to Dr. Rowe, the president of the Society, or whether I should say nothing about it and request that Miss Bradley say nothing. It would be tragic if Perry's professional reputation were to be damaged by a single evening's misadventure; and before long all of Boston would be talking.

In his present state, however, he is likely to tell everyone about it himself.

At Montague House the poor man was unable to sleep. He would have kept me up all night had I had the stamina to endure his excitement.

There *are* spirits! There have always been spirits!

His entire life up to the present time has been misspent!

And of course, most important of all . . . there is no death!

He paced about my hotel room, pulling at his beard nervously. At times there were tears in his eyes. He seemed to want a response of some kind from me but whenever I started to speak he interrupted; he was not really listening.

"Now at last I know. I can't undo my knowledge," he said in a queer hoarse voice. "Amazing, isn't it, after so many years . . . so many wasted years . . . Ignorance has been my lot, darkness . . . and a hideous complacency. My God, when I consider my deluded smugness! I am so ashamed, so ashamed. All along people like Mrs. A—— have been in contact with a world of such power . . . and people like me have been toiling in ignorance, accumulating material achievements, expending our energies in idiotic transient things. . . . But all that is changed now. Now I know. I *know.* There is no death, as the Spiritualists have always told us."

"But, Perry, don't you think. . . Isn't it possible that . . . "

"I *know,*" he said quietly. "It's as clear to me as if I had crossed over into that other world myself. Poor Brandon! He's no older now than he was *then.* The poor boy, the poor tragic soul! To think that he's still living after so many years . . . Extraordinary . . . It makes my head spin," he said slowly. For a moment he stood without speaking. He pulled at his beard, then absently touched his lips with his fingers, then wiped at his eyes. He seemed to have forgotten me. When he spoke again his voice was hollow, rather ghastly. He sounded drugged. "I . . . I had been thinking of him as . . . as dead, you know. As dead. Twenty years. Dead. And now, tonight, to be forced to realize that . . . that he isn't dead after all . . . It was laudanum he took. I found him. His rooms on the third floor of Weld Hall. I found him. I had no real idea, none at all, not until I read the note . . . and of course I destroyed the note . . . I had to, you see: for his sake. For his sake more than mine. It was because he realized there could be no . . . no hope . . . Yet he called me cruel! You heard him, Jarvis, didn't you? Cruel! I suppose I was. Was I? I don't know what to think. I must talk with him again. I . . . I don't know what to . . . what to think. I . . . . "

185

"You look awfully tired, Perry. It might be a good idea to go to bed," I said weakly.

" . . . recognized his voice at once. Oh at once: no doubt. None. What a revelation! And my life so misspent . . . Treating people's *bodies*. Absurd. I know now that nothing matters except that other world . . . nothing matters except our dead, our beloved dead . . . who are *not dead*. What a colossal revelation . . . ! Why, it will change the entire course of history. It will alter men's minds throughout the world. You were there, Jarvis, so you understand. You were a witness . . . "

"But . . . "

"You'll bear witness to the truth of what I am saying?"

He stared at me, smiling. His eyes were bright and threaded with blood.

I tried to explain to him as courteously and sympathetically as possible that his experience at Mrs. A——'s was not substantially different from the experiences many people have had at séances. "And always in the past psychical researchers have taken the position . . . "

"You were *there*," he said angrily. "You heard Brandon's voice as clearly as I did. Don't deny it!"

" . . . have taken the position that . . . the phenomenon can be partly explained by the telepathic powers of the medium . . . "

"That was Brandon's *voice*," Perry said. "I felt his presence, I tell you! *His*. Mrs. A—— had nothing to do with it . . . nothing at all. I feel as if . . . as if I could call Brandon back by myself. . . . I feel his presence even now. Close about me. He isn't dead, you see; no one is dead, there's a universe of . . . of people who are not dead . . . Parents, grandparents, sisters, brothers, everyone . . . everyone . . . How can you deny, Jarvis, the evidence of your own senses? You were there with me tonight and you know as well as I do . . . "

"Perry, I don't *know*. I did hear a voice, yes, but we've heard voices before at other sittings, haven't we? There are always voices. There are always 'spirits.' The Society has taken the position that the spirits could be real, of course, but that there are other hypotheses that are perhaps more likely . . . "

"Other hypotheses indeed!" Perry said irritably. "You're like a man with his eyes shut tight who refuses to open them out of sheer cowardice. Like the cardinals refusing to look through Galileo's telescope! And you have pretensions of being a man of learning, of science. . . . Why, we've got to destroy all the records we've made so far; they're a slander on the world of the spirits. Thank God we didn't file a report yet on Mrs. A——! It would be so embarrassing to be forced to call it back . . . "

"Perry, please. Don't be angry. I want only to remind you of the fact that we've been present at other sittings, haven't we? . . . and we've witnessed others responding emotionally to certain phenomena. Judge T——, for instance. He was convinced he'd spoken with his wife. But you must remember, don't you, that you and I were not at all convinced . . . ? It seemed to us more likely that Mrs. A—— is able, through extrasensory powers we don't quite understand, to read the minds of her clients, and then to project certain voices out into the room so that it sounds as if they are coming from other people. . . . You even said, Perry, that she wasn't a very skillful ventriloquist. You said—"

"What does it matter what, in my ignorance, I said?" he cried. "Isn't it enough that I've been humiliated? That my entire life has been turned about? Must you insult me as well . . . sitting there so smugly and insulting *me?* I think I can make claim to being someone whom you might respect."

And so I assured him that I did respect him. And he walked about the room, wiping at his eyes, greatly agitated. He spoke again of his friend, Brandon Gould, and of his own ignorance, and of the important mission we must undertake to inform men and women of the true state of affairs. I tried to talk with him, to reason with him, but it was hopeless. He scarcely listened to me.

". . . must inform the world . . . crucial truth. . . . There is no death, you see. Never was. Changes civilization, changes the course of history. Jarvis?" he said groggily. "You see? *There is no death.*"

25 March 1887. Cambridge.
Disquieting rumors re Perry Moore. Heard today at the University that one of Dr. Moore's patients (a brother-in-law

of Dean Barker) was extremely offended by his behavior during a consultation last week. Talk of his having been drunk . . . which I find incredible. If the poor man appeared to be excitable and not his customary self, it was not because he was *drunk,* surely.

Another far-fetched tale told me by my wife, who heard it from her sister Maude: Perry Moore went to church (St. Aidan's Episcopal Church on Mount Street) for the first time in a decade, sat alone, began muttering and laughing during the sermon, and finally got to his feet and walked out, creating quite a stir. *What delusions! What delusions!* . . . he was said to have muttered.

I fear for the poor man's sanity.

31 March 1887. Cambridge. 4 A.M.

Sleepless night. Dreamed of swimming . . . swimming in the ocean . . . enjoying myself as usual when suddenly the water turns thick . . . turns to mud. Hideous! Indescribably awful. I was swimming nude in the ocean, by moonlight, I believe, ecstatically happy, entirely alone, when the water turned to mud. . . . Vile, disgusting mud; faintly warm; sucking at my body. Legs, thighs, torso, arms. Horrible. Woke in terror. Drenched with perspiration: pajamas wet. One of the most frightening nightmares of my adulthood.

A message from Perry Moore came yesterday just before dinner. Would I like to join him in visiting Mrs. A—— sometime soon, in early April perhaps, on a noninvestigative basis . . . ? He is uncertain now of the morality of our "investigating" Mrs. A—— or any other medium.

4 April 1887. Cambridge.

Spent the afternoon from two to five at William James's home on Irving Street, talking with Professor James of the inexplicable phenomenon of consciousness. He is robust as always, rather irreverent, supremely confident in a way I find enviable; rather like Perry Moore before his conversion. (Extraordinary eyes—so piercing, quick, playful; a graying beard liberally threaded with white; close-cropped graying hair; a large, curving, impressive forehead; a manner intelligent and graceful and at the same time rough-edged, as if he anticipates or perhaps even hopes for recalcitration in his listeners.) We both find conclusive the ideas set forth in Binét's *Alterations of Personality*—unsettling as these ideas may be to the rationalist position. James speaks of a *peculiarity* in the constitution of human nature: that is, the fact that we inhabit not only our ego-consciousness but a wide field of psychological experience (most clearly represented by the phenomenon of memory, which no one can adequately explain) over which we have no control whatsoever. In fact, we are not generally aware of this field of consciousness.

We inhabit a lighted sphere, then; and about us is a vast penumbra of memories, reflections, feelings, and stray uncoordinated thoughts that "belong" to us theoretically, but that do not seem to be part of our conscious identity. (I was too timid to ask Professor James whether it might be the case that we do not inevitably own these aspects of the personality . . . that such phenomena belong as much to the objective world as to our subjective selves.) It is quite possible that there is an element of some indeterminate kind: oceanic, timeless, and living, against which the individual being constructs temporary barriers as part of an ongoing process of unique, particularized survival; like the ocean itself, which appears to separate islands that are in fact not "islands" at all, but aspects of the earth firmly joined together below the surface of the water. Our lives, then, resemble these islands. . . . All this is no more than a possibility, Professor James and I agreed.

James is acquainted, of course, with Perry Moore. But he declined to speak on the subject of the poor man's increasingly eccentric behavior when I alluded to it. (It may be that he knows even more about the situation than I do—he enjoys a multitude of acquaintances in Cambridge and Boston.) I brought our conversation round several times to the possibility of the *naturalness* of the conversion experience in terms of the individual's evolution of self, no matter how his family, his colleagues, and society in general viewed it, and Professor James appeared to agree; at least he did not emphatically disagree. He maintains a healthy skepticism, of course, regarding Spiritualist claims, and all evangelical and enthusiastic religious movements, though he is, at the same time, a highly articulate foe of the "rationalist" position and he believes that psychical research of the kind

some of us are attempting will eventually unearth riches . . .
revealing aspects of the human psyche otherwise closed to
our scrutiny.

"The fearful thing," James said, "is that we are at all times
vulnerable to incursions from the 'other side' of the personality. . . . We cannot determine the nature of the total personality simply because much of it, perhaps most, is hidden
from us. . . . When we are invaded, then, we are over-
whelmed and surrender immediately. Emotionally charged
intuitions, hunches, guesses, even ideas may be the least
aggressive of these incursions; but there are visual and au-
ditory hallucinations, and forms of automatic behavior not
controlled by the conscious mind. . . . Ah, you're thinking I
am simply describing insanity?"

I stared at him, quite surprised.

"No. Not at all. Not at all," I said at once.

Reading through my grandfather's journals, begun in East
Anglia many years before my birth. Another world then.
Another language, now lost to us. *Man is sinful by nature.
God's justice takes precedence over His mercy.* The dogma
of Original Sin: something brutish about the innocence of
that belief. And yet consoling. . . .

Fearful of sleep since my dreams are so troubled now.
The voices of impudent spirits (Immanuel Kant himself
come to chide me for having made too much of his catego-
ries!), stray shouts and whispers I cannot decipher, the faces
of my own beloved dead hovering near, like carnival masks,
insubstantial and possibly fraudulent. Impatient with my
wife, who questions me too closely on these personal matters; annoyed from time to time, in the evenings especially,
by the silliness of the children. (The eldest is twelve now and
should know better.) Dreading to receive another lengthy
letter—sermon, really—from Perry Moore re his "new position," and yet perversely hoping one will come soon.

I must know.

(Must know *what?*)

I must know.

10 April 1887. Boston. St. Aidan's Episcopal Church.
Funeral service this morning for Perry Moore; dead at
forty-three.

17 April 1887. Seven Hills, New Hampshire.

A weekend retreat. No talk. No need to think.

Visiting with a former associate, author of numerous books. Cartesian specialist. Elderly. Partly deaf. Extraordinarily kind to me. (Did not ask about the Department or about my work.) Intensely interested in animal behavior now, in observation primarily; fascinated with the phenomenon of hibernation.

He leaves me alone for hours. He sees something in my face I cannot see myself.

The old consolations of a cruel but just God: ludicrous today.

In the nineteenth century we live free of God. We live in the illusion of freedom-of-God.

Dozing off in the guest room of this old farmhouse and then waking abruptly. *Is someone here? Is someone here?* My voice queer, hushed, childlike. *Please: is someone here?*

Silence.

Query: Is the penumbra outside consciousness all that was ever meant by "God"?

Query: Is inevitability all that was ever meant by "God"?

God—the body of fate we inhabit, then; no more and no less.

God pulled Perry down into the body of fate: into Himself. (Or Itself.) As Professor James might say, Dr. Moore was "vulnerable" to an assault from the other side.

At any rate he is dead. They buried him last Saturday.

25 April 1887. Cambridge.

Shelves of books. The sanctity of books. Kant, Plato, Schopenhauer, Descartes, Hume, Hegel, Spinoza. The others. All. Nietzsche, Spencer, Leibnitz (on whom I did a torturous Master's thesis). Plotinus. Swedenborg. *The Transactions of the American Society for Psychical Research.* Voltaire. Locke. Rousseau. And Berkeley: the good Bishop adrift in a dream.

An etching by Halbrech above my desk, "The Thames 1801." Water too black. Inky-black. Thick with mud . . .? Filthy water in any case.

Perry's essay, forty-five scribbled pages, "The Challenge of the Future." Given to me several weeks ago by Dr. Rowe, who feared rejecting it for the *Transactions* but could not, of course, accept it. I can read only a few pages at a time, then push it aside, too moved to continue. Frightened also.

The man had gone insane.

Died insane.

Personality broken: broken bits of intellect.

His argument passionate and disjointed, with no pretense of objectivity. Where some weeks ago he had taken the stand that it was immoral to investigate the Spirit World, now he took the stand that it was imperative we do so. We are on the brink of a new age . . . new knowledge of the universe . . . comparable to the stormy transitional period between the Ptolemaic and the Copernican theories of the universe. . . . More experiments required. Money. Donations. Subsidies by private institutions. All psychological research must be channeled into a systematic study of the Spirit World and the ways by which we can communciate with that world. Mediums like Mrs. A—— must be brought to centers of learning like Harvard and treated with the respect their genius deserves. Their value to civilization is, after all, beyond estimation. They must be rescued from arduous and routine lives where their genius is drained off into vulgar pursuits . . . they must be rescued from a clientele that is mainly concerned with being put into contact with deceased relatives for utterly trivial, self-serving reasons. Men of learning must realize the gravity of the situation. Otherwise we will fail, we will stagger beneath the burden, we will be defeated, ignobly, and it will remain for the twentieth century to discover the existence of the Spirit Universe that surrounds the Material Universe, and to determine the exact ways by which one world is related to another.

Perry Moore died of a stroke on the eighth of April; died instantaneously on the steps of the Bedford Club shortly after 2:00 P.M. Passers-by saw a very excited, red-faced gentleman with an open collar push his way through a small gathering at the top of the steps . . . and then suddenly fall, as if shot down.

In death he looked like quite another person: his features sharp, the nose especially pointed. Hardly the handsome Perry Moore everyone had known.

He had come to a meeting of the Society, though it was suggested by Dr. Rowe and by others (including myself) that he stay away. Of course he came to argue. To present his "new position." To insult the other members. (He was contemptuous of a rather poorly organized paper on the medium Miss E——of Salem, a young woman who works with objects like rings, articles of clothing, locks of hair, et cetera; and quite angry with the evidence presented by a young geologist that would seem to discredit, once and for all, the claims of Eustace of Portsmouth. He interrupted a third paper, calling the reader a "bigot" and an "ignorant fool.")

Fortunately the incident did not find its way into any of the papers. The press, misunderstanding (deliberately and maliciously) the Society's attitude toward Spiritualism, delights in ridiculing our efforts.

There were respectful obituaries. A fine eulogy prepared by Reverend Tyler of St. Aidan's. Other tributes. *A tragic loss . . . Mourned by all who knew him* . . . (I stammered and could not speak. I cannot speak of him, of it, even now. Am I mourning, am I aggrieved? Or merely shocked? Terrified?) Relatives and friends and associates glossed over his behavior these past few months and settled upon an earlier Perry Moore, eminently sane, a distinguished physician and man of letters. I did not disagree, I merely acquiesced; I could not make any claim to have really known the man.

And so he has died, and so he is dead. . . .

Shortly after the funeral I went away to New Hampshire for a few days. But I can barely remember that period of time now. I sleep poorly. I yearn for summer, for a drastic change of climate, of scene. It was unwise for me to take up the responsibility of psychical research, fascinated though I am by it; my classes and lectures at the University demand most of my energy.

How quickly he died, and so young: so relatively young. No history of high blood pressure, it is said.

At the end he was arguing with everyone, however. His personality had completely changed. He was rude, impetuous, even rather profane; even poorly groomed. (Rising to challenge the first of the papers, he revealed a shirtfront that appeared to be stained.) Some claimed he had been drinking all along, for years. Was it possible . . . ? (He had clearly enjoyed the wine and brandy in Quincy that evening, but I would not have said he was intemperate.) Rumors, fanciful tales, outright lies, slander. . . . It is painful, the vulnerability death brings.

Bigots, he called us. Ignorant fools. Unbelievers . . . atheists . . . traitors to the Spirit World . . . heretics. Heretics! I believe he looked directly at me as he pushed his way out of the meeting room: his eyes glaring, his face dangerously flushed, no recognition in his stare.

After his death, it is said, books continue to arrive at his home from England and Europe. He spent a small fortune on obscure, out-of-print volumes . . . commentaries on the Kabbala, on Plotinus, medieval alchemical texts, books on astrology, witchcraft, the metaphysics of death. Occult cosmologies. Egyptian, Indian, and Chinese "wisdom." Blake, Swedenborg, Cozad. *The Tibetan Book of the Dead.* Datsky's *Lunar Mysteries.* His estate is in chaos because he left not one but several wills, the most recent made out only a day before his death, merely a few lines scribbled on scrap paper, without witnesses. The family will contest, of course. Since in this will he left his money and property to an obscure woman living in Quincy, Massachusetts, and since he was obviously not in his right mind at the time, they would be foolish indeed not to contest.

Days have passed since his sudden death. Days continue to pass. At times I am seized by a sort of quick, cold panic; at other times I am inclined to think the entire situation has been exaggerated. In one mood I vow to myself that I will never again pursue psychical research because it is simply too dangerous. In another mood I vow I will never again pursue it because it is a waste of time and my own work, my own career, must come first.

Heretics, he called us. Looking straight at me.

Still, he was mad. And is not to be blamed for the vagaries of madness.

19 June 1887. Boston.

Luncheon with Dr. Rowe, Miss Madeleine van der Post, young Lucas Matthewson; turned over my personal records and notes re the mediums Dr. Moore and I visited. (Destroyed jottings of a private nature.) Miss van der Post and Matthewson will be taking over my responsibilities. Both are young, quickwitted, alert, with a certain ironic play about their features; rather like Dr. Moore in his prime. Matthewson is a former seminary student now teaching physics at the Boston University. They questioned me about Perry Moore, but I avoided answering frankly. Asked if we were close, I said *No*. Asked if I had heard a bizarre tale making the rounds of Boston salons . . . that a spirit claiming to be Perry Moore has intruded upon a number of séances in the area. . . . I said honestly that I had not; and I did not care to hear about it.

Spinoza: *I will analyze the actions and appetites of men as if it were a question of lines, of planes, and of solids.*

It is in this direction, I believe, that we must move. Away from the phantasmal, the vaporous, the unclear; toward lines, planes, and solids.

Sanity.

8 July 1887. Mount Desert Island, Maine.

Very early this morning, before dawn, dreamed of Perry Moore: a babbling, gesticulating spirit, bearded, bright-eyed, obviously mad. Jarvis? Jarvis? Don't deny me! he cried. I am so . . . so bereft. . . .

Paralyzed, I faced him: neither awake nor asleep. His words were not really *words* so much as unvoiced thoughts. I heard them in my own voice; a terrible raw itching at the back of my throat yearned to articulate the man's grief.

Perry?

You don't dare deny me! Not now!

He drew near and I could not escape. The dream shifted, lost its clarity. Someone was shouting at me. Very angry, he was, and baffled . . . as if drunk . . . or ill . . . or injured.

Perry? I can't hear you—

. . . our dinner at Montague House, do you remember? Lamb, it was. And crepes with almond for dessert. You remember! You remember! You can't deny me! We were both nonbelievers then, both abysmally ignorant . . . you can't deny me!

(I was mute with fear or with cunning.)

. . . that idiot Rowe, how humiliated he will be! All of them! All of you! The entire rationalist bias, the . . . the conspiracy of . . . of fools . . . bigots . . . In a few years . . . In a few short years . . . Jarvis, where are you? Why can't I see you? Where have you gone? . . . My eyes can't focus: will someone help me? I seem to have lost my way. Who is here? Who am I talking with? You remember me, don't you?

(He brushed near me, blinking helplessly. His mouth was a hole torn into his pale ravaged flesh.)

Where are you? Where is everyone? I thought it would be crowded here but . . . but there's no one . . . I am forgetting so much! My name—what was my name? Can't see. Can't remember. Something very important . . . something very important I must accomplish—can't remember—Why is there no God? No one here? No one in control? We drift this way and that way, we come to no rest, there are no landmarks . . . no way of judging . . . everything is confused . . . disjointed . . . Is someone listening? Would you read to me, please? Would you read to me?—anything!—that speech of Hamlet's—*To be or not*—a sonnet of Shakespeare's—*any sonnet, anything*—*That time of year thou may in me behold*—is that it?—is that how it begins? *Bare ruin'd choirs where the sweet birds once sang.* How does it go? Won't you tell me? I'm lost—there's nothing here to see, to touch—isn't anyone listening? I thought there was someone nearby, a friend: isn't anyone here?

(I stood paralyzed, mute with caution: he passed by.)

. . . *When in the chronicle of wasted time*—*the wide world dreaming of things to come*—is anyone listening?—can anyone help?—I am forgetting so much . . . my name, my life . . . my life's work . . . to penetrate the mysteries . . . the veil . . . to do justice to the universe of . . . of what . . . what I had intended? . . . am I in my place of repose now, have I come home? Why is it so empty here? Why is no one in control? My eyes—my head—mind broken and blown about—slivers—shards—annihilating all that's made to a . . . a green thought . . . a green shade—Shakespeare?

Plato? Pascal? Will someone read me Pascal again? I seem to have lost my way. . . . I am being blown about—Jarvis, was it? My dear young friend Jarvis? But I've forgotten your last name. . . . I've forgotten so much . . .

(I wanted to reach out to touch him—but could not move, could not wake. The back of my throat ached with sorrow. Silent! Silent! I could not utter a word.)

. . . my papers, my journal—twenty years—a key somewhere hidden—where?—ah yes: the bottom drawer of my desk—do you hear?—my desk—house—Louisburg Square—the key is hidden there—wrapped in a linen handkerchief—the strongbox is—the locked box is—hidden—my brother Edward's house—attic—trunk—steamer trunk—initials R. W. M.—Father's trunk, you see—strongbox hidden inside—my secret journals—life's work—physical and spiritual wisdom—must not be lost—are you listening?—is anyone listening? I am forgetting so much, my mind is in shreds—but if you could locate the journal and read it to me—if you could salvage it—me—I would be so very grateful—I would forgive you anything, all of you—Is anyone there? Jarvis? Brandon? No one?—My journal, my soul: will you salvage it? Will—

(He stumbled away and I was alone again.)

Perry—?

But it was too late: I awoke drenched with perspiration.

Nightmare.
Must forget.

Best to rise early, before the others. Mount Desert Island lovely in July. Our lodge on a hill above the beach. No spirits here: wind from the northeast, perpetual fresh air, perpetual waves. Best to rise early and run along the beach and plunge into the chilly water.

Clear the cobwebs from one's mind.

How beautiful the sky, the ocean, the sunrise!

No spirits here on Mount Desert Island. Swimming: skillful exertion of arms and legs. Head turned this way, that way. Eyes half shut. The surprise of the cold rough waves. One yearns almost to slip out of one's human skin at such times . . .! Crude blatant beauty of Maine. Ocean. Muscular exertion of body. How alive I am, how living, how invulnerable; what a triumph in my every breath . . .

Everything slips from my mind except the present moment. I am living. I am alive, I am immortal. Must not weaken: must not sink. Drowning? No. Impossible. Life is the only reality. It is not extinction that awaits but a hideous dreamlike state, a perpetual groping, blundering—far worse than extinction—incomprehensible: so it is life we must cling to, arm over arm, swimming, conquering the element that sustains us.

Jarvis? someone cried. *Please hear me—*

How exquisite life is, the turbulent joy of life contained in flesh! I heard nothing except the triumphant waves splashing about me. I swam for nearly an hour. Was reluctant to come ashore for breakfast, though our breakfasts are always pleasant rowdy sessions: my wife and my brother's wife and our seven children thrown together for the month of July. Three boys, four girls: noise, bustle, health, no shadows, no spirits. No time to think. Again and again I shall emerge from the surf, face and hair and body streaming water, exhausted but jubilant, triumphant. Again and again the children will call out to me, excited, from the dayside of the world that they inhabit.

I will not investigate Dr. Moore's strongbox and his secret journal; I will not even think about doing so. The wind blows words away. The surf is hypnotic. I will not remember this morning's dream once I sit down to breakfast with the family. I will not clutch my wife's wrist and say *We must not die! We dare not die!*—for that would only frighten and offend her.

Jarvis? she is calling at this very moment.

And I say *Yes—? Yes, I'll be there at once.*

Born in 1938 in New York and educated at Syracuse University and the University of Wisconsin, Joyce Carol Oates is an English teacher, currently at Princeton. Her first book By the North Gate, *was published in 1963. Strongly influenced by William Faulkner, Oates sets many of her works in her fictional Eden County. She has been called "the finest Southern writer that ever came out of the North."*

Mrs. Timm expected some of the pupils at her new school to be difficult, but she was not prepared for the boy who could only come to school at night.

THIRTEEN

The Dark Boy
August Derleth

Mrs. Judith Timm came to teach at District No. 9 well past the midterm, and not without some trepidation. Just before setting out, she had had a brief, anonymous note which said only, *"Don't come."* She was sure it had been sent by her predecessor, but that lady had gone by the time she arrived; so she settled down a little uneasily with two spinsters, Miss Abigail Moore and her sister, Miss Lettie, who lived just down the road from the schoolhouse. Like most of the parents of children who came to No. 9, they were uncommunicative people.

But they were pleasant enough. And the school was pleasant, if a little old-fashioned, still, with its lamplight instead of electricity. But then, few farms in this isolated part of Vermont had electricity, and the schoolhouse had less use for it than the farms did. Miss Abigail, who was on the Board of Education, was as tall and gaunt as her sister was short and plump; she explained that Miss Mason, who had been teaching at No. 9, was a nervous woman, and not well.

"Nervous as a cat," she said. "It fair gave one the creeps, it did. I don't think she liked children. She was younger than you, and, of course—"

"I never had any children," said Mrs. Timm. "My husband died not long after we were married."

"But you're not so old," protested Miss Lettie.

Oh, yes, I am, thought Mrs. Timm. Desperately old. "I'm thirty."

"Well, the real young ones don't have any sense, and

199

that's a fact," said Miss Abigail primly. "I've never known it to fail. You like the schoolhouse?"

"Yes. It's airy and has a good many windows."

"We had them put in. Of course, we don't have the electricity, but then, we don't use it much at night, you see, and we have to keep expenses down."

They seemed eager to help, despite a natural reserve. But there was something unspoken in the air. Mrs. Timm did not want to ask about the anonymous warning she had received. She could wait and bide her time. She had a cozy room downstairs in the old house where the sisters lived; from it, she could look right down the road and see the schoolhouse past the long row of old soft maples which were now in late March in the full of their yellow and maroon blossoms, with the first leaves just beginning tenderly to uncurl.

The schoolhouse was of red brick. It must have been fifty years old. But the women of the district had kept it immaculate inside, and the men who could use tools had kept it up; so it looked older outside than in. She had seventeen children, spread through all the grades, and three more who came irregularly, since they were needed at home to help in the fields, now that the land was opening up once more after the winter. The children were all from the old families; it seemed there were no others. There were Perkinses, Browns, Potters, Fields, Mahans, Jefferses, Moores, and not a name that wasn't English in origin. The children were attentive; if anything, they were a little too grave with a gravity she attributed to their natural tendency to wait until time betrayed the nature of their new teacher.

"I hope I won't disappoint you after Miss Mason," she said on her first day.

They did not seem to need her assurance; they seemed quite willing to take her on her own terms, and despite their watchful gravity, she was inspired with more confidence than she thought she would have. She ordered them all in her mind, marshaling them into groups and grades so that she would soon know where each belonged, and on the evening of her first day at school, she discussed the children with the Moore spinsters, who told her about their backgrounds.

"How many have you again?" asked Miss Abigail.

"Seventeen—and then the three they say come from time to time."

A glance flickered between the sisters.

She enumerated them, one after another, and came out with sixteen. "That's funny," she said, "I seem to have forgotten one's name. He's the dark boy in the fourth grade, I think."

"Oh, yes," said Miss Lettie. "I think, Sister, it's coming on for rain tonight. Shall we close the shutters?"

"But the moon's shining," protested Mrs. Timm.

"I feel rain," said Miss Lettie.

Mrs. Timm did not close the shutters over the windows of her room. Moonlight flooded the earth outside, and the night was warm. Not a cloud was in the sky. When Mrs. Timm stood at the window of her darkened room just before getting into bed, she looked down to where the moonlight gleamed from the schoolhouse windows. Was someone prowling about there? Or was this not, after all, her responsibility? She decided that it was not and got into bed.

The schoolhouse gave no evidence of vandalism next morning. Mrs. Timm reflected that, in this quiet country, fears for the safety of the building from night-walkers were groundless. She settled down to count her charges as they came in—sixteen. The dark boy was missing. Perhaps he, too, had had to help out at home. If it were possible to hold classes in the evening, it might assure more of the country boys a modicum of education.

That evening she returned to the schoolhouse after supper. Curiously, the spinsters tried to dissuade her. Miss Mason had not done it. Before her, Mr. Brockway had not done it. There ought not to be so much work. Perhaps the Board could make it lighter. Their assiduity was pathetic and absurd.

"I like to work," explained Mrs. Timm. "It keeps my mind off other things."

"What other things?" asked Miss Abigail bluntly, her dark eyes keen on her.

"Myself," answered Mrs. Timm simply.

Could I say to them, I am thirty, I don't feel old, I wish I had a home and children of my own? Could I say to them, each time I see them I ask myself whether I will be as they are in another twenty or thirty years? But the answer was surely self-evident. The Moore sisters were so inured to habit that even the departure of someone else from custom disturbed them; they viewed her going with misgivings plain on their homely faces.

She set out for the school while it was still dusk; the evening air was filled with the spring carols of birds; the wind blew softly out of the west, aromatic with the smell of earth freed again from winter. A moon burgeoned into the darkening heaven, and the evening star shone low in the west. The schoolhouse was set in a grove of tall maple trees—"sugar maples," the people called them; they bowered the small building and the twilight clung about them.

She set to work compiling neat records for every pupil, an onerous but not difficult task. The lamp threw a pale yellow flower of light over the worn old desk. *"Birch, Mary,"* she wrote, and followed her name with her age, the names of her parents, and other pertinent data. She worked rapidly, and presently she was well into the fourth grade. Then she remembered the dark boy who had not been in school today. She would have to leave a blank card for him. She went on.

But the thought of the dark boy haunted her. He had been so quiet, so withdrawn, and yet there had been such an appealing air about him, like someone lost. Despite the winsomeness of the smaller children, this boy of nine or so touched upon her long-suppressed maternal instincts as none other did.

She was aware suddenly of being watched. Looking up, she saw a face peering in from the darker side of the school building, that side opposite the moon, which opened toward a woods of some depth, beyond which lay the home of one of her irregular pupils, a small boy named Edward Robb. In a moment the face was gone. She was briefly alarmed, but almost simultaneously she realized that the face was that of a boy.

The face reappeared. She looked steadily in its direction

and saw that it was faintly familiar—the slight, sensitive mouth, the dark brooding eyes, the curled hair, the scar on his forehead, over the left temple. The dark boy, of course. He had finished his work and had been drawn to the light in the schoolhouse. She half rose, beckoning him in; but he was off like a deer, too shy to be drawn in at this unusual hour.

He did not return.

When she got back home, she found Miss Abigail waiting up for her. The old lady was clearly apprehensive, and studied her face as if she were looking for some sign of travail.

"I waited up because I didn't know but what you might want something to eat when you came in," said Miss Abigail.

"No, I think not, thank you."

"Well, there's hot tea, if you want some."

"If it's ready, I'd like a cup."

"I thought you would."

When they were seated in the spare kitchen, the older woman asked, "How did the work go?"

"Very well."

"As long as you weren't disturbed, I suppose you made good progress."

Was it a question that the older woman asked? It sounded more like that than a statement.

"Oh, one of the boys looked into the window while I was at work, but he didn't come in."

The older woman's eyes were intense on her. "Which one?" she asked in a voice that was little more than a whisper.

"That dark boy—I've forgotten his name. It takes a while, you know, to get used to pupils in a new school."

The older woman's gaze lingered. What was brooding in her eyes gave way to an uncertain tranquility. She drank her tea slowly.

"It must be lonesome working there at night. I don't expect you'll have to do much of it, will you?"

Was it a simple question she asked, or a plea she made? Mrs. Timm was disconcerted; she could not tell.

"I don't know," she said. "I don't think so."

The older woman concealed her relief well.

It was strange, thought Mrs. Timm when she was once again in her room, but the solicitude of the spinsters was almost parental. She found herself responding to it, with the response of one long in need of affection. It was understandable that they should be lonely, too, living isolated here, their farm land rented to a neighbor who seldom came in, limited in their social life to the few events which took place in the neighborhood.

On the following day, school had hardly begun when she answered a knock on the door and found herself facing a dark-eyed, black-haired man in his middle thirties, holding one of her irregulars by one hand.

"You the new teacher?" he asked.

"Yes, I'm Mrs. Timm."

"I'm Tom Robb. Brought my boy over. Don't care much about his comin' to school, but the law says he's to come; so here he is. I need him some days. He won't be regular."

"Of course. I know." She turned to the boy. "This is Edward, isn't it?"

"Yes, it's Edward. And I don't want him on any ladders, understand?"

What a peculiar request! she thought fleetingly. "I don't think we'll have to put Edward on a ladder, Mr. Robb," she said.

She met his eyes squarely. There was something in them, too, which baffled her. Perhaps it was this wall of mystery which had disturbed her predecessor. His eyes burned at her; he looked a little wild, resentful, brooding—all this lay in his eyes, together with a kind of defiant misery.

She opened the door wider. "Would you like to come in, Mr. Robb?"

He was startled and surprised. "No, thank you, ma'am." He relinquished his son's hand and pushed him forward. "You just take Edward now. He'll come home directly school's over." Hesitantly, he added, "You'll have to overlook things now and then."

"If Mrs. Robb—"

"The boy's mother died three years ago."

"Oh, I'm sorry, Mr. Robb."

"That's all right, ma'am. You couldn't know."

204

"It's the same way with me," she hastened to add in expiation. "My husband died, too, six years ago."

He smiled wintrily.

Not until after he was gone did she think about his resemblance to the dark boy. Perhaps his name, too, was Robb. The man, clearly, had some prejudice against education; it stood out in his defiant, resentful manner. He had not been discourteous, as if he recognized that she only represented a system he disliked, and was not herself the author of it. But he did not seem an uneducated man, and his dislike was inexplicable. He was a man not ill-favored in appearance, she thought on reflection, but, like his son, he needed caring for. Or is it my imagination? she asked herself.

That night again, the dark boy looked in at her. All day he had been absent; but so had three other boys in the upper grades. She knew they had had to take advantage of the balmy weather and work in the fields. Doubtless the dark boy, for all that he could not be more than nine or ten at most, had done so too.

This time she slipped out the door when he moved back, so that when he came up to the window once more, she was there beside him almost before he knew it. His dark face looked up at her out of the night.

"Won't you come in?" she asked.

He followed her silently, but did not go far beyond the door, keeping away from the light. There he stood, gazing at her with his brooding eyes.

"I've been looking back into the records," she said, trying to be friendly, "and I guess your name is Joel, isn't it?"

He nodded.

"You've been in the fourth grade two years," she said gently.

He nodded again.

"Wouldn't you like to learn faster, Joel?"

"Oh, yes," his voice came in an urgent hushing.

He is as shy as a deer, she thought. Her glance fell upon the scar on his forehead. It was angry, still, as if but half-healed.

"How did you hurt yourself?" she asked.

205

But almost instantly, almost as if he himself had answered, she knew how he had come by it.

"You fell off a ladder, didn't you?" she asked. "Here in school?"

He nodded.

Certainly he was Tom Robb's son. Perhaps it was because of what that resentful man had told her that she had known so surely what had happened to Joel. He had been hurt badly, so much was clear. His hurt was part of his father's withheld fury, the pent-up anger against schooling, the wild defiance that shone in his eyes.

At the same time she was aware of something more, a kind of hunger emanating from the boy. It touched her. He needed affection, he needed the care of the mother who had died, he needed more than his father's anger at destiny and his resentment. He needed it desperately, as something to keep him from his solitude and isolation. Her maternal instincts welled up.

"Come closer, Joel," she said persuasively.

He took a hesitant step forward, but he was trembling, poised for instant flight.

"Are you afraid of me?" she asked.

He shook his head.

"I'm not afraid of you," she went on. "I can teach you. If you can't come daytimes, I can teach you at night."

She stood up. Instantly he turned and was gone like the wind. The door yawned blackly where but a moment before he had passed; the moonlight lay on the floor as if no shadow but that of the trees had obscured it even for a moment.

She ran to the door, calling him. But no sound answered her save the wind's hushing in the maple trees and, far down the road, a dog barking, a cow lowing.

When she reached home, the hour was late. She had waited in vain for the dark boy to return; he had not come. Yet she could have taken oath that she had seen his face peering in at her from time to time, that he had been skulking along behind her on her way from the schoolhouse.

Despite the lateness of the hour, both the Moore sisters were still up. They sat in a kind of tension which seemed to abate a little as soon as she was in the house and it was plain that she had come to no harm. She was touched.

"You shouldn't have waited up," she chided them gently. "You make me feel guilty to keep you waiting."

"Not at all," said Miss Abigail. "We just wanted to make sure. After all, we have our responsibilities."

"And we don't take them lightly," added Miss Lettie, her pale blue eyes fluttering.

"It's such a quiet, peaceful night," she said.

"And you weren't disturbed?" inquired Miss Lettie anxiously.

She laughed. "Who would disturb me?" Then, casually, she added, "Except, of course, that fourth grade boy. Think of it—two years in the one grade! Does his father keep him at work so much he can't come to school enough to pass? I should think the law—" She stopped, amazed at the grimness of Miss Lettie's stare, a grimness more artfully concealed by Miss Abigail.

"What boy?" asked Miss Lettie in a voice that squeaked with fear.

"That dark boy—I've forgotten his name. But he looks like Tom Robb; he must be one of his boys. Or his brother, if he has one."

"Oh!" cried Miss Lettie. "I told you, Abbie! You'll have to move the schoolhouse. You'll have to get a new place."

"Hush, Lettie! Go on, Mrs. Timm."

"I did manage to get him in tonight, and I talked with him a while. He seems so pathetically eager for attention and affection, but he's so shy! I suppose he misses his mother. His father—"

Miss Lettie got up, her handkerchief pressed against her mouth. She left the room, her eyes wild.

Mrs. Timm was amazed. She looked toward Miss Abigail. "Whatever have I said?"

"You must overlook my sister's emotionalism, Mrs. Timm," said Miss Abigail in an unsteady voice. "Did the boy speak to you?"

"Only a little. He answered most of my questions with a nod—just as if, why, as if he were afraid to speak."

"Mrs. Timm, may I ask you a question? I don't want to seem impertinent—"

"Why, of course."

"Did you know Miss Mason?"

"No."

"Did you ever speak to her, or correspond with her?"

"No, I didn't. But wait—"

Now was the time, Mrs. Timm thought, the time to inquire about the anonymous note she had received. She went hurriedly to her room and came back with it. She laid it down before Miss Abigail, whose eyes lowered to it.

"I don't know who sent it," explained Mrs. Timm. "I thought it might have been Miss Mason."

"Yes. It looks like her handwriting." Miss Abigail folded the note and handed it back to Mrs. Timm. "Poor woman! Perhaps we did her an injustice."

Mrs. Timm was more mystified than ever. She was beginning to feel a guilty bond of sympathy with Miss Mason. There was no explanation of the mysterious conduct of the spinsters; it baffled her. She sat for a long time in her moonlit room and sought some solution to the riddle. There was none; she sank only deeper into perplexity. If all the people of this rural community were as strange as the Moore sisters and Tom Robb, she could understand why a sensitive young woman such as Miss Mason must have been could not have stood up against them. How tense, how strange they all were! As if they labored under some problem which was insoluble.

In the morning she sought in vain for any sign of the sisters' nocturnal distress. She set out for school earlier than usual because she had made up her mind that something must be done for the dark boy; he must be helped, and there was only one way in which to do it. She herself must talk to Tom Robb.

She found him in his barn. He had just finished milking and the cows had been turned out. He had no sooner caught sight of her than he spoke, his voice cutting across her "Good morning, Mr. Robb."

"I need Ed myself today," he said. "He can't come."

"It wasn't Edward I came to see you about," she answered. "I wanted to talk about your older boy—the one with the scar on his forehead. Joel."

He dropped the pail he had in his hand. In one great stride he loomed immediately above her, his eyes blazing. He caught hold of her arms and shook her savagely, shouting at her, "What are you talking about! Why are you tormenting me like this? Why can't people leave us alone?" in a voice that was wild with despair and grief and anger.

She was too astonished and frightened to protest. She was passive in his grasp, recognizing instantly that there was no wriggling out of his strong hands. His temper passed; he let go of her, put one hand up to his forehead, and fell back a step, breathing hard. "Sorry," he muttered thickly. "I guess I lost control."

She repressed her indignation at sight of his eyes; there were tears there. She forgot her bruised arms.

"What have I said, Mr. Robb?"

He turned his eyes full upon her, suspicion rising in his sober gaze. "Don't you know?" he asked. "Didn't they tell you?"

"No one hereabouts tells me anything," she said simply.

"Didn't they tell you my boy, Joel, fell off a ladder in the schoolhouse and cracked his head open? It started to heal over—but it never did. He died two years ago. Ed's all I got left." His voice was chokingly hoarse.

For a piercing moment she thought the floor would give way under her. She fought for control.

She put one hand on his arm. "I'm sorry. I didn't know. But it explains everything. I've seen him."

"I have, too. What can I do?"

"You're afraid of him," she said simply.

He nodded dumbly, his eyes miserable.

"I guess maybe that's the trouble," she said. "He comes every night when I'm at the schoolhouse. Perhaps it's a mistake to be frightened."

But it was only his patent misery and need that held down her own chill fear. Once out of sight of the snug little Robb home, where he could not see her, she leaned breathlessly against a tree. There is no dark boy, she said to herself. Somehow, her imagination had played a dreadful trick on her. Dead two years! They had never taken his name off the records. Just stopped in the middle of the fourth grade. No dark boy! She repeated it over and over.

But she could not convince herself. That first day he had been sitting in the corner seat. She remembered asking his name; he had not given it. She remembered asking another boy, who only looked toward the seat and shook his head. How grave the children had been that day! And each night—Oh, no, it could not be!

When she returned to the Moore house for supper that evening, she was determined to face the spinsters with her discovery.

"Why didn't anyone tell me the schoolhouse was haunted?" she asked quietly.

"Oh!" cried Miss Lettie, looking accusingly at her sister. "I told you, Abbie—"

"Hush, Lettie," said Abigail with authority. "Is it?" she asked Mrs. Timm.

"The dark boy—Joel Robb. You knew."

Miss Abigail shook her head. "No, I didn't know. I've never seen him. Neither has Lettie. It's only what we've heard. Only a very few people have seen him. Miss Mason said she had. After that, Mr. Robb confessed he had. Perhaps we've done both of them a grave wrong, because you couldn't have known. We made sure Miss Mason was gone before you came. But that first day, of course, the children reported that you spoke to an empty seat—that was why, you see, we were so apprehensive. I suppose you will want to leave." She spoke with regret.

Mrs. Timm's first impulse was to say yes, she wanted to go. But she did not give it voice. "No," she answered. "I have no intention of leaving. If Mr. Robb has lived with that ghost for two years, I guess it won't harm me any. I'll try to be more careful in front of the children, and we'll say no more about it."

The two old women looked at her with no attempt to conceal their incredulity.

How could I have been so tranquil? she asked herself later, as she sat in the moonlit schoolhouse, waiting. She knew he would come. He must come now. But she had to fight down fear; it was only natural that she should wait now with trepidation and anxiety. The wind in the maples, lashing the thin twigs high up heaven, the occasional clouds which shadowed the moon, the isolation and loneliness of the countryside, the night's deep silence—all combined to supplant the afternoon's somnolence with eeriness.

Quite suddenly he was there, his face at the window, the scar black against the night. This was the test, she knew. For a moment she hesitated. Then she smiled and raised her hand to beckon him in.

He came in as before, slipping silently into the dimly lit room to stand shyly near the door. How tenuous he was! Now that she knew, it was plain.

"Hello, Joel," she said easily. "Did you come to learn tonight?"

He nodded. Scarcely a movement of air. How could she have misunderstood?

"Sit down."

He went back to the corner seat, the same seat in which she had first seen him, the one he had had when—There he sat, almost invisible in the shadows. He was himself no more than shadow.

"Shall we read a story tonight, Joel?" she asked.

Did he answer "Yes" or not? She could not be sure. But with each word she uttered, her uneasiness diminished a little and finally fell away from her, and the affection she had felt for this lost ghost returned. She read to him, interrupting herself from time to time to speak to him directly. She finished a story, and went on to another.

The door, which had stood ajar, for the night was warm, swung open a little farther. She looked up.

Tom Robb stood there, his hands clenched at his sides, his face turned to the corner seat.

"Your father's come to take you home, Joel," she said quietly.

A half-strangled exclamation came from Tom Robb.

She bent over and blew out the lamp. In a moment the reflected glow of the moonlight lit the room. She stood up.

The boy sat where he was, unmoving, a shadowy outline in shadow.

She walked down and over to where Tom Robb stood.

She put her hand in his and turned to the corner where the dark boy sat. The seat was faintly visible through him.

"Will you come home with us, Joel?" she asked.

She felt, rather than saw, him glide out of the seat toward them. She held out her hand. She felt the man at her side begin to shrink away, and tightened her hold on his rough fingers.

"Please, Tom," she said.

He relaxed.

The boy came on slowly, hesitantly, fearfully. He came almost up to them; there he stopped.

She turned without a word and walked out of the schoolhouse, still holding to Tom Robb's hand. Without looking around, she knew the boy was following.

In this fashion they walked through the woods back to the farm in the valley beyond, she and the stumbling man and the evanescent boy who had once walked this way like any other growing child.

At the house he was gone.

Robb flung himself into the house, exhausted. He sat down at the kitchen table, put his head down on his arms, and sobbed.

"Two years of it," he cried. "It like to drove me crazy. They all said I was crazy—every one of 'em. They ran Miss Mason out. They'll run you out the same way, you'll see."

She stood for a moment looking compassionately down at him. She put one hand gently on his thick dark hair. How soft it was! And inside, he was soft, too, she knew.

"I'd better go now," she said.

He turned and grasped one of her hands. "Don't go, Mrs. Timm!"

"I must," she said. "But nobody's going to run me out. I aim to stay. I expect to be back here."

"But if . . ." He hesitated. "When you tell them you aim to stay, they'll say you're crazy, too. They'll say you're out of your head."

"Then that'll make two of us," she answered tranquilly.

He looked past her to the windows. "Has he gone?" he asked.

"If you could just get used to not being afraid of him," she said, "you'd never notice him. I did, before I knew. Now that I know, it doesn't make any difference. He's just lonesome. And so are you. And, if it comes down to it, so am I. Most people are. After all, you're his father; he's got a right to look for some affection from you. I must go now, Tom."

He looked at her with challenge and wonder in his eyes. "You called me 'Tom'!"

"I'd better get used to it," she said. "Good night."

Outside there was nothing but the moonlight.

He came out after her. "I can't let you walk home alone, Mrs. Timm," he said gruffly. "If you don't mind, I'll walk you back."

"I don't mind at all."

Born in Wisconsin in 1909, August Derleth sold his first story, "Bat's Belfry," to Weird Tales *when he was only fifteen. Educated at the University of Wisconsin, he wrote more than one hundred books and three hundred short stories of mystery and the supernatural. His Sac Prairie Sage, books detailing a fictionalized account of Wisconsin history, made him a respected regional writer. In 1939, he formed Arkham House with Donald Wandrei, to preserve the then little-known work of his mentor and friend, H. P. Lovecraft. Derleth died in 1971.*

Acknowledgments

"This Is Death" by Donald E. Westlake. Copyright © 1977 by Barrie & Jenkins; copyright © 1978 by Donald E. Westlake. First appeared under the title "In the Death." Reprinted by permission of the author.

"On 202" by Jeff Hecht. Copyright © 1981 by Jeff Hecht. Reprinted by permission of the author.

"The Devil and Daniel Webster" by Stephen Vincent Benét. From *Selected Works of Steven Benet*. Copyright © 1936 by The Curtis Publishing Company. Copyright renewed © 1964 by Thomas C. Benét, Stephanie E. Mahin, and Rachel Lewis Benét. Reprinted by permission of Brandt & Brandt Literary Agents, Inc.

"Emmett" by Dahlov Ipcar. Copyright © 1990 by Dahlov Ipcar. Published in *The Nightmare and Her Foal and Other Stories* by Dahlov Ipcar; North Country Press, P. O. Box 641, Unity, Maine 04988.

"The Changing of the Guard" by Anne Serling. Copyright © 1985 by Anne Serling. Reprinted by permission of the author and the Rod Serling Trust.

"Herbert West—Reanimator" by H. P. Lovecraft. Copyright © 1922 by H. P. Lovecraft. Reprinted by permission of the agents for the author's Estate, the Scott Meredith Literary Agency, Inc., 845 Third Avenue, New York, New York 10022.

"A Friendly Exorcise" by Talmage Powell. Copyright © 1990 by Talmage Powell. A version of this story appeared in *Alfred Hitchcock's Mystery Magazine*, March, 1968, copyright © 1968 by HSD Publications Inc. Published by arrangement with the author.

"Safety Zone" by Barry N. Malzberg. Copyright © 1990 by Barry N. Malzberg. An original story, published by arrangement with the author.

"The Phantom Farmhouse" by Seabury Quinn. Copyright © 1923 by *Weird Tales*. Reprinted by permission of the agents for the author's Estate, the Scott Meredith Literary Agency, Inc., 845 Third Avenue, New York, New York 10022.

"Night-Side" by Joyce Carol Oates. Copyright © 1990 by the Ontario Review, Inc. Reprinted by permission of the author.

"The Dark Boy" by August Derleth. Copyright © 1957 by Mercury Press, Inc. Reprinted by permission of the agents for the author's Estate, the Scott Meredith Literary Agency, Inc., 845 Third Avenue, New York, New York 10022.